The Trinity Quilts

To Ethel —
May God bless you & yours today and always!
Lynne Wells Walding

Lynne Wells Walding

ISBN 978-1-64299-221-2 (paperback)
ISBN 978-1-64299-223-6 (hardcover)
ISBN 978-1-64299-222-9 (digital)

Copyright © 2018 by Lynne Wells Walding

All rights reserved. No part of this publication may be reproduced, distributed, or transmitted in any form or by any means, including photocopying, recording, or other electronic or mechanical methods without the prior written permission of the publisher. For permission requests, solicit the publisher via the address below.

Christian Faith Publishing, Inc.
832 Park Avenue
Meadville, PA 16335
www.christianfaithpublishing.com

Printed in the United States of America

Previous works of Lynne Wells Walding

Pastor McAlester's Bride

Witt Gregory, a man after God's own heart, is tempted
almost beyond his endurance to claim
the love of his life in order to *save* her
from her pastor husband.
Witness a Spiritual battle between
mortal love and Divine love.

Winnoby Cabin

Satan hasn't given up on the McAlester
family. Their faith is a constant
annoyance to him, so he lures them to a
peaceful mountain community, hoping to
"bring them down" for good. The Evil
One's minions set out to stop the
McAlester's influence on the few remaining
faithful citizens—and, at any cost,
stop Casey from writing the book
God has called her to write.
Big mistake!

Ian's Song

Annie has a happy marriage and a lovely
country home in the Piney Woods of
East Texas. Until one day when her idyllic
existence comes to a crashing halt, and
her whole world begins to fall down around her ears.
Once a faithful lover of God, Annie blames
Him for her misfortunes. The Lord
sends a very unlikely candidate
~ a womanizing, hard-living Tennessee truck driver ~
to draw the poison from her soul.

Dedication

My husband and I have a dear friend named Jake.
He's bought multiple copies of my first
three books, but after reading
the third one, *Ian's Song*, he asked my
husband why authors only
name *bad* guys Jake. "Why aren't good
guys ever named Jake" he asked.
I decided right then my next novel
would have a hero named Jake.
So, Jake Bradford . . . this one's for you.
The protagonist is named Jake. He's a hero and a good guy.
Like you.

Post Script: At 89 years of age, our dear
friend and brother-in-Christ,
Jake Bradford, moved on to Heaven to be with the Lord
before this novel made it to print. He
had received an advance copy,
and though I doubt he had a chance to read it,
he knew it had been dedicated to him.

Jake is survived by his lovely wife of 50
years, Betty Jo Myers Bradford,
three adult children, multiple grandchildren
and great-grandchildren.
Plus extended family and many friends
who will miss him greatly.
Rest in Peace, Jake.

Acknowledgements

Thank you, my good friend, Sheryl Shuler of New London, Texas, for the loan of your beautiful hand-crafted quilt as an inspiration for the cover of this book. Your work is exquisite.

And a big thank you to my first readers; my husband, Dee (who wasn't given a choice in the matter), Billy Barnett, and Kelly Gilbert. Your input is invaluable.

And to Becky Williams, my BFF, for your confidence in my ability to accomplish what I set out to do, even when I have my doubts. Perhaps I should say *especially* when I have my doubts.

A special thanks to every friend, family member, and faithful reader who "nagged" me to hurry up and get this work on the market.

To all of you . . . you are the wind beneath my wings.

Part 1

Chapter 1

January 1979, Texas Panhandle

Sam saw the brightly lit truck-stop sign in the distance, and his eyes automatically dropped to the gas gauge.

One-quarter tank. And a long way between these little Texas Panhandle towns. Better stop.

The rig was filthy, and he was tired. In no mood for anything but to get home, take a shower, grab a bite, and fall into bed. But home was still several hours away, and he'd skipped supper.

He uttered a quick prayer his bank card wouldn't be rejected as he slipped it into the slot in the diesel pump. Money was always tight, but this had been an unusually expensive run.

His card was accepted. He released a long breath. After he finished fueling the rig, he headed for the restrooms. The aroma of fried chicken wafted from the restaurant. In a rare moment of self-pity, Sam decided to have a bite to eat—and pay the two guys who'd asked for the job to give the rig a quick wash. They needed the work, and he needed something warm in his stomach. At least that's what he told himself. Even though he'd never hired out to have it washed before, it sounded like a plan tonight, time wise. In the morning, he had to be ready to leave the house at a moment's notice should a job become available. And a clean rig was essential.

After eating, he thanked the men who were patiently waiting by his rig and paid them their agreed wages plus a little extra for a job well done. Then he moved his big, white, shiny-clean—if old—pride and joy from the washing bay to the huge parking lot located behind the multipurpose building. Considering his finances, he probably shouldn't have hired the guys, much less *tipped* them. But they grabbed their money and headed straight for the restaurant. So, yes, it was the right thing to do in this case. The Bible says, "For as you do it unto the least of the Brethren, you have done it unto Me." And hadn't God always provided for the needs of his little family?

He left the diesel engine running and jogged back in for a few more minutes to get a refreshing shower. It was going to be a real luxury to get home already fed and bathed. He could tiptoe into the bedroom and drop directly between the fresh sheets he knew would be on his bed without waking the family.

Sarah looked over the row of rigs. She knew some of them had men sleeping over the cab. She really didn't want to wake anyone. Being awakened from a much-needed rest wouldn't put anyone in the mood to help her. And she *had* to have a ride.

A super-sized white vehicle caught her eye. A Peterbilt. She'd heard of them. It was so clean and bright it seemed to sparkle in the moonlight that drenched the lot—like an automotive celestial being waiting to sweep her away from her miserable existence into a world of beauty. If she was lucky, it would be headed in the right direction to take her far away from the back roads of this small Texas Panhandle town where she'd been raised in poverty and want.

She set her shabby little suitcase on the driver-side running board. No one would be able to enter the cab without noticing. Then, very carefully, she climbed on the warm hood, curled up, and pulled her lightweight coat around her. In her coat pocket, she'd pinned all the money she had in the world. Nineteen dollars and fifty-six cents she'd saved from odd jobs. Odd jobs Papa didn't know about—or he'd have taken the money from her.

She'd walked almost ten miles from home to the highway, carrying her small, heavy bag. She was hungry and cold, and her legs and shoulders ached. It was almost enough to drown out the fear she felt—not so much about running away—but about being *caught* by Papa. He would be so angry when he realized she was gone. And Mama wouldn't say a word in her defense. No, not a word. Any attempt Mama might make at defending her would only make Papa angrier.

Sarah whispered a little prayer to a God she'd only heard of, but hadn't yet met, that the truck driver she'd singled out wouldn't be too mean. She curled into the fetal position, and within minutes, the sound and gentle vibration of the ancient engine had lulled her to sleep on the warm hood of a stranger's shiny old rig.

At first sight, Sam felt a flush of anger. He was very particular with his rig. Certainly didn't like someone climbing on the hood. But as he got closer, he could see the offender was a mere girl. Fourteen or fifteen, maybe.

He looked up at her slight figure, sound asleep and looking a lot like the pictures you see on brochures asking for donations for poverty-stricken children. He cleared his throat and tried to keep his booming voice at a gentle level. "Child, what are you doing on the hood of my rig?"

The voice of an ogre.

Sarah sat up with a start, yipped, and positioned herself to slide off the hood and run for her life.

"Hold it. You'll break your neck. Climb down carefully. The same way you got up." He extended a heavily tattooed arm to assist her decent. "Here, let me help you." Reluctantly, Sarah took his hand. Then wiggled loose when she was on the ground.

He held up her bag. "This yours?"

"Yes, sir. I'm sorry. I didn't know where else to plunk it down, so you wouldn't leave without me." She raked her choppy-looking dark hair from her wide, fear-filled eyes.

"I think I'd have noticed you on the hood, child." He shook his head and sighed deeply. "And what makes you think I'll take you with me when I go? You have any idea how much trouble that could get me into, little lady?" He didn't want to frighten her, but hers was not a good plan. It could only have been conceived by a young and naive mind. Wherever she'd come from, she'd have to go back.

"I'll escort you home—in a taxi. That's the most I can do for you. What's your name?"

"My name's Sarah and I won't go home. And you can't make me. Just go ahead and leave. I'll find someone else to give me a ride." She'd already snatched her bag and turned away from him.

"Just a minute, young lady." He put his hand on her shoulder, noticing how frail she really was. "Do you know how dangerous it is to hitch a ride at a truck stop? Most the guys are decent. Even nice. But you're choosing a pig in a poke. You have no way of knowing what kind of man you might be getting a ride with . . . or what plans he may have for *you*."

Sarah huffed softly and eked out a small fake smile.

"Does that amuse you?" He didn't feel like having a know-it-all kid yank his chain tonight. "You think you're qualified to judge a man's nature without even knowing him?"

His gruff voice raised a few decibels. "Why, young lady, you could be *raped*."

A sound emitted from Sarah's throat that could have been a giggle—or a gasp.

Lord, give me patience. "So you think that's funny, too, do you?"

She hung her head. "No, sir, I don't think it's funny at all. It's just that . . . it's just that . . . I've already . . . well, that's why I'm running away."

Chapter 2

Nine weeks earlier on a Friday night

The homecoming game was exciting. The Plainsville Pirates had squeaked out a narrow victory at 34–32. Even better, some of the popular girls had spoken to her tonight. They'd noticed her, and, well, it was almost as if they *liked* her. She'd be home in plenty of time to satisfy Papa's strict curfew. Sarah seemed to have a new bounce to her step. Yes, life was good.

She could still smell the expensive perfume Allison Wilson had spritzed on her when she went to the restroom at half-time. Allison Wilson—Homecoming Queen—had actually smiled at her and said, "Want some?" Before she could speak, Allison squirted some in Sarah's hair, before using it on herself. She turned to Sarah as she was leaving. "See ya."

Sarah was on cloud nine. On her way to the game, she'd taken her hair out of the tight bun Papa always made her wear. When she took out the last hairpin, the dark curls cascaded around her shoulders and down her back. Then, with the rubber band she'd hidden in her skirt pocket, she gathered her generous mane into a loose ponytail. *All the girls wear ponytails.* At the game, she even got a few compliments on it. Now, it flounced from side to side as she walked at a quick pace down the dark road home, smiling to herself.

This has been the best day of my life.

As she neared her home, the pavement ended, and the road narrowed. If only she didn't have to pass the run-down, spooky Frederick's shack. She knew it wasn't really haunted and all the scary stories were nonsense, but it had been empty for years, and the rumors about strange happenings and weird noises that emanated from the rickety old building always crept to the surface of her mind when she passed that way, especially on a dark night like tonight.

She found herself tiptoeing past the shack, as though to not draw attention to herself, should any ghosts be hanging around. *Nothing to be afraid of. No such thing as ghosts. Nothing to be afraid of. No such thing as ghosts.* She chanted the words in her mind in rhythm with her footsteps. Holding hairpins in her mouth, she worked quickly with both hands, pulling her hair back into a tight bun as she moved past the shack. Couldn't let Papa see her with a ponytail. He'd go ballistic. He was already furious that Mama had given her permission to go to the game.

Sarah thought she heard movement in the underbrush. *It's my imagination.* Yet she quickened her step.

There it was again.

This time she knew it wasn't her imagination. Someone was following her. She spit out the hairpins, dropped the mass of curls she was shaping in to a bun, and kicked off her misfit, second-hand shoes, the better to run, just as someone from the darkness behind her threw a blindfold over her eyes. It jerked her neck and brought her to a dead stop, almost causing her to fall backward. She screamed and clutched vainly at it. With a yank and a grunt from behind, a knot dug into her scalp. At the same moment, a hand clapped over her mouth. She was dragged, kicking and squealing, through the underbrush that choked out the long, rugged walkway to the Frederick's front door.

She heard her captor kick the door open. A musty, dank odor overwhelmed her senses as he dragged her across the threshold. She tried to bite the hand that was clamped tightly over her mouth, which only made her nemesis laugh and squeeze harder. She struggled vainly against the strong arm clamping her arms to her sides and almost squeezing the breath from her. It was hard to think beyond the pounding fear clenching her heart, and every breath she managed was rancid and sour.

The door slammed shut, and she heard the sound of an old skeleton key turning in the rusty lock.

With his attention divided between her and the door, Sarah managed to twist loose from his grip. But, blindfolded, she was helpless to run. Her hair was tangled in the blindfold, and before she could get it off, he'd grabbed her again. Pulling her against him, he began ripping at her clothes. She fought like a tiger. With fingernails and knees, she went after her tormentor. He yelped in pain, and she could feel his blood on her fingertips. Infuriated, he shouted an obscenity and ruthlessly shoved her away from him. She felt herself spinning helplessly across the room, where she hit the opposite wall at full force. Blackness enfolded her.

Crumpling like a discarded rag doll, Sarah slithered to the floor.

Chapter 3

When Sarah next opened her eyes, the first dim light of morning was seeping through the window, barely illuminating the room. She was lying on a smelly old couch. The sweet smell of Allison's perfume still clung to her and mingled with the rancid smells of the old shack.

Apparently alone, she moved to sit up and pain shot through her body. Her hair tumbled down her back in a tangled array of matted curls. The blindfold had been thrown across the room, a lock of her dark tresses still tangled in the knot. She felt the painful spot on the back of her head and discovered crusty dried blood. Whoever her attacker was, he was very angry at her for resisting. Guilt flooded her soul. This wouldn't have happened if she'd kept her hair in a tight little bun. If she'd not smiled at people at the game, revealing her dimple. Papa had warned her about the dangers of flaunting her long hair and fetching smile.

She tried to stand and fell back onto the couch, the room spinning. She sat for a moment before she tried again, attempting to recall every detail of last night. But she had no recollection beyond being thrown across the room.

When she finally stood and took a few shaky steps, every move was painful. She realized her worse fears about what may have happened after she lost consciousness were indeed true, and a wave of nausea overwhelmed her. She tried unsuccessfully to hold it in until she was outside.

When she reached the front door, it was unlocked, the old key still in it.

She found her second-hand shoes in the road. No point in looking for the hairpins. But without them, Papa would figure out what she'd done with her hair.

The walk home was agonizing. And as if she was not already hurting enough, she knew Papa would be waiting for her with his belt.

The sun was peeking over the horizon when she stumbled through the door of her shabby home. Papa was sitting a few feet back, directly in front of the door in a straight-back chair, with his belt furled and ready to mete out her due punishment.

"Look at you. You hussy! Your best dress . . . ruined. Hair over your eyes, makeup smeared all over your face. Harlot! You've shamed your mama and me." He stood and brought the belt across her legs, leaving a red whelp on her left calf.

Sarah squealed and tried to swallow the pain. "Papa, please . . ."

Another blow, this time through her wrinkled skirt to her thighs. A whimper of agony escaped her lips.

"Papa, let me explain. It was horrible."

"Sin always is."

"Someone . . ." She turned away when she saw the leather strap raised for another blow.

"Didn't bother to learn his name?" he screeched and landed a blow across her back. "Don't walk away from me. You have the stench of sin all over you."

She turned and faced him, wincing as she grabbed the belt when he lashed out at her again. She hung on with both hands. "Listen to me. Let me explain. I was . . ."

He pulled her to him with the belt, slapped her across the face with his free hand, and turned to stride out of the room. He spun around to face her, his features bloated with uncontrolled anger. "I don't care what you have to say. That hair. That dimple your mama thinks is so fetching. Man traps. That's what they are. You swing your hips and flip your hair—I warned you about that hair—and then you complain when a man calls your bluff. Well, you better hope your lover was careful. I ain't raising no bastard child." He slammed the door behind him.

Mama was standing in the kitchen doorway, watching. Hard eyes burning into Sarah's shame. She'd put water on to heat. Shaking her head, she carelessly and wordlessly stripped her young daughter to the buff, right there at the kitchen sink. "Now look what you've done. He'll be 'hell on wheels' till this blows over, thanks to you."

Sarah stood like a sheep led to slaughter, gritting her teeth in pain as her mother dispassionately bathed her whelps and abrasions and applied an ointment.

"Mama," Sarah pleaded, "I was attacked, and I'm pretty sure he . . . he . . . violated me."

Mama shot her a disbelieving stare. "You don't even *know?*"

Sarah picked at her fingernails. "No, Mama, I was unconscious."

"Yeah, right. Unconscious. Hmmph."

Sarah squirmed under Mama's rough touch. "I want to report what happened to the police. And see a doctor."

Mama crossed her arms in front of her. "We can't afford no doctor, and I don't *need* no doctor to tell me your man had his way with you. And we ain't involving the police in our private affairs. You know, you ain't the first pretty young thing to succumb to a man's pleading."

Mama wouldn't look Sarah in the eye. "I was still kinda hopin' you'd marry *up*. But that's pretty doubtful after a shenanigan like this. Best we forget the whole mess. Just stay out of Papa's way, ya' hear?"

She left Sarah standing there with only a towel around her. "Now get dressed and clean up this mess."

On Monday, Sarah went back to school. Her beautiful hair gone—chopped off by Papa. The same popular girls who had spoken to her at the game now huddled together and snickered when she passed by. Even Allison Wilson looked the other way when they passed in the hall.

But worst of all, the boys taunted her mercilessly. Every one of them wore a large Band-Aid on his left cheekbone in solidarity with the only one among them who'd shed blood from Sarah's desperate attempts to escape.

She walked down the hallway unsmiling, her eyes straight ahead. But the remarks persisted.

"When's it *my* turn?"

"What about the rest of us? Ain't we good enough for you?"

And the most hurtful one of all. "You been asking for it, you know."

Chapter 4

Standing at the door of his rig, Sam listened in disbelief. "Oh my good Lord, I'm sorry." He closed his eyes and muttered a small prayer asking God to give him the right words.

"Your mother must be very frightened of your father."

"Yeah, she won't cross Papa no matter what. Told me many times, a woman's place is wherever her man wants her to be. In front of the stove or in the bed."

Sam touched her choppy hair. Cut half an inch long in some places, four inches in others. "And the long hair? What happened to it?"

"Papa chopped it off and forbid Mama to do anything more to it."

"What about the guy who did this to you? Have you any idea who he was?"

Sarah squirmed. "As I was leaving the stadium, a car followed slowly a few yards behind me for a block or two. Then it speeded up and whizzed by."

"Did you get a look at the car?"

"I'm sure it was a guy from school. But I kept my eyes straight ahead. And when he passed me, I looked the other way. I guess that was a dumb thing to do."

"A natural reaction, Sarah. But why are you so sure it was someone you knew?"

"The whole school knows about it, and I sure didn't tell anybody. And the guys . . . they keep asking me when do *they* get a turn. And they all wore Band-Aids where I scratched the one who did it. And besides . . . he blindfolded me. There would've been no reason to unless I knew him."

Sam nodded, more or less to himself. This little girl was no dummy.

"I can't believe the school didn't conduct an investigation."

"The teachers and principal don't know anything about. And wouldn't rock the boat if they did."

He put his hand over hers, but she pulled away.

"You didn't try reporting it to the school authorities?"

"Wouldn't do any good. Rich folks run the school board. Their kids run them. And they do as they please." She wrapped her arms around herself and shivered. "Besides, Papa would have beat me good, if I had."

Sam thought about that statement for a moment and sighed. "How old are you, Sarah?"

She didn't answer and looked like she was about to bolt. He took her gently by the arm. "Little lady, I want to help you, but you've got to tell me how old you are."

"I'll be seventeen in . . . uh, four months. I'm not lying, I swear."

Perhaps she could be sixteen, now that he'd had a good look at her. She was small and frail, but her eyes reflected countless ages of sorrow.

Sam stood silent for a while. Finally, he cleared his throat and blurted out what he was thinking. "Sarah, your father . . . what kind of a man would punish his daughter for being raped and tell her she'd shamed the family? I just can't get my brain wrapped around that."

"Mister—the kind who's poor, has always been poor, and is trying to be somebody. When I was little, he used to say I was real pretty and I'd marry somebody rich and move him and Mama up to the right side of the tracks." She felt of her chopped off hair and sighed. "Then he got religion and decided being pretty was of the devil.

"Papa said now I'll get real popular and have lots of suitors. But none that want to marry me. Only ones who want *you know what* from me. Because I'm used goods. Even God can't look on me now."

Sam grabbed his gut. He hoped she couldn't see the disgust in his eyes. He turned his head for a moment, thinking for sure he was about to lose the fried chicken he'd just eaten. "Please don't believe that lie, Sarah. God loves you. Always has, always will."

"Don't know about that, mister. Sure doesn't seem like it." Sarah's shoulders drooped, and she sighed a bone-deep sigh. "I'm so tired. Do you have a bed in your rig?"

"It's full of stuff, Sarah, but you can sleep on the seat. By the way, my name's Sam. You can call me Uncle Sam, if you like. That's what my nieces and nephews call me. And I have a bunch of them."

He walked over to the passenger door and bid her climb in. Taking her bag from her, he closed the door behind her and walked to the front of the rig and around to the driver's side. Climbing in, he tossed her bag behind the seat and turned to her. "What made you choose *my* rig to wait at?"

"Because it was so clean. I love things that are clean and white. It looked so pure next to the others. Like an angel truck."

A chill ran down Sam's spine. Tonight was the first time he'd *ever* had his rig washed on the way home. It usually arrived home filthy dirty. Had his brainy idea about saving time in the morning actually been a word from God? He was well aware that with God, there are no coincidences.

"Sarah, I know it's asking a lot, but do you think there's any chance you could go home and do your parents' bidding. Stay there where you have a roof over your head and food to eat. And leave in a year or so when you'd be better equipped to take care of yourself?"

"Not a chance, mist-Uncle Sam." She turned her head away from him. And Sam had to strain to hear her next words.

"I'm going to have a baby."

Chapter 5

Sarah watched Sam as he searched for the door and window locks on his armrest in the near dark of the cab. And she jumped in spite of herself, when the door locks clicked. *Now the passenger side can only be opened from the driver's side.*

"You don't think maybe a baby in the house would soften them up a bit?" Sam asked as he began fiddling with the gear shift.

"Maybe it would if I got to keep it. But how much worse would it be for me to have a baby—if they're ashamed of me for getting raped? Besides, I don't have any doubt they'd make me have an abortion. And I just can't take a chance on that."

He didn't reply. He just looked at her. In the dim light of the dash, his eyes were dark and unreadable. What was he thinking behind that furrowed brow?

This huge stranger she'd chosen was pulling out onto the highway. Picking up speed. And she was going wherever he was going. *No backing out now. And no point in thinking about how big and mean looking he is. As Papa always said, I've made my bed. Now I gotta lie in it.*

Sarah kicked her shoes off and pulled her feet up under her as Sam maneuvered the huge rig, merging into the oncoming traffic.

The matter seemed to be settled. She'd found a refuge. And he'd accepted responsibility for her safety. At least on a temporary basis. Until he could figure out what God wanted him to do with her. It was obvious He had assigned him the job. And in spite of his own family's financial distress, God would provide.

Sam tried not to give in to the anger he felt for her piece-of-dreck father.

They hadn't gone ten miles before he could hear Sarah's soft breathing. She was curled against the door, seatbelt straining, but sound asleep. Sam double-checked her door lock. Then felt directly behind his seat until he came up with the soft comforter Vivi had insisted he take with him. He lovingly tossed it across this woman/child, next to him to cover her shoulders and her legs. He heard her breath a soft, contented sigh.

She hadn't even asked where he was headed.

In a couple of hours, he'd be home. Not exactly the home he'd always dreamed of. No wife and no children of his own. But he'd willingly taken in his sister, Vivian, and her six children.

Vivi had never worked outside the home, and they had no insurance when her husband was killed in a farm accident. So she and the kids were in really bad straits. Add to that the grief of losing a husband and father, they needed immediate help. It worked out well, though. Vivi was an excellent housekeeper and mother. And he adored the kids like they were his own. They were a happy—if unusual—family. Now he was adding another member. Hopefully Vivi could stretch the house *and* the budget to accommodate one more child.

Following State Highway 15, he headed east. There were still a few lights on in each of the little towns as he crept through them in the dark of the night.

His eyelids were getting heavy by the time he reached the turnoff to his house. Sarah was still sleeping soundly. Probably the first good sleep she'd had in weeks. When he hit the rough dirt road, she was jostled awake. Her words were slurred. "Where are we?"

"Almost there."

"Almost where?"

"That's for me to know and you to find out," he said in jest. It was an expression his mother had always used, and it was meant to be amusing.

Chapter 6

There'd never been any good-natured joshing around in her family. So Sarah had never heard the expression before. To her, it sounded creepy.

She laid her head back down but didn't close her eyes. Her heart started beating faster. They'd turned off the main highway and there was nothing—no houses, no lights, no fences—in sight. Only the headlight beams of the monster truck she was *locked* in, piercing the night and fading into the emptiness ahead. They rounded a curve. Then passed one lone scrubby looking tree. The road was getting rougher and narrower. It reminded her of her own neighborhood. Sam looked like he was lost in thought. He stared straight ahead, his hard-featured face dark and menacing in the sickly blue light of the dash.

For him to know and me to find out?

Sarah made out a faded sign that read PLEASANT ACRES. Ahead, among shoulder-high weeds, at what appeared to be the end of the road, a run-down, abandoned shack with a sway-back roof came into view. *Oh, please, no. Let this be a bad dream.*

Had she made a terrible mistake trusting this man who wanted her to call him Uncle Sam? Had she fallen for the oldest trick in the world?

Why had she smiled at him when he warned her about the danger of hitching a ride at a truck stop? She wasn't sure, except maybe because it felt good to have someone care about what might happen to her. Even if he was a stranger. Big and mean-looking and all covered with tattoos. Or maybe he had just enough goodness in him to forewarn her of what was going to happen if she climbed into that cab and hit the road with *him*. When she didn't take his hint and run, he began to make his own plans for her. After all, she was "used goods."

Sam slowed to a stop in front of the shack and killed the engine.

"Here we are." He smiled across the seat at Sarah.

Opening his door, he grabbed his flashlight and slid out to make room for her to slide past him. "Sarah, get out on this side. I'll help you down and light the way."

Seeing her only chance of escape, Sarah scooted past him, fairly flew off the seat, and hit the road running.

"Sarah. Wait. What's gotten into you?" Sam took off after her. She was headed for the wilderness. If she made it that far, he might never find her in the thick brush.

She was fast for her size. But she was no match for Sam's long legs. He caught up with her just as she approached the edge of the thicket and grabbed her around the waist. "Sarah, Sarah. Be still. You can't run off into the wilderness. Wild animals abound around here."

She kicked and screamed. "I'd rather be ripped apart by wolves than go in that shack with you." She tried to rake her nails down his face, but he caught her hand.

"Let me go."

He had no choice but to clamp both of her hands in one of his gargantuan fists. With the other arm, he swung her over his shoulder. She wailed like a trapped animal.

"We're not going into any shack, child. Look over there."

A bright porch light snapped on across the dirt road from the run-down shack. A woman's voice rose over Sarah's screams. "What is all the racket?"

Sarah's eyes focused against the brightness to see a pleasingly plump and rather attractive, middle-aged lady standing on the covered porch of a small, neat, white house. Her screams abated, and she went limp. Why struggle against this giant? They will do whatever it is they want to do with her. Tears filled her eyes. As always, she had no control over her fate.

The motherly looking lady hurried toward Sam and Sarah. "Sam Blake, what in God's name are you doing to that child? Put her down. I said put her down . . . now!"

"No can do, sis. She's trying to run away. She's frightened and homeless. But I don't know what brought *this* on. We were getting along fine, and suddenly she's as wild as a feral cat. Just open the door and lock it behind us. I'll put her down when we get inside."

Vivi walked with a slight limp. But she hurried to do as Sam had asked. Sam carefully threaded his way through the door so as to not clunk Sarah's head on the door frame. He strode across the living room and set her down on the couch as gently as possible, while his sister closed and locked the door behind him. Then Vivi handed her brother the key as she slipped past him and plopped down on the couch. She put her arms around the quaking young girl. Sarah buried her face in Vivi's shoulder and collapsed into pitiful sobs.

Sam was pacing the floor. Stopping abruptly, he turned to Vivi. "I hate to ask you to do this, sis . . . but please wake the kids and have them come in here to meet Sarah. We've got to convince her she's safe here. Surely a passel of happy, friendly kids can do that."

Vivi hesitated. "You go wake them, Sam. You can bring them up to speed. I don't want to let her go right now. She's clinging to me like a drowning kitten."

When Sam stepped down the hallway, Vivi stroked Sarah's unsightly, lopped-off hair. "There, there, little one.

No one in this house will ever harm you. We'll do nothing but love you. Please give us the chance." Sarah's frail body was pressed tightly against Vivi's generous bosom. Her breathing slowed, and she seemed to be soaking up the love she was being offered.

A few minutes later, six sleepy-eyed kids came to her, one at a time, to welcome her to their home. When four-year-old Penelope asked her if she'd like to share her bed, Sarah smiled broadly—and revealed the beautiful dimple in her right cheek—for the first time since that fateful night when she was attacked.

Penelope's bright eyes implored her. "I don't take up much room."

"She's right about that," Vivi offered. "Her bed is against the wall, and every night she hugs the wall. She says it's her most comfortable position. But you can sleep in my bed tonight if you'd rather."

If they only knew. Anything would be better than the palette on the floor Sarah had slept on most of her life.

Speaking her first words since they'd pulled out of the truck stop parking lot, Sarah reached out to Penelope. "I'd love to sleep with Penelope, if she really wants me to." Penelope jumped into her arms, knocking the breath out of poor Vivi.

It was one in the morning before everyone settled down. Sarah in the girl's room with Penelope and Vivi's other two daughters. The boys snuggled in their beds down the hall. Vivi in her own room, and Sam on the floor directly in front of the girls' bedroom door. His bedroom would remain vacant tonight because he was taking no chances on Sarah running away again. God had assigned him the job of sheltering a young lady in need. And Sam never shirked a responsibility.

The next morning

The house was bright and immaculate. Nothing like the shack Papa had started years ago and never quite finished. She could see no cobwebs—no dust bunnies. No broken window panes with paper stuffed in opening.

Vivi's children were in their rooms getting ready for school. Sarah ventured into the living room with Sam and Vivi, wearing borrowed cuddly pajamas and fuzzy house slippers.

"I like your house," Sarah said quietly.

"Dad built this house. Vivi and I were raised here. Would you believe we had neighbors on all sides? Neat lawns and modest but well-kept homes. When our neighbors started moving to Amarillo, where the money was, Dad wanted to buy their land but couldn't afford it. No one has ever made a claim on any of it. Probably most of the folks are gone by now. So it's all grown over with scrub bushes and weeds." He reached over and pulled Vivi to his side. "But between Sis and the kids, I can be proud of our little homestead. And one of these days, I'm going to get a tractor and clean up the whole neighborhood. It can never be legally ours . . . but we might as well keep it neat."

Sam continued, "Vivi got married right out of high school, and I moved away for a while. But when Dad got sick, I came home to help keep things running smoothly. Our folks never got well enough to live alone again, so I just stayed. Vivi had five kids and one on the way when her husband was killed in a farm accident. Mom and Dad had already gone to be with the Lord by then, so she and the kids moved in here with me. We've been one big happy family ever since."

He motioned to Sarah and Vivi to move to the kitchen. "I had to add a couple of rooms to accommodate everyone, and I'm not the carpenter Dad was. But it's still hanging together and Vivi does a great job of keeping it looking good. So I guess you'd say we are really blessed."

"Oh yes," Sarah cooed. "I just love it."

Sam looked her beaming face. His house was so modest. She must have been raised with nearly nothing to be so impressed.

"So, Sarah . . ." Vivi chimed in. "We have four bedrooms. The three girls share a bedroom, as you know. The three boys share one, and Sam and I each have our own. And we'll figure out some way to give you a private place to sleep as well."

"It really is nice. But my being here would mess everything up," Sarah stammered. "I won't be staying."

Vivi put her hand over Sarah's. "Please stay for a while, at least. This world is no place for a young one like yourself to be alone. Let us help you. Let us be your family."

Sarah's lower lip quivered. "I've never . . . no one has ever . . . I mean . . ."

"Well, you do now," Sam said with finality.

Her second night there Sarah had a bath in an old-fashioned claw-foot tub before bed. And put on a band new pair of soft pajamas Vivi had laid out for her. She'd never owned a pair of pajamas nor slept in such a comfortable bed nor such a clean house. She buried her nose in her pillow and breathed deep. It even *smelled* clean.

Sarah climbed carefully out of bed to not wake Penelope or the other two children, and walked to the bedroom door.

At home, she locked her door every night. It was only a thumb bolt, but it kept Papa out. She never knew when he was going to lose his temper. And she was usually the scapegoat.

But this bedroom door had no lock. Sam's nieces had no reason to be afraid of him and no need for a lock on their door. *Too bad this is only a dream. Ms. Vivi has three girls to raise. And she seems like a very proper lady. When she finds out what kind of girl I am, my stay here will be over.*

Chapter 7

Sarah was being as still as she could, sitting on a high stool. Vivi's scissors clicked in syncopated rhythm as she deftly trimmed and evened out the mess Papa had made of Sarah's naturally curly tresses. Vivi was talented with a scissors, and you could hardly tell some spots were a little too short. "You've been here almost a week, Sarah. And we've not talked about your situation yet. When is your baby due, sweetheart?"

Sarah cast her eyes Vivi's direction without moving her head. "I was hoping Uncle Sam wouldn't tell you until I got a chance to know you better. Maybe make you like me more."

"Sam didn't tell me. Do you really think after having six of my own I can't recognize the signs?" She smiled and put her hand on Sarah's knee. "You don't have to *make me* like you, darling. That was instantaneous." Vivi wrung her hands. "I do wish you'd tell me the whole story of how you happen to be *here*, instead of being under your parents' protection and guidance."

"My parents don't know . . . or care. They're mad at me for getting myself raped. I'm sure if they knew, they'd make me get an abortion." Her voice cracked. "And I won't do that."

Vivi put down her scissors and pulled her close. "Go no further, little one. That's all I need to know. Because I know Sam, I knew you were special. Now I know you're a *very* special person, loved by God, and sent our way to be loved on this side of heaven. With His help, we'll come through this okay—together."

Vivi left the room momentarily and returned with a box of tissue. She pulled one out for herself and held the box out to Sarah. "We may need a lot of these over the next few months. Small price to pay for the life of a precious child."

Sarah took the tissues, then turned her gaze to the floor. "Aunt Vivi, why did Uncle Sam pick me up? Why didn't he leave that responsibility to someone else? It's obvious he has an awful lot of responsibility already."

"He was afraid, Sarah."

"Afraid? Of what?"

"Afraid you'd climb in the seat of some semi and never be seen alive again."

Sarah found this puzzling and illogical. "He didn't know me, and he wouldn't have known if that *did* happen, so what difference does it make?"

"Just the thought that it might have happened would have never given him a moment's peace for the rest of his life. From the moment he saw you as a vulnerable child—and that's how he sees you, you became his responsibility. Our only job now is to relax and see how God plays this out." Vivi took the cloth from Sarah's shoulders, brushed little hairs from her back, and ran a comb through her hair. She stepped back to admire her handiwork. "You have beautiful hair, Sarah."

Sarah blushed and murmured a thank you.

Vivi held out her hand. "Hop down. Gotta sweep up, then it's time to take the kids to school. Wanna ride along?"

On the ride back from the school, Sarah began sharing with Vivi some of the lurid details of her night of horror.

THE TRINITY QUILTS

It brought on a new torrent of tears. Vivi started looking around for a place to stop. She pulled into a roadside park and turned off the engine. Turning her whole body in the seat to be fully facing Sarah, she put her hand on the youngster's shoulder. "You're okay now, darling. Sam and I will be here for you for as long as you need us . . . and beyond. You're a part of *our* family now." She pulled the beautiful woman/child close to her.

After a few moments of tender embrace, they parted and Vivi spoke up, "You never did tell me when the baby's due." Before Sarah could answer, Vivi blurted out, "Oh my, have you seen a doctor yet, darlin'?"

Sarah turned her head and looked out her window. "Couldn't do that in our small town, Aunt Vivi. Word would get around before I got out of the doctor's office. Besides I don't have any money. I found a home pregnancy test in Mama's bureau. She and Papa sure didn't want any more kids. They were always saying they shouldn't have had me." Sarah's lower lip quivered. "But Mama had a scare last year, and she still had the test stuff lying around."

"Well, soon as we get to the house, I'm going to make you an appointment with a doctor in Amarillo. It's not safe to go too long without some confirmation and advice from a doctor."

Sarah swung her head around to look at her. "No, please. I don't want to go to a doctor. He might find something wrong with me."

"That's what doctors are for, sweetie. Are you worried you have something wrong?"

"Well, I was never checked out after . . . you know. What if *he* had something?"

"It's not likely. Especially if he *is* a high school boy from a well-to-do family like you believe. But it would be wise to be sure. You don't want any harm to come to the baby."

They pulled back onto the road. Vivi started several times to ask something but always ended in silence.

"What is it, Aunt Vivi?"

"I don't want to put any pressure on you, sweetie . . . but have you given any thought to what you're going to do after the baby comes? You know you're welcome to stay with us as long as you want, and I hope you will. But everyone needs to have a plan. A goal. Back to school, maybe? For your diploma. I can help out with the baby. In fact, I'd love that. I haven't held an infant in so long. Too long."

"No. No more school for me. And . . . and . . . Aunt Vivi"—Sarah gave her head a slow, sad shake—"I'm not . . . going to keep the baby."

"I'm sorry. I'd just assumed. You say you're vehemently opposed to abortion . . . I just thought . . ."

"I am. I hate abortions. Some of the teachers say it's a woman's choice what she wants to do with her body. It's like the baby doesn't count for anything. I love my baby. Oh, I love it so much, but . . . I . . . oh, I don't know how to say it. I don't want you to think I'm . . ."

"Just say it, darling. I love you no matter what."

"Well, I used to want to know who it was . . . I was a virgin until he . . . and I really wanted to be a virgin when I married. He took that from me. And from my husband, if I ever *do* marry."

"Oh, you'll fall in love and marry one day, dear one. God has the right fellow out there for you. I'm sure of that. Just allow Him to work in your life."

Well, I'm not so sure about *that*. God doesn't seem to like me much. But anyway, I wanted to have my attacker arrested. See him punished—really punished bad—for what he did." She dropped her gaze to her tummy and laid one hand over it. "That was before I found out I was pregnant . . ." Sarah fell silent for a long moment.

"Go on." Vivi had to pull off the road again to take both of Sarah's hands in hers.

"But now I just want my baby to have a good life. He or she should never have to know it came to be in such a horrible way. I want it to think it was a product of love." She pulled a tissue from Vivi's tissue box. "If I try real hard and pretend, sometimes I can even convince myself my baby is a product of true love. Aunt Vivi, I can't even have that dream if I find out who the father is."

"Well, you have a good point . . ."

A red light was flashing in the rearview mirror.

⁂

Vivi watched in her side mirror as a policeman slowly get out of his patrol car and walked toward her vehicle. Turning her head to look out the window at him, she recognized him as an old friend on the force.

"Officer Statton, did I do something wrong?"

"Hey, pretty lady." He put his hand on the window frame and smiled. "No, you haven't done anything wrong. I don't think *you* could ever do anything wrong. But I've seen you pull off the road a couple of times, and I thought I'd better see if everything was okay."

He fleetingly glanced Sarah's way, seemingly much more interested in flirting with Vivi.

"Oh, we're fine, Officer. But thank you so much for your concern."

"Anytime. Just be careful out there." He patted the window frame, turned on his heel, and picking up the pace, he jogged back to his patrol car. Something was coming over the radio.

Vivi waited for him to pull out, sirens blaring, before she returned her gaze to Sarah. "Go on, sweetie."

Sarah cleared her throat. "Well, what if I keep my baby and it grows up to look just like it's father and *that's* how I find out the horrible truth? Would I ever be able to look at my own child without reliving the horror of that night? Would I be able to give it the kind of joyful love it deserves?"

"Those are tough questions, honey. I don't know how to answer them."

"Well, Aunt Vivi, I haven't thought of much else since I found out I was pregnant. And I know the answer. I have to look for a couple who wants a child very badly. And would take very good care of it. A family that would see to it their child had every advantage, and education, and lots and lots of love." She wiped her eyes on another tissue, sat up straight, and looked past Vivi—toward the road. Determination steeled her gaze. "And I have less than seven months to find them."

Chapter 8

One month later

Sarah was lying quiet as a mouse in the Murphy bed Uncle Sam had built for her in the laundry room. It wasn't much, but it gave her more privacy at night than she had in the girls bedroom. Privacy, running water, and easy access to the bathroom right across the hall. It was much nicer than her bedroom in the shack Papa had put up. Come morning, she'd lift the foot of the bed up and make the whole thing disappear into the wall. Voila! It's the family laundry room again.

She heard the big rig pull in and saw the lights flash across the living room wall through the wee crack she'd left in the door of her tiny retreat. And heard the big whoosh sound the huge white vehicle always made when Uncle Sam released the brake.

His door key sounded in the lock, and the front door creaked open. He was obviously trying to not awaken anyone. But Sarah knew his sister had been sitting in the dark in the living room waiting for him for over an hour. Vivi'd seemed preoccupied all day, and Sarah was worried she'd done something to upset her.

Vivi rose to meet Sam at the door with her index finger to her lips. Then took him by the hand and led him into the kitchen. She was short and plumb, and he was so big and lanky. It was hard to imagine they were brother and sister. Sarah wished she'd had a brother. That night probably wouldn't have happened if she had. Her big brother would have protected her.

She got up and tiptoed to the wall vent, through which sounds from the kitchen were easily heard. Trembling, for fear of what she was about to hear, she laid down on the floor with her ear to the vent.

○○○

Vivi laid her hand over Sam's. Her voice was low and a little hoarse, like she'd been crying—a lot.

"Sam, I hate to trouble you with this. But the money is just not stretching far enough, and I don't know what to do. You know the insurance company refused to cover Sarah's doctor's appointments, let alone the vitamins she takes . . . and really needs. The poor child was borderline malnourished."

She stood up and went to the sink to put on a pot of coffee.

"That alone we could probably handle." She looked over her shoulder at her brother. "But now Dr. Jackson wants Sandra to start taking a new medication that's not covered either. And every class in school is starting a new program that requires the kids to buy supplies. Mrs. Edmiston said it would 'only cost six dollars per month per child.' *Only!* With six kids that comes to thirty-six dollars a month. Thirty-six dollars we don't have."

Sam looked troubled. "Do they *have* to participate?"

Vivi lit the burner under the pot and turned to him. "Well, no, but it will put them at a big disadvantage if they don't."

"Do we have anything left in savings?"

"Enough to last maybe another two months, if you get a good job or two." She sat down, put her elbows on the table, and rested her head in her hands. "Here's what I'm thinking. I need to get a job. Sandra's old enough to watch the other five kids after school. And I'm sure Sarah would pitch in any way she could."

Sam heaved a sigh. "No, I don't want you working. You're just not in good enough health to work a full-time job and run a household, too. And part-time wouldn't pay enough to cover your truck expenses." He chewed on his lower lip and looked down at the tabletop. "I'm sorry I haven't been able to do better for you and the kids, sis."

Aggravated at himself, he slapped the edge of the table, rose quickly, and walked to the cabinets to take down a couple of cups.

Vivi put her forefinger to her lips. "Don't wake the kids, Sam."

"Sorry." Turning around, he leaned against the countertop, his face a portrait of discouragement. He spoke softly. "I have a better idea. I'll sell the rig and get a regular job. That way I'll be at home every night."

"I can't let you sell your rig. It's your pride and joy."

"Aah, it's just an old piece of junk I've become abnormally attached to, sis. We both know it won't bring a lot of money. But it could help to put us on top of the situation."

"You're right. It wouldn't bring anywhere near what it's worth. Sam, you've kept that old thing in tip-top shape. I'd put it up against anything on the road. And I won't let you sell it." She put her hand over his. "And don't apologize. You've given us a great life. We wouldn't trade it for anything in the world. The kids love you like a dad."

"Oh, sis, I don't know. I'm so tired right now I can't think straight. Let's just have a cup of coffee. Both of us can pray about it and sleep on it. In the morning after a good night's sleep, I've no doubt God will give us the answer."

Sarah crept back into bed.

Why has it never occurred to me that I'm a financial burden on the only people in the world who care about me? I can't let Uncle Sam sell his rig. It means too much to him. He's always saying someday he can make a really good living with it. When that big break comes.

She tossed and turned, but sleep wouldn't come.

I don't think they'd let me take a job. Besides, what do I know how to do? And how would I get to work without a car. I could use Aunt Vivi's pickup, but then she'd be stuck here with six kids and no vehicle. Uncle Sam wouldn't allow that.

The clock in the hall struck 2:00 a.m.

They were doing okay until I came along. It's not fair. They try to do good, and what does it get them? They're always praying to God, but I don't think He's listening. If He's even there at all.

The constant tick-tock of the clock seemed to get louder and louder.

I've got to do something to help them. But all I am is a burden.

The clock struck 3:00 a.m.

Sarah slipped out of bed, straightened the covers, and lifted the bed up into the wall. All as silently as the moon and stars that shined in the window. She wiggled out of her pretty pajamas and put them in the soiled laundry basket. Then dug through her folded clean clothes stored in another laundry basket—there was no room for a chest of drawers. She picked out the dress she had on the night Sam picked her up. Most of the rest would fit the other girls in time. And, after all, Uncle Sam had bought them. She couldn't take them.

At 3:10 a.m., Sarah took a sheet of paper down from the kitchen shelf. By the glow of the single nightlight over the sink, she wrote these words:

THE TRINITY QUILTS

Dear Aunt Vivi,

I love all of you more than I can say, but the time has come for me to find that family I spoke of. My baby's family. Please don't try to find me. This is something I must do. Give my love to Uncle Sam, Sandra, Misty, Penelope, Billy, Mark, and Butch. I will write you when I can.

Love, Sarah

She laid the note in the middle of the kitchen table and placed the salt shaker on top of it.

Three minutes later, Sarah was standing on the front porch, her tattered old bag in one hand, her shoes in the other, and her ragged coat over her shoulders. They'd never let her spend any of her money, although she offered it. So she still had a grant total of nineteen dollars and fifty-six cents stuffed in a coat pocket. Still safety pinned shut.

She'd managed to get out the front door without waking anyone. Tears stung her eyes. She blotted them with one of Aunt Vivi's always-handy tissues and sat down on the front step to put on her shoes.

The only things she took with her she hadn't had when she arrived were her vitamins and a tiny cross pendant Vivi had given her. Vivi would want her to take the vitamins, and she'd be hurt if she left the pendant behind.

Then she bravely took the first step *away* from the only happiness she'd ever known.

Chapter 9

Upscale suburbs in Dallas, Texas

"Please don't cry, Beth. We'll try again. I'm just so sure God is going to bless us with a baby. Remember my dream?"

Beth looked up at her handsome husband of ten years and slowly shook her head. "I don't want to try again, Rob. I'm tired. Three miscarriages in three years. Your dream was just that . . . a dream. Let's just get on with our lives and not live in this fantasy world anymore, where we have a houseful of kids." She laid back down on the pillow and turned her head away from him. "You know I'd be willing to settle for only one child. But it just isn't going to happen."

Rob glanced at his Rolex. He was running late, but Beth needed him this morning. "I'm going to call the office and cancel my appointments for today."

She turned back to face him and attempted to smile. "Oh, no, you're not, Rob. Your patients depend on you. You get yourself out of here. I'll be okay."

"Darling, I can't leave you alone feeling like you do."

"Don't worry about me. I'm hurting. But I know you are too. And as much as I'd love to be resting in God's arms right now, I would never take my own life. Of all people, you should know *that*. Now go."

Rob leaned down and brushed her plenteous auburn hair from her damp forehead. Kissing her before he straightened up, he had a fleeting moment of doubt. Immediately he asked God to forgive him for being weak in the faith. But she was so lovely and so good and so full of love for the Lord. It was hard to fathom why He wasn't blessing her with the children she desperately longed to have.

Rob often felt *he* was letting her down. He was a pediatrician, for goodness' sake. She surely expected him to have an answer to her inability to carry a baby to full term. But her body defied any knowledge he possessed—and that of his peers. Everything would be rocking along just fine, and suddenly her body seemed to simply reject the fetus.

He just had to believe there was at least one baby in their future. He'd once hoped for a couple of sons—dreaming one of them would follow his footsteps in the medical field. Beth had been hoping for a daughter or two. She'd been an only child who'd always dreamed of having a sister.

God had greatly blessed them financially and spiritually. Theirs was truly a marriage made in heaven. Their unanswered prayers for a child to call their own was the only fly in the ointment. And Rob was determined to find a solution.

Today I will begin the search for an unwed mother-to-be. When I find that person, then and only then, I'll broach the subject with Beth. I can't build up her hopes, only to let them be dashed again.

In his mind's eye, he could picture her right now, laying on her side, as she always did, gazing out the big window, and down at the path that led from the den to her garden—a path now bereft of her loving care.

She used to sit on the garden bench with a cup of tea, admiring her hard work and spending time with the Lord. But she hadn't felt like tending her garden in a long while.

Dear Father, please bless us with a child. Help me, God, to find an unwanted baby we can love and nurture, and teach Your ways.

～⚭～

Less than a quarter of a mile from Sam and Vivi's house, Sarah's steps slowed as though her resolve may be weakening. Then she broke into a run. Overhead, two dark shadows followed her down the road toward the highway. "Lookie, she's making a run for it. First stroke of luck we've had since Mr. Goody Two Shoes picked her up at the truck stop."

"Don't you mean Mr. Ugly Two Shoes?" His companion chortled. "By the looks of him, that guy really should be one of *us*."

The demon of fear grunted in agreement and drew a long breath. He dove down and blew it slowly in Sarah's face. His companion snapped a twig simultaneously, and Sarah whirled around to look behind her. Unheard by her, the demons both emitted a horrendous shriek of laughter.

"She's a little skittish, isn't she?"

One after the other in rapid succession, the two demons dove at her, blowing their rancid breath in her face. Taking turns, they whispered in her ear that she was promiscuous, worthless, used, and damaged. And no one would *ever* want her—or her child of sin.

She stumbled in a deep rut in road and fell forward. Picking herself up from the dirt, she searched the sky—her frightened eyes darting this way and that. She clamped her hands over her ears, trying desperately to blot out the voices.

"Let's do it again. She'll be a basket case before she gets to the main road. Probably run out in front of a vehicle . . .

and we can take her home with us tonight. Think of the reward we'd get for *that*."

The demon of fear dove at her face and fanned his leathery wings furiously. Sarah's hair billowed in the odious breeze. She fell to the ground, whimpering. Down on her knees in the dirt, she remembered something Sam had done one evening when, for some reason, Vivi had become very nervous and frightened.

"I'm not going to let them make you fearful, sis." Sam had announced. "We've put your problems in God's hands, and He'll see us through." Then he waved his fist in the air and shouted, "In the name of *Jesus*, be gone."

Vivi had immediately calmed down, and smiling at her brother, she whispered, "Thank You, Jesus." And she walked to the kitchen to begin supper as though nothing had happened.

Sarah lifted herself to a standing position. She stretched her slim body as tall as she was capable of doing and yelled into the darkness. "Leave me alone. In the name of *Jesus*, be gone!"

Totally caught by surprise, both demons were hit in the gut by a force like that of a speeding freight train and sent hurdling into the distance, screeching and bellowing. Sarah listened. She heard the sounds of night birds, and an occasional car passing on the highway ahead. But the gruesome voices were gone. Continuing down the road in perfect peace, she marveled at the near-euphoric feeling that enveloped her at the mention of His name.

Could Uncle Sam be right? Maybe there is a man named Jesus and maybe He really does watch over me.

She loved to hear Sam talk about the Lord because of the tender look that filled his eyes and swept over his entire being. Tender look—Uncle Sam. An oxymoron if there ever was one. He was a man who looked really tough and mean yet was so gentle. And something about the mention of the Lord changed his countenance from thuggish to saintly in the blink of an eye.

However, as much as she loved Uncle Sam, she still couldn't understand his devotion to a God who seemed to have forgotten him, at least where finances were concerned. But nonetheless she kept repeating Jesus's name—to be on the safe side—until she saw headlights crossing in front of her. She was almost to the highway.

The traffic on Highway 15 was very light at 4:30 a.m. She quickly ran across the road to walk east with the oncoming traffic. But when Sarah saw lights approaching, she dropped down low, almost in the ditch, so she wouldn't be seen. Her scolding from Uncle Sam regarding hitchhiking was still fresh in her mind after all this time.

When the sun came up, she could no longer hide from the increasing traffic, and she had to make a decision. About every third driver stopped to ask if she needed help. Even though she insisted she was fine, some of them were just as insistent she accept help. Then a cop car pulled off the road in front of her.

The officer got out of his vehicle and walked back to meet her.

Sarah froze. It was Aunt Vivi's friend, and admirer, on the force—Officer Statton.

"I hear you're having a problem, little lady."

"No problem, Officer. I just can't convince people I don't want any help. Did someone complain?"

"No, no complaints. Just concern. Where are you headed?"

"To the next town."

"And what town might that be?"

"I'm sorry, I don't know the name of it. But I don't think it's very far." Sarah clutched her tattered old bag tight and began fidgeting with the hem of her thin coat.

"You seem a little nervous, young'un. Runaway, maybe?" He looked closely at her. "Wait a minute, I know you from somewhere, don't I?"

Sarah kept her eyes on the ground. "I don't think so, sir."

"Oh, yeah. Indeed, I do. But where? Have you been brought in to the station in the last couple of weeks?"

She shook her head and looked up at him. Trying to figure out what her next move should be.

"Stay right where you are . . . no, on second thought, walk over to the squad car with me. I want to see if you've been reported missing."

Sarah lagged behind. She knew her folks wouldn't have reported her. But Uncle Sam may have, if they're awake and have found her note. Nibbling on her nails, she worried that at any moment Officer Statton may remember where he'd seen her before.

"Come on, kid." The officer opened the squad car door for her to get in. Reluctantly, she obeyed. He slammed the door and stayed outside the car with his back to her, talking on his radio and turning from time to time to look at her.

Finally, he opened the door and looked at her a long time before speaking.

"Well . . . no Amber alerts on the likes of you, but I think it would be prudent for me to take you back to town. It's early. Maybe you haven't been missed yet." He stuffed his husky body behind the wheel and started the engine. "We can sit around a while and see if anything comes in on you."

"Please, Officer. I don't want to go back there. I'm not doing anything wrong."

"I didn't say you were, young lady . . . but with all the evil going on in this world, we just can't be too careful now, can we? Why I remember a time when—"

He was interrupted by an urgent call on his radio.

"Shooting underway at Saddler's Bar in Pierceville. Officer down. All units respond."

"Six in the morning and the drunks are still at it. Out, child, I'll tend to you later. Stay put. You hear me? I *mean* it now. Get out of sight and stay put."

He pulled over and stopped. Sarah jumped from the vehicle. He gunned the engine, throwing dirt behind him, and made a U-turn in the middle of the highway. Then sped west on Highway 15, sirens screaming.

She sat down on the side of the road, her heart beating like a rock band drummer.

That was close. I can't take a chance that he'll come back and find me. Sooner or later he'll remember where he's seen me. And it could be even worse if he doesn't *remember. They could trace me back to Mama and Papa. I'd rather take my chances hitchhiking.*

She began walking backward so she could see the traffic headed her way. The first car that approached stopped.

"Where you headed?" A bearded man in his late thirties or early forties, wearing a muscle shirt with underarm hair poking out both sides, leaned across the front seat and beckoned her to the window.

"Anywhere east." Sarah's voice was trembling, but what choice did she have?

He grinned. "Hop in."

Chapter 10

Vivi's hands were shaking. "Sam, come quick. Hurry."
Sam dropped the boot he was getting ready to put on and ran sock-footed to the kitchen. When he got to there and saw see her sitting at the table, he was slightly miffed. "What in heaven's name is the hurry, sis? I thought you'd hurt yourself."

"She's gone."

"Who? What are you talking about?"

Vivi held out the piece of paper with Sarah's flowing handwriting on it. Sam grabbed it and began reading.

"Oh, dear Jesus. What would make her do a thing like that?" He plopped down in the chair next to Vivi. "Did you two have a falling out or something?"

"No. No. We got along great. I love that girl so much. Only thing I can think is she overheard us last night. And decided she was a burden."

"I thought she was in bed. We weren't talking very loud."

"We've never used the laundry room for a bedroom before. Maybe sound travels from here to there."

Sam bolted to the laundry room. The bed was raised, and everything was in place. He was across the hall from the bathroom. Beyond that a couple of walls separated him from the kitchen. His eyes scanned the room for a clue. And there it was. The vent.

He shouted to his sister. "Vivi, sit at the table and talk to yourself. I think I know what happened." He stretched out on the floor and put his ear to the vent.

Vivi began reciting the Lord's Prayer. "Our Father who art in heaven. Hallowed be Thy Name . . ."

Sam called back. "Thy kingdom come, Thy will be done . . . I can hear you through the vent. Oh, Vivi, what are we going to do? Her heart must be broken." He strode back to the kitchen.

Vivi was up and pacing. "First thing we have to do is call the police."

"Sis, she specifically asked us not to look for her. She's having a baby . . . and she wants to find a family to adopt it. Where could she find a family like that around here?"

Vivi put her hand on his shoulder. "Right here. In this house. I'd take that baby in a heartbeat. But I know that's not what she wants. She's been poor all her life and she doesn't want that for her child. And I can't blame her." She resumed pacing. "But out there all by herself, there are so many terrible things that could happen to her. We've got to notify the police, Sam. We've got to find her . . . and then *help* her find the family she's looking for."

"I guess you're right. Although she did promise me she wouldn't hitchhike anymore. Which begs the question, how is she going to get anywhere?"

"Exactly."

"Last stop. All out for Shattuck, Oklahoma."

Sarah's ride with the man in the muscle shirt was about to come to an end.

She bolted from her sleeping position. Interrupted from a horrible nightmare just in time. "*Where*, Oklahoma?"

"Shattuck, my sleepy damsel. I'm going south a ways further. If you want to continue east, we must part ways." He grinned his very silly bearded grin.

In spite of his looks, Chauncey had turned out to be a pretty nice guy. A talker who entertained her until she could no longer keep her eyes open. Then he started singing. The last song she remembered hearing before dozing off was "I'll Fly Away."

She'd never heard it before. But after fifteen miles of it, she just about had it memorized. Yes, Chauncey was a card. She could have done worse. A lot worse.

But Shattuck, Oklahoma? Would she ever find another ride there?

"Come on, gal. Gather your stuff and say goodbye, or you're going to Oklahoma City with me." He reached across her and opened her door, puckering his lips in a fake kiss.

"Chauncey, this is the middle of nowhere. I'm not getting out here. I'll go to Oklahoma City with you, okay?" She slammed the door in a final gesture.

He pulled back onto the road. "Suits me. But you know it might help if I knew your intended destination."

"Dallas or Houston. I haven't decided. What do you think?"

"Dang, girl. Why didn't you say so? I'll get you to OC, and from there, it's a straight shot by bus to Dallas on Interstate 35."

Sarah couldn't help but wonder if she had enough money for a ticket to Dallas. If she didn't, she'd just have to hitchhike again. Hadn't been too bad so far. Maybe her luck would hold out.

Chauncey slowed down again and pulled into a little cafe parking lot. "But first . . . some lunch."

Sarah unpinned her coat pocket and extracted a dollar bill. "Just buy me a bag of peanuts, please."

"Peanuts . . . piffle. Keep your dollar. I know you're hungry. I couldn't hear myself think for your stomach growling." He grabbed her hand, and together they walked into the cafe holding hands and singing "I'll Fly Away."

Heads turned.

People smiled.

They were an odd couple, indeed.

Chauncey lifted Sarah's spirits. She dreaded when the time would come to part ways.

The bus to Dallas was crowded and hot. And Sarah's seatmate was irritatingly friendly.

"So, missy, you're telling me this perfect stranger bought you a ticket from Oklahoma City to Dallas. No strings."

"Yes, ma'am."

"Call me Sasha."

"Well, Sasha, I'm not sure why he was so kind to me. He didn't look like a very kind person when we first met." Sarah wasn't really in the mood to chat, but she didn't want to be rude. "In fact, I was a little bit scared of him."

"Well, you know you shouldn't have been hitchhiking. That just makes extra work for God."

"How did you know I was hitchhiking?" Sarah tilted her head to one side.

"Oh, just a guess, dear one. And, for the record, your Chauncey could have been an angel. Angels can look any way they want to look, you know. They can be grungy-looking white dudes or a little old black ladies. Or even *dogs*, if that fits their plan. Didn't you know that, girl?"

"Angels?"

"You don't think God's going to let one of his little ones wander across the country alone without sending an angel to guide the way, now do you? Especially when she's carrying such precious cargo." The elderly black lady reached over and patted Sarah's tummy.

Sarah drew away from her touch. "How did you know? And how did you know Chauncey's name?"

"I know just about everything. Been around for a very long time."

She reached over and touched the little cross Sarah was wearing. "That's a very nice pendant you have. Hang on to it. One day you'll really appreciate it."

The bus was slowing down. Sasha stood and gathered her purse and her cane. "This is my stop. It's been so nice chatting with you, Sarah. Perhaps we'll meet again someday."

Sarah watched her walk down the aisle and haltingly lower herself down the steps to the front door of the bus. She was so tiny she disappeared behind the cushioned back of the first seat. The door opened, and someone from the outside threw a bundle of mail in.

"Nobody getting off here today, Ted?"

The driver shrugged. "Slow day today, pal. I stopped just for you."

Puzzled by that exchange, Sarah tried to watch and wave to Sasha as the bus pulled away. But she was nowhere to be seen. How did she move so fast, walking with a cane?

Sarah made her way to the front of the bus. The driver's ID plaque read Ted Tanner, twelve years service. Sarah cleared her throat. "Mr. Ted, the little black lady who just got off—is she a regular?" Without taking his eyes off the road,

Ted assured her no one had gotten off the bus since they left Oklahoma City. "Perhaps your friend is in the rest room."

"But . . . I saw her . . . I mean I thought I saw her . . ." Her voice trailed off. Silently she threaded her way back to her seat, through luggage and stretched-out legs. The little old lady had dropped something on the seat. A tiny pamphlet explaining God's plan of salvation. Sarah picked it up and looked around for a place to dispose of it. Seeing no place to throw it without littering the aisles more than they already were, she stuck it in her bag to throw away later.

Chapter 11

"Sam, I know you must be worried sick about her. I saw you in town with her a time or two, and she seemed like a real sweet young lady. But if she left of her own free will and even left a goodbye note . . . there's not a whole lot I can do. She isn't related to you, and it's up to her parents whether they want to let her roam the countryside."

"But, Pete, her parents don't care. That's the whole problem."

"Sam, I'm sorry. My hands are tied." Pete looked down at his desktop and mumbled something about how tough it is to have to ignore what you know is a bad situation.

"Thanks, my friend. I understand. But just keep your eyes and ears open, will you? Let me know if you hear anything at all." Sam walked back out to the pickup truck and climbed behind the wheel.

The truck belonged to his sister, but when they went somewhere together, he always drove. A habit they formed years ago. Being three years older than Sam, the chore of teaching "little brother" to drive had fallen to Vivi. When they went anywhere together, he always begged her to let him drive, because he needed the practice. It became the most natural thing in the world for her to head for the passenger side if he was along. Now that she'd gone through so much with her husband's death and fighting debilitating illness, Sam took it upon himself to be "big brother." And the title fit him like a glove.

Vivi laid her knitting on the seat beside her. "What did he say, Sam?"

"Just what we expected. No APB. No traffic stops. There's not a lot he can do. His hands are tied." Sam plopped into the driver's seat and leaned his head against the back. "He did say he'd have all his men on the lookout for her, though. Strictly as a personal favor."

"That's good of him." She put her hand on his arm. "Try not to worry, little brother. She's a pretty capable young lady. She took her vitamins with her. And her cross pendant. She said she'd write when she could. I'm optimistic we'll hear from her before long."

Sam heaved a long sigh, sat up straight in the seat, and cranked the engine. "Yep. That's about all we can do now. Just wait and pray."

Before Sam could pull out, there was a knock on the tailgate. Officer Statton rushed around to the passenger side window. "Miss Vivi, I think I saw the girl you're looking for. She was walking east on Highway 15 just after sunrise this morning. A lot of people called in, concerned, so I drove out to check on her. I knew I'd seen her before, but for the life of me, I couldn't place her. It just dawned on me a moment ago when the chief told me about her, I'd seen her with you."

"Where is she now?" Hope lit Vivi's eyes.

Officer Statton averted his eyes. "Ma'am, I got called to a location where live shots were being fired. I couldn't take her with me, so I told her to hide herself and wait for me." He looked up, his eyes moist. "She was a determined little thing. When I got back, she was gone. I imagine she took the first ride she could get, just as soon as I was out of sight."

Fresh tears filled Vivi's eyes. "I'm sure you did all you could. She's in God's hands now. But thank you for telling me."

THE TRINITY QUILTS

Sam and Vivi drove home in worried silence. Each raking over every word they'd said last night at the kitchen table. And each knowing in their hearts she'd be home right now if they'd not had that conversation.

∽༄∽

Lunch with Chauncey was the last meal Sarah had eaten, and it was past 10:00 p.m. when the bus finally lumbered its way into the Dallas bus depot. Only one clerk was on duty and he was on the phone.

"Be with you in a moment," he mouthed to Sarah. One moment dragged into five and five into ten. Yet the conversation continued. She found a seat at a small table close to the concession area and sat down. She put her forearms on the table and rested her head on them. And promptly fell asleep. When she awakened, the depot clock said 3:00 a.m. The young clerk had been replaced by a very old man, who sat behind the counter and stared at her. They were the only two people in the building.

When she approached the counter, he smiled. "Get your nap out, sweetie?"

She hung her head, embarrassed. "Sir, I need to use the restroom."

He reached under the counter and retrieved a large paddle with a key dangling from the end of it. "You'll need this. It's at the end of that hall," he said, pointing a crippled old finger.

The cold water felt good on her face. She rummaged around in her tattered bag until she found a comb. A few swipes through her tangled locks and she was ready to get out of the restroom. It smelled of mold and piney disinfectant. But she didn't move fast enough. Her empty stomach rolled, and she retched into one of the three sinks lining the grimy wall.

It took nearly a roll of paper towel, but she got it clean. She cleaned not only the mess she'd made, but what looked like a years-long accumulation of gunk. The sink sparkled next to the two remaining filthy ones. She felt pleasure in having done it. Sarah loved for things to be clean and dreamed of one day living in a neat little cottage with spotless floors and windows. It was her one idiosyncrasy. Perhaps the result of being raised in absolute squalor.

Growing up, she'd secretly earn a little bit of money doing chores or running errands for neighbors. Clutching her small treasure of fifty or seventy-five cents in her fist, she'd run to the old mercantile store to buy, not candy or ice cream, but sweet-smelling soap or shampoo to keep herself, her clothes, and her hair clean. The family only used the rough lye soap Mama made, because Papa said perfume was *of the devil*. So she hid her treasure in the old shed behind the house and took it to their tiny bathroom only after Papa and Mama were asleep.

She opened the rest room door, and the old man from behind the counter was right there waiting for her. "I'm sorry. I was getting worried about you. Are you okay?"

"I'm fine. Just a little . . . a little tired." No sooner were the words out of her mouth than she swayed slightly and a wave of dizziness engulfed her head and chest. She turned to the old man. "I think I'm . . . going to . . ." His face became a shapeless blur, and Sarah's knees buckled. The old man was able to ease her fall.

Sarah opened her eyes to dim lights and clean white walls. "Where am I?"

THE TRINITY QUILTS

"In the hospital, dear." A lovely lady in dark-blue scrubs took her hand. "Do you remember what happened?"

"The bus depot, I think. I remember talking to an old man, and everything kind of went blurry on me." Sarah looked down and realized someone had stripped her clothes and she was wearing only a hospital gown. "What's going on? I'm not sick."

"The doctor will be in to see you in a moment." The nurse scooted out and closed the door behind her.

Dr. Rob McKinley volunteered at the hospital two nights a week. A young man with a successful practice, he was a favorite with the staff. He had a calming effect on everyone he spoke with. When he entered Sarah's room, his bedside manner was put to the test.

Sarah was near a state of panic. "I can't be here. Please give me my clothes and let me out of here."

"Whoa, young lady. No one's going to hurt you. We'd just like to know why you fainted at the bus station." Doctor McKinley ignored her pleas, gently took her hand, and examined her fingernails. Next he checked her arms, apparently for needle tracks.

"Please, doctor, I'm just hungry. That's all. The smell in the bus station and being so hungry kinda got to me."

"Are you sure that's all? Do you have any conditions we should know about?

Her heartbeat increased at his question. *They mustn't find out I'm pregnant, underage . . . and unmarried.*

"No, no. I'm fine. Please give me my clothes. I've got to . . . I've . . . got to . . ." The doctor's face was beginning to blur. *No. Not again, please.*

She awakened with an IV in her arm. Dr. McKinley was sitting beside her bed looking concerned. The smell of food overwhelmed her senses. *Oh God, I'm so hungry.*

"Here you go. Take a spoonful." The doctor was holding a spoon to her mouth. She did as he said. Noodle soup.

"Is that good?"

She didn't speak but nodded her head, and he fed her a second spoonful.

"Do you feel strong enough to feed yourself?" he asked, pulling the rolling food tray in front of her.

She nodded again and took the spoon he offered her. It was all she could do to not lift the bowl to her lips and drink it down.

"I'm Dr. McKinley. Please tell me your name, dear."

Between swallows she blurted, "Sarah. Do you have any crackers?"

He laughed aloud and pressed the call button. "Sounds like you're feeling a lot better."

He was still smiling. "And your last name is?"

She hesitated again. *If I give him my last name, he may be able to trace me to Papa and Mama. I know Uncle Sam won't mind if I use his name.*

"Blake. My name's Sarah Blake."

A nurse popped in. "Yes, Dr. McKinley?"

"Jane, would you get Miss Sarah Blake another bowl of soup and some crackers?"

"Be glad to. She must be feeling better."

"I'd say so."

When the nurse left, Dr. McKinley's demeanor changed. Entwining his fingers, he captured Sarah's attention with a very serious gaze. "How old are you, Miss Sarah Blake?"

He keeps using my whole name, like he doesn't believe me. "Almost eight . . . almost seventeen."

THE TRINITY QUILTS

"And how far along are you?"

"What do you mean?"

"I think you know what I mean, young lady," he spoke softly. "When is your baby due?"

"I'm not preg . . ." His gaze stopped her. *He knows. He's a doctor.* "In about six months, I think."

He tilted his head. With an expression of compassion, he prodded her. "Well, let's see if we can get more accurate. What was the date of your last menstrual period?"

"I don't know. I've never felt the need to keep track of it. I was a virgin, until . . ." Her voice dropped off and she stared at the two peaks in the sheet, created by her toes.

"Have you only been with a man once?" The concern in Dr. McKinley's eyes deepened.

"Yes, sir. Just one time." Tears gathered in her eyes, and she began to tremble.

He pulled his chair closer and covered her hand with his. "Tell me about it . . . were you raped, Sarah?"

She hesitated. *It's time to unveil the lie. This man is a doctor. He may know the family I'm looking for.* She'd rehearsed her story, but she hadn't expected anyone to guess she'd been raped. She could feel the heat rising in her cheeks.

Finally, she responded. "Rape? Oh no, it . . . it wasn't like that. I . . . no, sir. I mean . . . I had a boyfriend. We were very much in love. We'd planned to get married. We'd actually planned to wait. But it just . . . happened. Then, a week afterward, he was killed in a terrible accident. When I told my parents I was pregnant, they wanted me to get an abortion, but I refused. So they kicked me out. I'm from a very small town, so I came to Dallas to find a family for my baby."

He doesn't look like he believes me. Maybe I should have faked tears when I told him my boyfriend had died.

An unreadable expression lit the doctor's eyes for a split second, then they seemed to sort of *glaze over*. No expression at all. He entwined his fingers over and over in a nervous gesture. It was as though he was restraining himself from saying something. Something really important. Perhaps he was resisting the urge to scold her for having been promiscuous. Papa said she was. Maybe the doctor thought so too.

Shortly after her explanation, he seemed impatient to leave. "Okay, dear. Your soup should be here any minute. I'm going to leave orders to give you a mild sedative. I want you to get a good night's sleep, and we'll talk more in the morning." He was already on his feet.

He turned and left without another word.

Sarah was devastated. He seemed to want to get away from her. He probably thought she was a tramp.

I messed up. He knew I was lying. I gotta do better if I'm ever going to find a good family.

He'd practically run out of the room. Dr. Rob McKinley didn't know whether to laugh or cry. Had God answered his prayer this quickly? This girl was young and sweet natured. Too thin, but lovely in a slightly tomboyish fashion. Certainly not a very good liar. She'd hesitated much too long before denying she was raped. But she was very much pregnant.

The urge to discuss her with Beth was overwhelming. But first he had to get to know her better. He had to know if she was sincere in her desire to find a family for the baby. He couldn't bear it were he to bring more heartache on Beth.

He stopped at the nurse's station. Jane was still on duty. He grabbed Sarah's chart and scribbled some instructions.

"Jane, I've ordered a sedative for Sarah Blake in room 208. Would you please see that she receives it soon? And, Jane, she's a brave and headstrong young lady who may decide she doesn't need to spend the night. I know this is an unusual request . . . but would you please remove her street clothes from her closet and put them in the supply closet temporarily?" He rubbed his chin and smiled. "I don't want her to feel like a prisoner. Hopefully she'll just think her clothes have been misplaced. And, headstrong or not, I rather doubt she'd venture out in her hospital gown."

The next morning

Rob sat on the side of the bed. "Beth, honey. It's time to get up. You asked me to remind you of the lady's meeting at church today. Do you feel up to going?"

Beth roused, turned to her husband, and graced him with a drowsy, half-hearted smile. "Oh, Rob. What time is it? How long have you been up?" She looked beautiful even first thing in the morning with her generous mop of hair all mussed. Maybe even more so than when it was neatly combed.

He leaned over and kissed her on the forehead. "It's eight o'clock. As I recall, the meeting starts at nine thirty. What's your pleasure? A cup of coffee before your shower or a couple more hours of sleep?"

"My pleasure would be more sleep," she said, sitting up, "but coffee and a shower are what I need." She swung her feet around to the side of the bed and leaned down to get her slippers.

Not fast enough.

Her adoring husband was kneeling before her with her slippers in his hand. "Here, baby, slip them on. I'll get you a cup of coffee while you get ready for your shower."

While Beth took her time putting on her robe and walking leisurely to the master bath, Rob hot-footed it into the kitchen to get her coffee. *I've got to make my phone call while she's in the shower. Surely Adam's in his office by now.*

He poured himself a cup also and tapped on the bathroom door with his slippered toe. "Beth, open up. Got your coffee."

The door opened a crack. "I'll take mine in the shower with me, if you don't mind." Beth reached out for the cup and disappeared around the stone corner, into the mammoth stone and glass shower before Rob could get in the door. All he saw was a glimpse of one shapely leg as she swept around the corner. The stone was chest high on him and glass the rest of the way to the ceiling. But she was much smaller. So all he could see through the steamy glass was the nape of her slender neck and a head full of long auburn curls pinned on top of her head.

"You're no fun," he teased. "I'll be waiting in the kitchen. Need to make a couple of calls before I get dressed." He tried to appear to be in no rush, but the minute he closed the bathroom door, he broke into a trot. He grabbed his cell phone as he passed the chest-of-drawers and speed dialed his attorney, Adam Liotta. Adam could give him some pointers on the best way to approach the subject of adoption with Sarah Blake.

Adam answered. It was still too early for his secretary.
"Adam, this is Rob McKinley."
"Hey, Doc, what can I do for you this morning?"
"I need to talk to you about something important. But I don't want Beth to know about it. Not yet, anyway. It's kind of urgent I see you as soon as possible."

There was a long pause at the other end. Adam had known Rob and Beth since before they got married. Never once had they kept any secrets. "Sure, come on in as soon as you can. Marge isn't in yet . . . but as far as I know, I don't have anything on my agenda until ten o'clock."

Rob took a sip of coffee. "I need to appear unrushed to Beth. But I'll be there as soon as I can make it."

"Whatever. Take your time, Doc. I'll see you when you get here."

Rob disconnected and then deleted the call from his phone memory.

The shower was still running when he returned to the bedroom. With a deep sigh, he took off his robe and began to dress for the day. *Oh no, I forgot to cancel my appointments.*

The sound of running water ceased. Beth was finished showering. It was too late to call the office without taking a chance she'd walk in on him.

I'll have to call from my car phone on the way to Adam's office.

―――

Traffic was heavy this time of the morning. Rob pulled over to the curb to dial. When the phone started ringing, he pulled back into the flow of traffic. He'd been one of the first to have a speaker phone installed in his car. Not one to feel the need to "keep up with the Jones," he simply found the convenience of being able to talk with patients—and especially with Beth—while he was on the road too good to pass up.

The phone rang four times before his head nurse answered breathlessly. "Dr. McKinley's Office. How may I help you?"

"This is Rob. I need all my appointments for this morning cancelled. Is that going to be a problem?" *After I finished with Adam, I'll devote the rest of my morning to Sarah Blake.*

"A big one. Absolutely, Dr. Mac, but nothing I can't handle." He could hear the smile in her voice.

"I should be in by—" A horn blared.

Rob caught a peripheral glimpse of something to his left. He turned his head in time to see a blob of metallic red headed straight at him. Time seemed to stand still. The approaching vehicle swerved and fishtailed before the inevitable impact. The sound of metal against metal reached his brain nanoseconds before the sharp pain in his head. A woman screamed. Murky blackness overtook him.

"Dr. Mac... Dr. Mac... answer me. What happened? Are you okay? Dr. Mac..."

Chapter 12

"Where are my clothes?" Sarah paced from the bed to the closet to the hallway and back, clutching her hospital gown together in the back with one hand. "You can't make me stay here. I want to get dressed and get out of here." Her tone was urgent, but her voice was soft. She was talking to the walls.

The other bed in her room was empty. There was no one to hear her.

She pressed the call button. And the one on the empty bed. And waited. For what seemed a very long time.

In a totally uncharacteristic move, she called down the hall. "I want my clothes."

A nurse who'd been attending a patient across the hall stepped into her room. "Miss Blake, many patients are still asleep. They need their rest. Please keep your voice down."

A repentant teenager looked up at her with tears in her eyes. "I'm sorry. I didn't mean to be rude. It's just that I have to go and I can't find my clothes. Why aren't they in the closet?"

"Get back into your bed, dear." The nurse put her arm around Sarah's shoulder and walked her to the bed. "I want to talk to you."

Obediently, Sarah climbed back into her hospital bed and clasped her hands in front of her. "Why? Is there something bad wrong with me?"

The nurse sat down beside her. "No, Sarah, it's about Dr. Mac . . . uh . . . McKinley. He's a very special man. He was your doctor yesterday . . ."

Sarah glanced at the nurse's name tag. "Yes, I know, Miss Barbara. He seemed nice."

"Well, he's more than nice, honey. He's dedicated, kind, and insightful. Yesterday he asked the nurse on duty to hide your clothes from you so you wouldn't run away. He could be called down for that. But he took a chance, because it was important to him for you to not be out on the streets last night.

"And it seemed important as well that he see you again today. Why, we're not sure. All your tests came out good. Other than being pregnant and a little too thin, you seem to be in good health."

"Does *everybody* know I'm pregnant?" Sarah could feel her lower lip quivering and her cheeks flaming.

"It's on your chart, Sarah. Everyone who needs to know . . . knows."

"Did he say anything to you about how I got pregnant? I mean about my boyfriend . . . and . . ."

"He'd never share anything personal with anyone. But if you need to talk about it, I'm here for you."

Sarah looked down at her hands. "No, I'm good. Just wondering. Do you think he'll be here soon?" She turned her gaze back to Barbara. "'Cause I really need to get out of here."

"No, honey. He won't be here this morning at all." Her voice broke. "He's right here in the hospital . . . one floor down in ER."

"They needed his help in ER this morning?"

"I wish. No, he's there as a patient. He was in a pretty bad accident this morning. A driver lost control on the freeway and smashed right into the driver's side of Dr. Mac's vehicle." Barbara stood up and walked to the window. "He has head injuries and hasn't regained consciousness." She drew a deep breath and released it slowly.

Sarah could see Barbara was taking it hard. She got out of bed and walked over to the window next to Barbara. "I'm sorry. Would they let me see him?

"I'm afraid not, honey. Family only right now. But you can check back later in the day, if you like. With Dr. Mac unavailable, I have no reason to hold you here, so I'll go get your clothes for you now." Barbara straightened her shoulders and walked out into the hall without another word.

"Where's my cross pendant?" Sarah called after her.

"In the bedside drawer, dear."

Sarah had to walk past the nurse's station on the way to the elevator, lugging her old suitcase. There was no idle chatter and no friendly smiles. Dr. Mac's accident seemed to be on everyone's mind. She stopped to inquire about him just as Barbara hung up the phone.

"No change," she said to the ladies gathered around. "He's still unconscious. Beth is with him."

Sarah caught her eye. "Who's Beth?" She set her suitcase down.

"His wife, honey." She shot Sarah a tender look. "Are you ready to go?"

"Uh-huh. What do I do now? I only have nineteen dollars and fifty-six cents, and I really hate to give it up. I need it for my taxi."

"Normally, I'd send you by the financial office. But Dr. Mac told Beverly last night he'd take care of everything. So you're free to go."

Sarah wrinkled her brow. "Why would he do that? He doesn't even know me."

Barbara came from behind the counter and put her hands on Sarah's shoulders. "I told you he was a great guy. Now, where will you go, honey?"

"Oh, don't worry about me. I've got family in Richardson," she lied. "In fact they're probably pretty concerned about me. I should have gotten there yesterday."

Sarah forced a smile, picked up her suitcase, waved goodbye to all, and rushed to the bank of elevators. It was the first time she'd ever ridden in an elevator, except when they brought her in, and she wasn't conscious then. Nervous about what to do once she got in, she waited for a few moments, and when no one at the nurse's station was looking her way, she ducked through the door to the staircase.

Stairs she could handle.

She passed a hallway with an arrow pointing to the emergency room. Deliberately blotting out a vision of Dr. Mac lying unconscious on an emergency room bed, she forced her footsteps to continue toward the front entrance.

Two steps beyond, she slowed to a stop. *He's going to pay my hospital bill. Such a nice man. I really should go check on him.*

She bowed her head and swallowed hard. *But he's better off if I stay out of his life.*

Sarah resumed her determined walk toward the lobby. *Someday I'll look him up and pay him back.*

Out the big front doors onto the city sidewalk—with no earthly idea what her next move should be.

An "open" sign blinking in the window of a small cafe across the street, and down the block to her left, caught her attention. *I'll have a cup of coffee while I decide what to do next. That will make me look more mature. I'll put in lots of*

sugar and lots of cream . . . the way Vivi used to make it for me.
A lump filled her throat. She wished she hadn't thought of Vivi. Because there was no going back now.

Once again, she'd made her bed.

Chapter 13

Rob was finally assigned a room in ICU. Beth sat beside his bed holding his hand. It was only because of his position with the hospital and the affection they all felt for Beth she was allowed to stay. Her lips moved in silent prayer.

The door opened and closed behind her. "Mrs. Mac, why don't you take a break? Go home and get some rest. I promise I'll call you immediately if there's any change." Frank, Rob's PA, walked up beside her and laid his hand on her shoulder.

"Thanks, Frank, but I just can't. When he wakes up, I want to be the first person he sees." She patted the hand on her shoulder. "I hope you understand."

"Of course, I do. I've been with Dr. Mac for five years. I'd have to be blind to not see the beautiful cord binding you two together." He cleared his throat. "How about I see if I can dig up a cot and a couple blankets? Maybe you'll be able to catch a wink or two."

Beth looked up at him and displayed a very sincere, if sad, smile. "That would be great, Frank. Thank you so much."

She watched him walk away. Frank was a good friend. They'd forged quite a bond themselves in the last five years. Since she had no family to lean on, she was grateful he'd assumed the position of "big brother" to her in this, her personal tragedy.

She turned her attention back to Rob. *Oh, Rob, what were you doing on Stemmons Freeway on your way to the hospital? It's out of your way.* His cell phone vibrated from inside her purse, where she'd put it with his other valuables. She retrieved it and looked at the caller ID.

Adam Liotta. Rob's attorney. Why would he *be calling?*

"Hello, Adam, this is Beth."

The hesitation in his voice was a dead giveaway he hadn't expected *her* to answer the phone. "Hey-um, Beth. Uh . . . how have you been?" He seemed to grasping for his self-confidence, which *usually* preceded his handsome self by a mile.

"Fine, just fine, Adam. What can I do for you?"

Adam's office is on Stemmons Freeway.

"Just touching base with Rob. Hadn't heard from you folks in a while. I . . . uh . . . thought the four of us might get together sometime. Is Rob handy?"

"I'm afraid not, Adam. He was in an accident this morning. He's in ICU." Beth knew she sounded cold and uncaring, but this man . . . this man who was *not* a part of their social circle and who surfaced in their lives only when there was a problem . . . had never once called to chat or invite them out for an evening before. How strange he should pick today. The day Rob was involved in an accident *on Liotta's own turf.*

Adam Liotta was in a quandary. *This is awful. I know now why Rob didn't show up this morning. But now I'm afraid I've alerted Beth something is amiss. And he didn't want her to know.*

He fidgeted with his letter opener and struggled with a way to get off the line, before she could ask him any point-blank questions. Questions he couldn't answer.

But, then again, maybe she already knows . . . whatever it is . . . 'cause she sure seems distant. Or maybe she's in shock over Rob's condition. Oh Lord, I do hope he's going to be all right.

He stammered, "Is there anything . . . *anything at all* . . . I can do?"

Beth murmured, "No, I don't think so." She was speaking so low Adam could barely hear.

"Oh oh, my other line is ringing and my secretary's out. Have to get off now. I'll come by tonight to check on him. And please call if there's anything I can do, Beth."

He scribbled "Rob Mac in ICU" in big letters on his desk pad and mumbled what he hoped was an appropriate "goodbye" to Beth.

He wasn't sure why his hands were shaking so badly as he tucked his cell phone back in his jacket pocket. He'd handled many divorces . . . but never for a couple he'd grown so fond of—in spite of the infrequency of their association. And never for a couple who seemed so in love.

Tears filled Beth's eyes as she slipped the cell phone back in her purse.

Rob had contacted his attorney without her knowledge. And she could only think of three possible reasons. One, someone had brought a malpractice suit against him, or two, they were in serious financial straits. He wouldn't want her to worry about either of those. But neither of those scenarios seemed very likely.

Or, number three — he wanted a divorce. Adam Liotta had a successful business and family practice but was also well-known for his prowess in the divorce court.

Rob certainly had ample reason to want to be free of her—to marry again. Time and time again, she'd conceived and tried to carry his child to full term. Time and time again, she'd failed. And Rob wanted a son so badly. He deserved better than to be tied down to a barren woman for the rest of his life.

Chapter 14

Sarah nursed her cup of coffee for as long as she could, ignoring the gnawing in her stomach. Finally the memory of her last meal—the delicious soup and crackers—got the best of her, and she picked up the menu to look for the cheapest meal offered. The coffee had cost her a dollar thirty-five, so she was down to eighteen dollars and twenty-one cents, with no idea of how long it would have to last her.

There was nothing in the menu for less than seven dollars, so Sarah stood, carefully placed a twenty-one cent tip on the counter where the waitress would be sure to see it, and slipped out the door. With no idea where it would lead her, she began walking east, past a multitude of medical supply stores and small eateries. She knew it was east, because she was walking into the sun. It was a nippy morning, and the sun on her face felt good.

The savory smells emanating from the restaurants were wreaking havoc with her empty stomach. Sarah was glad when she finally got out of that district, although the buildings she passed now looked pretty run-down by comparison. She contemplated turning to go another direction but spied a small grocery store in the distance.

A little bell tinkled as she opened the door. The lady behind the cash register was reading a tabloid and didn't bother to look up but mumbled, "G'mornin'," in Sarah's general direction. The old hardwood floors were filthy and buckled, and the food in the hot food case looked shriveled and off-color.

"It's kinda dark in here." Sarah ventured. "I'm looking for the canned pork and beans. The easy-open kind. I don't have a can opener."

The cashier looked up from under the light of a single bulb that hung over the counter. "You wanna help pay the electric bill, I'll turn the lights on." Returning to her tabloid, she mumbled, "And we're outta pork and beans. Any kinda pork and beans.

"We got stuff to eat right here." She pointed a dirty fingernail at the hot food case.

"None of that is what I'm hungry for right now." Sarah kept her voice pleasant in spite of the revulsion she felt at the thought of eating any of that stuff. "I'll keep looking."

Sarah opened the door to leave, ringing the little bell.

Ms. Hospitality grumbled over her shoulder, "Soup kitchen right down the road about a mile. I've heard it's eatable."

Sarah had eaten some pretty humble meals within the walls of the shack Papa built. But they'd never been so poor they had to go to a soup kitchen. She looked around at the folks she would be sharing a repast with. Very shabby—some without sufficient clothing to keep them warm. Others looked like they didn't own a comb. Then she looked down at her own attire. And for the first time fully realized she looked no better. A new rip had appeared in her old dress and the sole was flapping on her left shoe.

Some without jackets huddled close to the old wood burning stove that warmed the building. It had seemed warmer outside than inside. Tucked in among taller buildings, the soup kitchen retained the cold. That was probably a good thing in the summer heat, because it was doubtful the building had any air-conditioning.

To Sarah's surprise, the volunteers who served her were very polite and kind. They almost made her forget for a time she was dirt poor, homeless, and pregnant. When they offered her seconds, she gladly accepted. She tried to donate a dollar, but the gentleman she offered it to curled her fingers back around the bill and said, "Maybe later, when you're on your feet." When she left, full and satisfied, several of them greeted her at the exit and invited her to come back—anytime.

Sarah walked to the end of the row of ramshackle buildings in search of a place to sit and try to come up with a plan. She'd managed to get away from her family, then reluctantly leave her new family, only to find herself totally alone with no inkling of what to do next. She was no closer to finding a family for her baby than the day she discovered she was pregnant.

And she was much further from being able to properly feed the wisp of life she carried within her. *This* weighed heavily on her mind. Her thoughts drifted to Uncle Sam and Aunt Vivi, and the vitamins they bought, even though they couldn't afford them. She reached to touch her pendant. Her neck was bare.

Puzzled, she looked around her, thinking it may have just fallen off. Then, crestfallen, she remembered where it was. *Oh, no. I left it in the drawer in my hospital room. I can't go back for it. I'm so sorry, Aunt Vivi. Maybe they'll put it in lost and found . . . and someday I can claim it.*

Nearing tears, she rounded the corner. A girl leaning against the side of the building reached out a tattooed arm to stop Sarah in her tracks.

"Where you staying?" Multiple lip rings jiggled when she spoke.

"I . . . I . . . don't know, really. But I'll find a place." Sarah was uncomfortable in this girl's presence, because she neither smiled nor looked Sarah in the eye.

"I gotta room. You can stay with me."

"Thank you, but I have some friends just down the road. I'm sure they'll take me in."

"You're lying. Ain't nothing down this road but woods. You too good to stay with me?"

"No . . . I . . ."

"Then come on." Grabbing Sarah's arm, she began walking back toward the grocery store. "I'm Sylvia. I eat at the kitchen every day and I ain't seen you before. Where you from?"

She was five or six inches taller than Sarah and skinny and dirty. Sarah wasn't sure she would recognize the odor, but she felt sure the girl had been smoking pot or something.

Sylvia jerked on Sarah's sleeve. "I said where you from?"

Sarah looked around the dingy neighborhood and shuddered. Reminded her of her old her neighborhood—it was just city squalor instead of country squalor. She missed Sam and Vivi's neat cottage. And she didn't want to divulge any more about herself than absolutely necessary to this weird girl.

"Texas."

"Well, duh, in case you didn't know it, you're still *in* Texas." Sylvia winked and revealed a mouth full of not very well-cared-for teeth.

Not a very pretty smile, but relieved at Sylvia's attempt to be friendly, Sarah let down her guard a little.

"West Texas."

"I guess that'll have to do. You don't talk much, do you?"

Sarah looked down at her shabby shoes. She realized she was being downright unfriendly. Out of necessity, she told herself. Then remembering she was no better off than this Sylvia person—no, in truth, worse off. At least Sylvia had a place to sleep. And she didn't look pregnant.

Sarah decided a change of attitude was in order. "Sorry. I'm from the country and everything is so different around . . ."

They were passing a short flight of stairs leading from the sidewalk to a weathered black door with a small peephole when Sylvia grabbed her arm and jerked her toward the steps. "Home sweet home, Bumpkin."

Sylvia led her about halfway down a dark hallway and stopped at a stained and battered door on the left. Behind the door was the drabbest and dirtiest room Sarah had ever seen. Roaches scattered when Sylvia flipped on the overhead light. Papa's shack was immaculate by comparison.

"Two dollars a night," Sylvia announced.

"Uh . . . is that what you pay?"

"No, Bumpkin. I pay four dollars a night. If you're going to be my roomy, it's going to cost you two." Shaking her head, she added, "I ain't Santa Claus."

So much for having found a friend.

"I only have eighteen dollars. If I give you two a day, I'll be totally broke in nine days," Sarah objected. "And I'm not going to be around that much."

"So what you think's gonna to happen? Prince Charming gonna rescue you and keep you in the manner you're accustomed to? Good luck with *that*." She laughed. "Tell you what. I'll let you stay a couple of days for one buck a day, while you try to find a job." Sylvia seemed proud of her generosity.

She's right. What had I hoped to find? How had I hoped to live with no income?

"Okay. I guess so. I really don't know what else to do." Sarah nibbled at her fingernails. Roaches creeped her out. Would she be able to live in this filth while she looked for "the family"?

"Well, check out my closet and see if there's anything of mine you can wear. Chance is having a party tonight . . . and you sure can't go lookin' like you do." She held out a hand. "But first, the rent, Bumpkin."

Sarah unpinned her coat pocket, pulled out a dollar, and handed it to Sylvia. "I'll pass on the party. I think I'll just get some rest." At the same time deciding if she hoped to hang on to what money she had left, she'd have to sleep in her coat at night.

"Chance works at a pizza joint. A party at his place means pizza all around. It's a long time 'til lunch at the soup kitchen tomorrow. You'd better rethink your plans."

Chance was squatting on some land about a mile from the apartment house in a tiny two-room run-down shack deep in the woods. He had no running water and no electricity. He rode his bike through a narrow path in the woods to and from work. But his place was clean, and he was rather personable. A few years older than the others and not bad looking at all.

He'd managed to steal six large pizzas from his employer, which he warmed up over a campfire in the overgrown clearing that surrounded his shack. Of the ten people who showed up for the party, three had brought some sort of liquor to drink. Two of *them* had obviously imbibed too much before they arrived.

Sarah had never been to a party before. Not even a childhood birthday party. She sat on the side of the single metal bed—which along with a rusty metal chair was the only furniture in the bedroom. She nibbled on a piece of pizza, listening to the laughter coming from the next room.

"Get in here and join the party, Bumpkin." Sarah's new roomy slumped against the door facing, already high. Sarah hoped Sylvia would be sober enough to find her way back through the woods to the apartment in the dark. Raucous music filled the air, but Sarah imagined they were too far from civilization for anyone to complain. She didn't respond to her the slurry invitation, and Sylvia floated back out of the room on her own private cloud of alcohol.

"Are you enjoying yourself?" Sarah hadn't noticed Chance enter the room until he was standing right over her, offering her another slice of pizza.

"Yes, yes. Very much." She accepted the pizza, having decided to save it for breakfast.

"You don't look like it." He'd brought an old TV tray for her. He set a drink down on it. "How about a drink?"

"No, thanks, I'm drinking water."

"Why?"

"I . . . I . . . just happen to like water better than alcohol." She smiled, not wanted to seem rude. She couldn't drink alcohol even if she'd wanted to. The baby.

"I bet you've never even tasted alcohol." He pushed the drink closer to her.

"Oh, yes. Many times," she lied.

"Then have just a swallow to prove it."

"Please don't ask me to. I don't want to." Tears were forming in her eyes.

His gaze softened. "Hey, take it easy. You're not like the others, are you? You're not a party girl."

"I . . . I . . . this is the first party I've ever been to. I'm really not comfortable with the loud music and the drinking." She turned her face from him.

Chance sat down next to her and gently turned her head to face him. "I can tell. But what I can't figure out is . . . what are you doing here?"

She smiled shyly. "Sylvia told me there would be pizza, and I was hungry."

Chance laughed aloud. "No, silly girl. I mean what are you doing living like this? You don't seem the type."

"It's a very long story, and I can't share it with someone I hardly know."

"I'd like to get to know you better. Maybe well enough you'd feel safe to tell me your story." He put his arm around her shoulder. Sarah stiffened and Chance released her. "Whoa, girl, I won't hurt you."

"I think you'd better get back to your party, Chance. I'm fine."

"And you're sure you don't want to join me. Maybe have just one little drink?"

"My Papa used to drink. He was always mean when he drank. I don't ever want to be like him."

Chance stood, shaking his head. "Okay, I'll get back to the party. But I'm not finished with you. I wanna be your friend." He put his hand on her shoulder. "On *your* terms." He turned his back and strode to the door. But turned to look at her before joining the crowd. Holding his drink up, he winked. "Till next time."

Chapter 15

Rob opened his eyes.

Beth was at his side before he could speak.

"Oh, darling, I was so worried." She pressed the call button. "How do you feel?"

"Wow. My head feels like a ping-pong ball at the end of a close game. Who won anyway?" He grinned sheepishly.

Nurse Barbara burst in the door. "Oh, praise God, you're awake."

The next hour or so was a bustle of doctors and nurses in and out, each one making the statement that he needed his rest but none willing to leave him in solitude for fear of missing the chance to be of help. Finally, things settled down, and Rob closed his eyes to doze for a while.

Beth took the opportunity rush home, take a quick shower, and change clothes. When she returned, he was just awakening again.

"Anything happen while I was out of it, sweetheart?"

"Not much. Scads of people came to see you. You have a pile of cards on the bedside table to look at when you feel up to it. And look at all the flowers." She gestured toward a windowsill and desk crowded with every color blossom under the sun. "The phone rang off the hook. Just the usual 'everybody loves Rob McKinley' stuff," she bantered.

"I'm only interested in how much you love me right now, Beth. Thank you for being here for me." He beckoned her over to his bed for an embrace.

She bent over to kiss him on the forehead and was overcome with tenderness and grief. She couldn't shake the dread she felt at the thought this man—her whole life—wanted a divorce. She knew it hadn't been an easy decision for him. He was loving and kind and so good to her. His desire for a child must be overwhelming for him to have come to this conclusion. And she knew his godly nature would make it almost impossible for him to bring up the subject. So it was up to her to help him find his release.

"Adam Liotta called and sent flowers."

"Oh?"

"He said he was going to visit but never did. I got the distinct impression he didn't want to see *me*."

It was then Rob remembered he was on his way to Adam's office when the accident happened. And he'd indicated to Adam he didn't want Beth to know. What had Adam said or done to spook Beth?

"Why do you think that, Beth? Adam has always been very cordial toward you."

"A little too cordial this time, Rob. He suggested we get together sometime for an evening out. Now, we both like Adam. But we all know we run in different circles. We've never so much as gotten a Christmas card from Adam and Gloria. I've haven't even *met* her. Perhaps you have."

Rob squirmed under his sheets. "No. No, I've never met his missus. And you think this sudden interest in getting together is indicative of . . . what?"

"It was his attempt to give himself a reason for having called. He was temporarily discombobulated when *I* answered *your* phone." She snatched a tissue and held it to her eye to stop an errant tear.

"Rob, be honest with me. What need do you have of Adam's services? The accident didn't take place on your way to your office . . . or to the hospital. You were way across town, in his territory. I think he called because he was expecting you, and you didn't show up. What were you doing there?"

Rob looked down at his hands. "I didn't want to worry you with it until I could see which way things were going."

"What things? Are you being sued for malpractice? Are we in financial trouble?"

"Oh, heavens no, sweetheart. It's something much more important than that."

Beth stood and turned her back to Rob. "Please don't call me 'sweetheart' when you're trying to break the *important* news to me that you want a . . . divorce. It's too painful."

"I want a *what*?" Rob attempted to swing his legs around to get out of the bed, but the pain was still too great. He fell back.

Beth swung around in time to see him sink back into the bed. "Rob! Stop that. You're know you need complete rest. I'm sorry I let this conversation begin with you still in ICU. But I know how badly you want a son. I figured you'd need help to even bring it up. And I . . ." She broke into heart-rending sobs. "I wanted to . . . make it as easy . . . for you as possible."

Rob hit the call button. Nurse Barbara was leaving for the day and just happened to be passing his door. "What's the matter, Dr. Mac?"

"Barbara, close the door behind you, pull a chair up close to my bed. Set my wife down in it and don't let her get up no matter what she does or says."

Beth allowed herself to be led to the chair. Gritting her teeth against what he was going to say to her—in front of another woman, she sat stiffly, her eyes pooled with tears. Barbara's hands rested on her shoulders.

"My beloved Beth. You are my life. You are my reason for living. There is nothing in this world that could ever influence me to ask you for a divorce. I would not want to have a child with any other woman. If we are never able to achieve parenthood, so be it. We will have each other till death do us part."

Both Beth and Barbara were crying now.

"You remember the day we took our vows before God? Well, I love you more now than I did then."

He paused, not wanting to tell her his reason for calling Adam, but knowing it was necessary in order for her to be completely convinced of his undying love.

"I met a young lady, a patient . . . pregnant and looking for a home for her baby. She was sweet and innocent." He looked up at Barbara. "You remember her, Barbara? Sarah Blake?"

Barbara nodded.

Rob reached over and touched Beth's hand. "She's a little tomboyish but very pretty, like you. And I'd hoped we could adopt her baby. I called Adam and made an appointment to find out the correct way to go about it. Then I was going to come to the hospital and talk to Sarah about it. But I didn't want to tell you until I could be sure she was sincere."

"Oh, Rob. Oh my God. How could I have been such a fool?" Beth attempted to get up, and Barbara held down on her shoulders.

Rob continued, "I need to go see her as soon as I can get out of this bed."

"Dr. Mac," Barbara stammered, "you've been out of it for a long time. Sarah's gone. Left the morning of the accident."

"Did you get an address, or anything where she can be reached?"

"She gave us a made-up address in Richardson. I don't think she had any place to go."

"Dear Lord, I don't know if I can find her now. But if you're willing, Beth, I'll take a sabbatical and I'll turn this city upside down looking for her."

Tears and mascara running down both cheeks, Beth attempted to rise again.

Rob smiled. "I think you can let her go now, Barbara."

Chapter 16

By two in the morning, Sylvia was too drunk to walk, much less find her way through the woods. And so were all the other partygoers. Some had already found their way to the couch and the chairs to curl up and sleep off their drunken stupor.

Chance had not had very much to drink. He'd been obsessed with Sarah all evening . . . neglecting his other guests, to look in on her every few minutes. Now he gathered every pillow, coverlet, and blanket he owned—save the one on the bed where Sarah had already fallen asleep—and threw them on the living room floor. He closed and locked the door to the bedroom, so no one would pile in with Sarah and found a vacant spot on the floor with the others. The living room was wall-to-wall bodies.

At 8:00 a.m., he gently awakened Sarah and offered her a ride home on his bike, while the others continued to sleep it off.

"I don't have a key to Sylvia's apartment, Chance."

"Sarah, Sylvia's apartment is never locked. This bunch is likely to sleep until two o'clock and you'll miss lunch at the soup kitchen. You really need to let me take you home." He started to pull her toward the door.

"Chance . . . I need to tee tee."

"Oops, of course. Let me show you where the outhouse is." He led her through knee-deep weeds about twenty yards behind the shack to a lean-to outhouse that looked like it was about to fall over. "Sorry about the accommodations. Not used to entertaining ladies." He rolled his eyes and grinned.

Riding through the woods, Sarah asked Chance to stop and let her off for a moment. She walked a few feet away and lost last night's pizza in the underbrush.

"You okay?"

"Just morning . . . I mean, I guess something I ate last night didn't agree with me."

Twenty minutes later, when he dropped her off in front of the apartment house, Chance got off his bike and executed a deep bow in front of Sarah. She giggled.

"Until we meet again, m'lady."

Back at his shack, Chance threw himself down next to Sylvia, who had migrated to the bed Sarah had vacated. "You were right, Sylvia. I think she's pregnant. She wouldn't drink anything last night and she had to toss her cookies on the way home." He gave Sylvia a high five. "I can't believe my luck." Chance was grinning from ear to ear.

Sylvia rolled over in bed and looked at him. "What's up, Chance? You yearning to be a daddy?" she chortled.

"Maybe."

"To Bumpkin's kid?"

"I could do worse."

"Yeah, right." Sylvia sat up and pulled her shoes on. "Hey, I missed lunch at the joint. What'cha got that I can munch on, on my way home?"

Chance opened a pizza box. "Something different—pizza."

"Ugh. Well, I guess it's better than going hungry." Sylvia grabbed a couple of pieces and headed out the door.

Chance yelled after her. "Tell Sarah I'll stop by after work."

He stepped back into his little shanty and began picking up the mess left by his "overnight guests." *Gotta clean up, in case Sarah wants to come over tonight.*

Chapter 17

"**S**o you see, Chance, I can't get serious about anyone until I've done what I came to do, and that's to find a home for my baby." Sarah was wearing a neat little shift dress Chance had bought at the Dollar General store for her. He'd surprised her with several cheap little outfits for her seventeenth birthday.

"I appreciate everything you do for me and I'll repay you some day. But the most important thing in the world to me right now is this baby."

"It's important to me too, Sarah. You know, we could get married and keep it. I'd love it like I was its real daddy."

"No, I've got my reasons why I can't keep it. And it's certainly not that I don't love it, because I do. But I want my baby to have a chance at a good life. Something I never had. And something you and I can't give it. You know, like where would we live with it? In your shack? No, Chance, I'm going to find a good family. And I have to get busy looking."

Her shoulders drooped when she looked into his pouty face. "Don't be that way. There's another reason—a bigger one—that I just can't tell you." Sarah still feared finding out who her attacker was by seeing familiar features in her growing child's face. More than anything, she wanted her baby to feel secure and loved and wanted. Because of who she was and how she got pregnant, she wasn't sure she could ever provide that security.

Chance knew he had to get her moved into his place and away from civilization before this *family* she was so obsessed about materialized. "Well, at least come live with me. You need to get out of this apartment building. It's a firetrap and a . . . a whore house. You don't belong here."

He had his important plans as well. Sarah wasn't the only one with dreams.

"You only have one bedroom, Chance. I'm afraid at some point you'll decide to share my bed, whether I like it or not. I just can't let that happen. It's not that I don't care for you . . . I do. Just not *that* way." Sarah stepped into the tiny kitchenette and put on a kettle of water for tea. A roach scuttled across the counter and behind the stove. Sarah shuddered.

Chance followed her. "I won't. I won't. I swear on a stack of Bibles. I'll never try to get you to . . . you know what. Never. Not unless you asked me to." He took the kettle from her hand, laid it on the countertop, and with both hands on her upper arms, he turned her toward him.

"You know you don't like living here. You hate the roaches and the filth. You have to *pay* to live in this dump." He gestured toward the stained and dirty walls. "And you know my place, humble though it is, is at least clean . . . and it's free. You'll be more comfortable and happier. Come on, Sarah. Don't be so stubborn."

She pulled away from him and put the kettle on the stove. Lighting the burner below it, she turned to walk into the next room, Chase right on her heels. "How would I get to town to look for the baby's family?"

"I'll take you in on my bike any time you want to go. We'll have it all taken care of before you get too big to ride on the handlebars. I promise you. I'll be a big help to you."

He watched her closely. He could almost see her indecision leaning toward his side of the argument. She'd give in soon. But he couldn't afford to get cocky. This might take yet another day or two of pleading. But he'd get his way in the end. He could feel it in his bones.

"She's weakening. Come on, Chance, me boy." The demon of lust was almost jumping up and down. "We can kill two birds, maybe three, with one stone. A conquest for Chance, a defeat for the good doctor and his wife. And then there's the baby. We could jump on it young and make it miserable for years to come."

"If we can just get her settled into that shack, the rest will be in the bag. And I'll get to have a little fun too." The demon of fear licked his chops. "Haven't had a go at her for weeks. I bet she misses me."

Sarah peered around Sylvia's filthy apartment. The wallpaper seemed dingier than usual. Almost like a film of soot hung between her and the walls. A shiver ran down her spine and she had the same ominous feeling she'd felt in the woods the night she ran away from Uncle Sam's. Like maybe she was being watched. By someone other than Chance.

His place—like he said—was just a shack. But the sun shines in the windows during the day giving it cheerful look. Like one of the cabins on "Little House on the Prairie." *I could make it look even homier with some curtains and a tablecloth.*

The tea kettle whistled, jolting Sarah from her reverie.

Chance had been watching her, calculating his next move. "Gotta go, baby." He touched her still-small belly. "Get lots of rest today and take care of our baby. See you this evening." He slipped out the door and Sarah padded to the kitchenette to make her tea. She didn't even notice Chance had said "our" baby.

Sitting down at the little table alone with her cup of tea, the apartment suddenly seemed almost pleasant. The heebie-jeebies she was feeling only moments earlier had lifted. Gone out the door with Chance. But she was running out of money to pay the rent, with no income in sight. She could live with Chance for free. And he would help her find a family. Oh my, it was such an important decision. She had to be sure she was doing the right thing.

Out of the blue, visions of Chauncey and Sasha flitted through her mind.

This apartment's not so bad. You could fix it up. Sasha seemed to be saying. *Don't make any rash decisions,* Chauncey whispered in her ear.

Drowning out their voices came the chant, *You'll never be able to get rid of the roaches.* Over and over, the evil ones bombarded her ears and her mind. *Roaches, roaches, roaches, roaches.* Sarah clamped her hands over her ears. A roach dropped from out of nowhere and landed inches from her cup of tea. She jumped back, knocking over her chair and spilling her tea.

Chance is right. I hate it here.

⁂

Flies were thick in the alley behind the pizza joint. Chance leaned against the brick wall outside the back door. "How much did you say this couple would pay for a healthy baby?"

Standing in the shadows where even Chance couldn't get a good look at him, the big man croaked "Seventy-five thou."

"What if I could guarantee it to be a beautiful baby? The mother is a real looker."

"Seventy-five thou."

"How much you gettin'?"

"Listen, punk. That ain't none of your business. You want the seventy-five or not?" Chance could tell he was getting antsy. Best not to push him over the edge.

"Sure. Sure. I want it." Chance moved a little closer. "But how can I be sure they'll keep their end of the bargain? Who are they anyway?"

A fist from out of the shadows punched Chance's shoulder. "Keep your distance if you want to keep your pretty face."

Chance backed up.

"They can't get a kid from any orphanage because of his, uh, shall we say his . . . occupation. I could tell you his name, but then I'd have to kill you." His humorless laugh came from the pits of hell.

Flies were everywhere. Like tiny, evil demons taking note of their progress in Chance's life. And enjoying the opportunity to dole out aggravation while they worked.

Waving his arms and swatting, the big man bellowed, "Where'd all these flies come from?"

"Duh. You're in an alley behind a pizza joint, standing next to a dumpster."

"Watch your mouth, kid."

Chance stifled a smile. The big man was tough, but he wasn't very bright.

"His broad wants a kid real bad." The big man swatted at a fly and cursed. "So let's just say he'll do whatever he has to do to get one. And he don't like to be double-crossed. So keep your nose clean."

"Okay. Yeah. What do I do next?"

"How long till you can deliver?"

"Five and a half or six months. Can't rush *that*, you know." Chance tried to emit a low chuckle that came out sounding more like a squeaky hinge.

"You better be on the up-and-up. I'm gonna clinch the deal with my client tonight. I'll be in touch. You got six months to deliver the goods. Keep the pregnant dame healthy is all I got to say. He don't take kindly to cancellations. Or complications. Now get lost. I gotta get away from these flies."

Chance stepped back into the kitchen. The smell of pizza was no longer pleasant to him. It made him sick. He deserved better.

Six months till I'm free of this joint.

Chapter 18

"Chance, I only have five months till the baby comes, and you haven't taken me into town *once* to look for a family."

"You got plenty of time. Don't nag me, or I won't take you at all."

"But you promised. You know how important it is to me." Sarah was near tears. Chance had changed since she moved to the shack with him. He left her home alone—a lot—and when he was home, he was either sleeping or playing his guitar.

He'd even taken the cute new outfits that hadn't been worn yet back to Dollar General. He needed the money, he said. He'd saved and scrimped enough to buy a small generator and a used electric guitar. His plan was to become a rock star.

She tried to follow him to town one day, but he rode so fast she quickly lost sight of him. The paths through the woods twisted and turned in all directions. After only a few minutes of trying to find her way alone, she realized she was hopelessly lost. It took an hour to get back to the shack. And her legs were scratched and bleeding from the briars.

It was chilly in the cabin, and Chance hadn't gathered any firewood. She found her coat thrown in one corner. There was no safety pin on the pocket anymore, and her money was gone. Sarah slipped the thin coat on to ward off the chill.

Next she searched in vain for her bag. Her pitiful little suitcase. But Chance had given or thrown it away. Or, if he could have sold it for fifty cents, she had no doubt he would have.

She rifled through the trash for anything of hers he may have thrown out and found the Gospel tract Sasha had left on the bus. She read it through once and then tucked it under a loose board in the floor. It became her lifeline as she faced each lonely day in a prison without bars. Her entire worldly possessions had been reduced to the clothes on her back and the little Gospel tract.

The only promise Chance kept, aside from not trying to sleep with her, was feeding her well. Every evening he brought home fresh fruit or vegetables and milk and fresh water to drink. He made sure she took her vitamins. Once a week, he'd bring home fresh fish. He wasn't interested in eating with her. He lived on fast food and candy.

Nor was he interested in sleeping with her. They hardly spoke. She was glad she didn't have to try to defend her honor, but she would have enjoyed some lively conversation with him once in a while. The way it used to be.

Before she moved in with him.

"Why did you tell me you wanted to marry me and be a father to my baby, when you won't even talk to me?" She shouted over the pounding and squealing of his guitar and the constant roar of his generator.

"I changed my mind."

"Well, I'm going back to the apartments. At least there I had someone to talk to occasionally. And I can walk to town."

He stopped playing and looked up at her. "You can't even find your stupid way out of the woods. How do you plan to get back to the apartments?"

Tears stung her eyes. "If you won't help me, I'll just walk until I come to something or someone. Anything would be better than the way I'm living here."

He walked to the door and looked out. "Well, it's almost dark. You can head out now, or we can talk about it in the morning." Sitting back down and picking up his guitar, the raucous noise resumed.

Sarah slept fitfully that night. Once in the night, she heard her door open. Chance looked into the dark room. Then walked over and touched her. She feigned sleep. Apparently satisfied she hadn't sneaked out, he left and closed the door.

Early the next morning, he peeked in. "Get up, Bumpkin, and go tee tee before we leave for the apartments."

"Really? You're taking me back?"

"That's what you want, isn't it?"

She hated being called Bumpkin, but she excitedly did as she was told. She'd decided she could live with the filth of the apartments better than she could live such a lonely existence. And, at last, she could begin her search.

When she got back in from the outhouse, Chance was waiting for her in the bedroom.

"I have a surprise for you. Come over here."

Hesitantly she moved closer to him at head of the bed, where he was holding his surprise for her behind his back.

He smiled "Now, close your eyes and put out your right hand."

Did our argument last night cause him to have a change of heart?

She hesitated.

Chance gave her his sad, repentant look, like he used to before he changed. "Come on, girl. I'm taking you back to the apartments. And I'm trying to make up with you. How can I if you won't close your eyes. I promise you . . . you're going to like it."

Excitedly, Sarah closed her eyes and put out her hand to receive his offering.

"Keep your eyes closed till I tell you to open them. This is my apology gift for being so mean to you." He held her hand gently and slipped something on her wrist.

Sarah smiled in spite of herself.

"Okay. Open your eyes." His gift made a ratcheting sound as he tightened it.

Sarah gasped. "Chance. No. Take it off."

The other end of her shiny new silver handcuff was attached to the metal headboard.

"Sorry. You can't be trusted anymore." Chance turned to leave the bedroom.

"Please, Chance, I'm afraid to be here alone, handcuffed to the bed."

"Afraid of the Boogieman?" He laughed. "I'll take them off when I get home, woman." He called over his shoulder. "I have to look out for my own interests."

From the doorway, he watched in amusement as she yanked and jerked at the handcuffs until her wrist began to get raw. Exhausted and defeated, she collapsed on the bed. "Oh, Chance, how could you do this to me?"

"There's a sandwich and a glass of water on the TV tray along with a few magazines. Relax and be glad you don't have to go to work like I do. I'll see you in six or eight hours."

After he closed and bolted the front door, Sarah waited a couple of minutes. Then she began screaming as loud as she could. "Help! Someone please help me." Over and over, until her throat was raw.

Chance could hear her. For a while. But as he pedaled deeper into the woods, the sound of her voice faded. Satisfied no one beyond a few hundred feet could hear noises from the shack, he put on the speed and hurried to the pizza joint. His only worry—she would struggle so hard she harmed his investment.

The baby.

He'd be glad when he had his money and was free of this woman and her baby.

He was sick and tired of worrying about seeing that she was well fed and cared for, with no reward for his efforts. More than once he'd seriously entertained the idea of joining Sarah in the bedroom. For a few minutes—or for the night. Now, more than ever. Only the thought he might be the cause of a miscarriage was powerful enough to keep him on his good behavior.

It certainly had nothing to do with his promise to her.

Chapter 19

Rob was standing at the nurse's station on the second floor. "Did any of you see which direction Sarah headed when she left the hospital?"

"No, Dr. Mac. We were all right here when she took the elevator."

A little red-headed nurse spoke up. "Actually, she didn't take the elevator. I saw her slip through the stairwell door. The stairwell would have taken her to the main street entrance if she followed her nose."

"Thanks, Red."

Rob literally ran down the hall to the stairwell. Taking the stairs three at a time, he emerged on the first floor just feet from the welcome desk. But his luck ran out there. No one remembered a pretty little dark-haired girl in a ragged dress emerging from the stairwell about three weeks ago.

Dejected, Rob walked out onto the city street and looked both ways. *She would have been hungry again.* Across the street and a couple of doors down the blinking "open" sign in a cafe window seemed to call to him.

"Yes," the waitress declared. "I remember her because she was quite thin, and I think she wanted to order some food but couldn't afford it. She put a ton of cream and sugar in her coffee and nursed it for a long time. She looked at the menu, then put it down. The poor little thing left a twenty-one cent tip." The waitress lowered her eyes and bit her lower lip—in deep thought. Raising her head, she pointed east. "I think she turned that way when she left. And she took off walking at a pretty determined pace."

Rob fished a ten-dollar bill out of his wallet. "This is from her, sweet lady. Thanks for your help."

"Oh, I can't take this." The waitress tried to stuff it back in his hand.

"Yes, you can. Do you know where this road leads if she kept going straight?"

"Far as I know, the street narrows and the neighborhood gets worse and worse. It ends up in some pretty nasty slums before you come to a big undeveloped and overgrown wooded area that covers miles and miles." She shook her head, woefully. "Sorry I can't be of more help."

"You've been a big help. Thanks again." Rob turned to leave.

"Wait. I almost forgot, there used to be a soup kitchen near the end of the road. Just a block or so before the road becomes impassable and the thick undergrowth takes over. Maybe she made it there. I hope so."

Rob took off at a run.

"Yes, there was a pretty little dark-haired girl who came here for a little while. Only a few days . . . maybe a week. She was always so polite and gracious." The lady smiled. "And she always accepted seconds. Then she stopped coming. I don't know what happened to her."

"Do you have any idea where she lived?" Rob wasn't a man to cry easily, but being so close and having just missed her was taking its toll on him.

"I think she stayed in an apartment building about a quarter of a mile that way." The kind lady pointed in the direction he'd just come from. "You must have passed it coming here. It would be on your left heading back. A really run-down, terrible-looking place. Painted a garish green with black shutters dangling at all angles from the windows."

When Rob pulled up to the apartment house, he shuddered at the thought of anyone, much less a little innocent like Sarah living there.

He bound up the front steps and thrust open the battered black door. Knocking on the first apartment door he came to, he was greeted by a young man with crusty brown hair. "Whatever you're selling, I don't want none." He closed the door in Rob's face.

But not before Rob stuck his foot in the door. "Oh no, you don't, young man. This is a matter of life and death."

When Rob described Sarah, someone from inside the apartment yelled out, "That sounds like Bumpkin. She moved out a couple of weeks ago."

"Do you know where she went?"

Everyone there knew she'd left with Chance. Though it seemed a pretty unlikely love affair, Chance had convinced them he and "his pretty" were honeymooning. And not to be disturbed.

A tall, skinny girl with bad teeth volunteered, "She left to move in with some guy. I think they moved out of town."

"Do any of you know the guy?"

"Nah." Every one of them shook their heads no. "Never saw him before."

Not one of them had dared to look Rob in the eye.

Chapter 20

"Thank you, Chance. Thank you. Thank you. Thank you." The demon of fear was beside himself. "Have you been out to the shack lately, worm." Fear loved to call the underlings "worm." They dare not challenge him. And the one that had been issued to him as a helper today was as worthless as a two-dollar watch.

"Of course you haven't. Well, you're going with me today. And you're going to learn some things no one . . . I said *no one* but me . . . I . . . me . . . whatever . . . is qualified to teach you."

He speeded ahead, leaving the underling struggling to keep up. They whizzed over thousands of closely huddled trees that were just beginning to sprout fresh green leaves. It could have been a beautiful sight to behold, but Fear was only interested in getting to the shack. Secluded, ramshackle, and spooky. That was more his cup of tea.

Screeching to a halt above the dilapidated structure, he hung in the air and waited for his wannabe assistant. "Here we are, *and there she is.* Our project of the hour." He pointed in the window at a frightened, frail girl who was just beginning to show some outward signs of being with child.

"She's afraid because, well, just look around you. All sorts of things could go wrong. A storm could brew and blow this shack away. A thief could come and find her, helplessly handcuffed to the bed." He cleared his throat. "This is my favorite. She's afraid someone will buy this land and have this shack dozed flat, with her inside."

"And so . . .," his helper muttered.

"And so . . . I do an excellent bulldozer. Watch this."

From deep within his throat emerged the sound of an approaching bulldozer. They watched as Sarah strained to look out the single window of her prison cell. But the sound came from the other side of the shack. It got louder and louder. Sarah struggled and screamed.

Fear dove at the building causing it to tremble. Then came a scraping noise, like a blade against the side of the building.

"Help. Stop. There's someone in here." Her voice was swallowed up by the thick, pungent air, and drowned out by the deafening rumble.

Fear was laughing so hard he fell forward and plunged downward into the side of the shack. Against the lone window in the bedroom. His form was plastered across the glass, throwing Sarah into dusky darkness. Shaking in fear and sobbing, she called out to God for help.

"This can't be happening, Lord. Please help me."

It isn't happening, child. You must learn to recognize your enemy.

Immediately her demeanor changed. She stood straight and raised her voice.

"I command you to leave. In the name of *Jesus*," she yelled at the top of her lungs, tears washing down her cheeks.

The underling was the first to go because of his small size. The demon of fear was right behind him and gaining on him as the force of the name of Jesus sent them tumbling and spinning across the opening and into the deep woods. The underling wrapped around a tree, and Fear, right behind him, hit him with full force. They both crumbled to the ground in a thousand pieces.

And Sarah got the first rest she'd had in days, secure in the name of Jesus.

An hour later, the sound of Chance working to unbolt the door awakened Sarah with a start.

Her emotions were a jumble. This young man she'd trusted with her future—and that of her child—had become her worst nightmare, *and yet her only hope*. She shuddered to think of what would happen to her if he was injured or killed in an accident one day. No one knew she was imprisoned deep in these woods. No one would come to rescue her. Ever.

※

It was now necessary for Chance to watch Sarah every moment she was not incarcerated. It became the daily routine for him to walk her to the outhouse in the morning and wait until she was finished. Then he would take her by the hand. Lead her through the weeds, back to the shack and into the bedroom where he forcibly handcuffed her the bed.

In the evening, he'd lock the door from the inside and free her long enough to cook a little meal in the tiny living room fireplace. And take another chaperoned trip to the outhouse. Then he handcuffed her on—sometimes outside to a tree—while he gathered water from the stream about fifty yards from the shack.

Before bedtime, he'd warm the water and stretch a sheet across the windowless end of the living room to provide a place for her to bathe. Let's face it, he was *working* for the money she would bring in. No one could call him lazy.

Sarah was grateful for the tub of warm water and the privacy to enjoy it. One evening after her bath, Sarah begged him to let her stay in the living room for a while. She sat next to him on the filthy old couch, leaned forward and bid him put the guitar aside and talk to her.

"I don't know why you're doing this, Chance. What good am I to you? Why won't you let me go? You could get your life back. You can't be enjoying the responsibility of keeping me a prisoner."

Chance didn't look up or put his guitar aside. "I have my reasons," he said over the repeated practicing of one chord that was alluding him.

"Please, please," she pleaded. "You must let me go to find a family for my baby. What will you do with the two of us? Will you keep my child a prisoner too?"

With an aggravated sigh, he laid his guitar down. "I *told* you *I* want the baby. I told you before you ever moved in with me. You see, I never intended to let you give it away." His voice took on a whiney tone and he avoided her eyes. "What? Did you think you could charm me into changing my mind? Not gonna happen. You're carrying *my* baby."

Oh God, it never occurred to me Chance truly wants a child of his own.

"I thought you understood." She put her hand on his jaw and turned his face toward her. "Look at me, Chance. That is not going to happen. We are not keeping this child only to have it live in poverty. I won't *let* that happen."

"Ha!" he snorted. "*You* won't let it happen. Since when do you have any say about *anything*?" He stood up, grabbed her arm, and dragged her to the bedroom. "All you have to do is see that this baby is born healthy. I'm in charge of everything else."

Sarah sank down on the side of the bed. Tired and listless, she let him lock the cuff on her tender, inflamed wrist.

"You're a fool, Chance. You're not in charge of anything. Don't you know I should be under a doctor's care?"

Without a word, he left the room for a moment, leaving Sarah waiting expectantly for his reply. Returning with a small tube of antibiotic ointment, which he kept in his jacket pocket, he pulled the chair closer to the bed.

"Dr. Chance at your service." He squeezed a little ointment on his right forefinger and began gently applying it to Sarah's sore wrist. It was almost as though he cared.

He spoke in a flat tone. "I've read up on it, Sarah. You're getting all the right food and vitamins. The baby will be okay."

His thoughtful treatment of her wrist and his earlier confession that he wanted to keep the baby confused Sarah. Her voice was soft. Almost tender. "Chance, you're acting like a crazy person. You're definitely not thinking very far ahead. Tell me . . . who is going to deliver the baby? You?"

He was only a couple of feet from her, his right ankle crossed over his left knee. His head down. It was obvious he hadn't thought about the delivery. "Maybe I can get Sylvia to help me."

Sarah reached out to touch his leg with her free hand. "No, please. So many things can go wrong. I need to be in a hospital for the birth. Please, Chance. Do that much for me."

If I can just get him to talk rationally about the birth of my baby, maybe I can make him see his plan to raise the child out here in the wilderness is not a good one.

Roughly knocking her hand from his leg, he raised his voice several decibels. "Nothing is going to go wrong. Why must you always harp on that subject? I know what I'm doing. You're eating good. Taking your vitamins. You're getting plenty of rest and a little sunshine. What could go wrong?"

Almost apologetically, she replied, "Well, for one thing, my wrist could get infected. I do appreciate your putting salve on it, though." She smiled and nodded her head slightly, trying desperately to restore the almost civil atmosphere of a few moments ago.

"Yeah, my pleasure," he retorted sarcastically. "I hope you don't get the idea it's because I give a crap. Just trying to keep you from getting sick before the baby gets here."

Still trying to calm him but with tears quickly rising to the surface, Sarah pleaded, "Oh, Chance, can't we just talk to each other without the animosity?"

He jumped up from his chair. "I'm getting a headache. I hate to be nagged." He blew out a long breath. "Okay. Okay. You want to know. I'll tell you. Surprise. Surprise. I've already got a family for the baby. So I'll tell them you think you need a midwife present. They got connections and dough. Won't be a problem."

A family! The subject of the delivery was blown from her mind. Sarah jumped to her feet, her arm yanked behind her. Eye to eye with her captor, she demanded, "Who? When do I get to meet them?"

"You don't. They want everyone to think the baby is theirs, the natural way. The old lady is going to wear a false belly when time comes to start showing. Probably already started wearing one. You *are* getting a little pudgy, you know." He smiled an evil grin and put his hand on her belly. Sarah shoved it away.

"Chance, please . . . please . . . tell me you're teasing. You can't do this to me." Sarah's breathing was coming in gasps.

"Oh, really? Watch me. Their agent is meeting me and the baby at a little cafe on the other side of Dallas after it's born. Your job will be done."

"No! Please, Chance. At least let me meet them so I can know what kind of home it will be going to."

"No can do. I don't even get to meet them. The family is rolling in dough. They just can't use the normal adoption channels."

"Why not?"

"Let's just say your baby's new father makes his living in a manner the law finds repugnant, so they try to keep a low profile. But that doesn't keep the old lady from having maternal instincts. Like you. You know what I mean?"

Sarah's mouth hung open. Words failed her and she felt like her heart was going to explode. She lunged at him so hard the bed moved. And her wrist began to bleed.

He turned to leave the room. Swinging around, he added, "So I have to follow the rules they set down—or else."

"Dear God, Chance. What do you mean 'or else'? What have you done?"

"I've stuck my neck way out. If I don't carry though now, there's a price on *my* head." He walked back to the bed and pushed her down on it. He turned the chair around. Sitting in it backward, he faced her and smiled smugly. "Like I said, it's *my* baby. You gave up all your rights to it when you moved in with me for free rent and food . . . all the while knowing I wanted it." He grabbed her free wrist as she lashed out at him. "It's mine and I can do what I want with it. And I just made the biggest money-making deal of my life. The deal that will get me out of this hell hole and into a real house. I'll never have to eat pizza again . . . and I'll be off that bike and into a cool car. Maybe one of those monster pickups. You may not know this, but healthy babies bring a bundle if you know the right people." He released her wrist and jumped back out of her reach.

A scream began in the depths of her being and ripped from Sarah's throat. "*Noooo!*" She strained helplessly to reach him with her free hand. "You're *selling* my baby? You can't do that. I won't *let* you." She collapsed on the bed, sobbing.

"There you go again, telling me what I can or can't do. Wake up, Bumpkin. You don't have a say in the matter. You sold your baby to me for a free meal ticket." He shook his head slowly, as though in sympathy. "Now it's mine to do with as I please."

"And what are you going to do with *me* afterward? You can't just toss me out. I'll be a thorn in your side forever. I won't let you get away with this. And I don't think you have what it takes to *kill* me."

He sat back down, just out of her reach. "You may be right. I probably don't have it in me to kill you."

Her hopes lifted, Sarah smiled. "Now you're making sense, Chance. Let me go now, and I promise I won't tell anyone anything about this."

He shook his head in mock sadness. "No can do. I've already made the deal. I'm locked in. If I go to the big man now and tell him it's off, he'll chop me into little pieces. And I'm the only one who knows where you are. So that wouldn't go too well for you either." He shot her a look of pure evil. "But don't you worry, I'll figure out *something* to do with you."

How did I ever believe he was a friend? I'm such a fool.

He turned to go, then whipped around. "Hey, I got an idea. Maybe I can find a house with a basement. That way I can keep you. We might even make another baby."

His laugh seemed to emerge from the pits of hell. He turned to leave and slammed the door behind him.

Sarah's water glass crashed into the back of the door as it closed. Water and glass detonated and spewed to every corner of the room.

"Not a smart move, Miss Sarah Blake." He mocked from the other side of the door. "Hope you don't get thirsty tonight."

She was right. He wasn't thinking very far ahead.

And he knew it. He plunked down on the couch. So many ifs.

What if her wrist gets infected? And what about when she needs to use the rest room more than twice a day? And who'll deliver the baby out here in the wilderness? I'm afraid the big man will consider a request for a midwife a complication. *But if the delivery goes south, I'm dead meat. But I sure can't involve Sylvia. I'd have to give her a cut. No, there's not enough to go around.*

And what am I gonna do with Sarah when this is over? I just told her I might keep her. Could be fun, for a while . . . but that's not really an option. I'd just be delaying the problem of what to do when I'm done with her.

I don't think I can bring myself to off her. Man, I gotta come up with something. Maybe someone else would like to have her.

That's it! She's young and pretty. And homeless. No one misses her now and no one would miss her if she fell off the face of the earth. Maybe . . . just maybe . . . she'll bring a good price.

The next morning, Sarah planned to make a run for it when Chance took her to the outhouse.

But as soon as he opened the door, he threw a broom at her. "Clean up your mess before I take you outside. Better do a good job, because you don't get to put shoes on this morning."

With a smirk on his face and his arms crossed, he watched as Sarah struggled to sweep up the broken glass with one hand. She could only reach the area close to where she got in and out of bed. He carelessly cleared a walkway to the door. Then made her walk barefoot in the cold to the outhouse. Her feet were freezing and she could barely walk in the brambles and rocks—much less run.

When they returned, she put up a valiant fight to keep him from putting the handcuffs back on. She scratched and bit and kicked. To no avail. Even with him holding back his ire, to keep from harming the baby, she was no match for him.

Chance was shaking by the time he got the cuff on. "I should pull your nails out by the roots, but I won't do that because I've figured out what to do with you when we're done here. And for that, I gotta keep you pretty."

"What are you talking about?"

"Don't have time to discuss it now. But it's gonna make me even richer.'

He threw her a kiss. "Be good today. I'm sorry I didn't have time to make you anything to eat or drink. You kept me up too late last night with your tantrum."

"What about the baby?"

"One day without food won't hurt it. Maybe this will teach you to be more obedient."

Obedient! She glared at him. "I'm losing it, Chance. Being imprisoned day after day is more than I can handle. I'll fight you tooth and nail from this point forward. Do what you must to me. But I won't make it easy for you anymore."

"Two can play that game, wench." He turned to leave. "I'll be home when I get home." He slammed the bedroom door so hard the window rattled. She heard him bolting the outside door.

She fell back onto the bed and cried herself to sleep thinking about Sam and Vivi and the kids. *Will I ever see them again?*

Chapter 21

Beth approached him tenderly. "Rob, I didn't think the day would ever come when I'd have to tell you this. But you need a shower. A long, soapy one. And a shave while you're at it."

"Sorry, sweetheart. Part of the disguise. Have you ever seen a homeless guy who looked like he just stepped out of the shower?"

"You're really serious about this, aren't you?"

"Never been more serious. God hasn't let me rest one minute where this girl's concerned. And He's impressed me with a great urgency, honey. Two lives are at stake here. Sarah's and her baby's." He turned to her, his eyes imploring her to understand. "I've got to find her, Beth."

He stroked his six-day beard. "This is driving me crazy, but I've got to look—and smell—the part. That's the only reason I'm sleeping in the guest room. You do know *that*, don't you?"

"Of course. But don't you think you're about ready."

"I'd like to have gotten started two days ago. But, remember, these kids have seen me clean-shaven, showered, and neatly dressed. I know they were lying. Sarah is still in the area, and I'm going to find her. There's no way that young lady would run off to live with some guy after only knowing him a couple of days." He scratched his head and looked down at his grungy fingernails. "Yuck! But I have to be sure they don't recognize me, or the whole plan will go down the tubes."

Last week, Beth had helped Rob streak his hair with gray. He normally wore it a little longer than average, and with the help of a scissors chop here and there, she managed to make it look badly neglected. Then they rubbed it down good with used motor oil. "Like Brylcreem," Rob joshed, "a little dab'll do ya."

For the next week, he hadn't bathed, shaved, or washed his hair. He literally rummaged through the dump to find a pair of ill-fitting pants, a filthy shirt, a stained and ripped suit jacket, and a pair of scuffed-up, ill-fitting shoes with holes in the soles. For the final touch, Rob found a pair of dingy and scratched, used eyeglasses with one stem held together with adhesive tape.

"Today's the day." Rob smiled at his image in the mirror the next morning.

But something was wrong. The gummy hair, the beard, the broken glasses, and filthy clothes all faded into the background. He still didn't look like a homeless derelict.

"My teeth. They're like spotlights shining back at me from a junkyard." He sighed a long, weary sigh. After not brushing for the past few days, he could hardly stand himself. But his teeth still looked too nice.

Rob had lost one bottom front tooth and the canine tooth next to it in a minor accident while still in college. His dentist fitted him with a flawless partial plate. In later years he'd always intended to get implants but had never gotten around to it.

No one but his dentist had ever seen him without his partial. Not even Beth. *Especially not Beth,* although she knew he wore a partial. She called him "her handsome prince." Why would he want to destroy her illusion by letting her see him with his front teeth missing, now—after ten years of blissful marriage?

But what choice did he have?

He took out his partial plate and smiled into the mirror again. Wrapping it in tissue and placing it carefully in the cabinet, he headed for the patio to show the woman he loved just how awful he was capable of looking.

They met for coffee on the patio. Beth drew in a sharp breath when he smiled at her. "Rob, your own mother wouldn't recognize you."

"I'm so sorry you have to see me like this, darling. I hope we can wash it all out of your mind when this is over. And I pray you don't stop loving me, now that you've seen the *real* me." Rob threw her a kiss. "I'd like to hold you, but . . ."

"Robert McKinley, don't you ever talk like that. I've never loved you more than I do right this minute."

"In that case, do we have any blueberry pie left?" He smiled an embarrassed smile. "I think a lovely blue stain on my remaining teeth would be a nice touch."

"One more sip, Beth, and I'm going to start the long walk to the slums where Sarah was last seen."

"Why don't you let me give you a ride as far as downtown? It's an awfully long way." She touched his cheek and shook her head. "I'm very worried about this idea of yours, Rob. If you get found out . . . who knows what could happen."

Rob took one last long slug of coffee. "I'm going to be walking everywhere for a while, sweetheart. Might as well get used to it. As far as being found out . . . I'll have nothing on me in the way of identification . . ."

"Not even your cell phone?"

"*Especially* not my cell phone. No wallet either. Only two or three wadded up dollar bills and a dirty comb." He stood and picked up his black trash bag containing an old homeless man's treasures. A filthy pillow, a ragged blanket, and a paint-stained piece of tarp.

"Oh, Rob. How will I know you're all right? I'm so afraid for you." She threw her arms around him in spite of his lack of hygiene.

"Don't be. God is with me. Just pray I get to Sarah in time." He stepped off the patio and made his way to the back gate and into the alley, past the garbage cans. He peeked in one as he passed it, for Beth's amusement. She shook her head, smiled sadly, and threw him a kiss.

Chapter 22

A couple of hours later, a bent-over Dr. Rob McKinley walked into the main door of the hospital where he worked, clutching his black trash bag in his grimy fist. The slight limp he'd acquired from walking so far in ill-fitting shoes only added to his new identity. He stopped a gentleman who happened to be rushing by and looked straight into his eyes—the eyes of one of his long-time colleagues.

The gentleman paused long enough to ask, "Is there something I can do for you, sir?"

"Heard there was a soup kitchen on this road. Do ya happen to know how much farther?"

"I'm afraid it's several more miles east of here. I doubt you can make it before lunch is served. But there's a cafe right across the street." The physician reached into his pocket and withdrew a ten-dollar bill. "Please . . . have lunch on me today."

Rob grabbed the ten like a starving man. "Thanks, mister. Pay you back when I get on my feet." He turned, managing to suppress a grin, and quickly shuffled to the exit.

I didn't realize Glenn was such a nice guy. Won't he be surprised when I pay him back?

The test had worked. If his colleagues couldn't recognize him, a bunch of kids he'd only met once would be a piece of cake.

Rob didn't have lunch on Glenn. Instead he folded the ten-dollar bill into a tiny square and hid it in a rip in the lining of his once-upon-a-time expensive right shoe. Arriving

THE TRINITY QUILTS

in the slum neighborhood where Sarah was last seen, he shuffled past the ugly green apartment building without looking to either side. But with his peripheral vision, he saw the Venetian blinds in the front apartment part enough to allow a pair of eyes to follow him. His heart stepped up a beat or two. It was the apartment he'd visited two weeks earlier.

There was a run-down boarding house on the other side of the street, with a sign proclaiming THREE DOLLARS A NITE in large red print. He turned and headed down the broken concrete walk. Clutching the banister as though it was his lifeline, he struggled up the creaking steps.

In his scratchiest voice, Rob muttered, "Do I get clean sheets for three dollars a night?"

From behind the desk, "Old man, you wouldn't know a clean sheet if it bit you."

"Ain't payin' three dollars for dirty sheets."

"Then let me show you to the door, your majesty."

Rob mumbled something about the man's ancestry and made his way back out the door. He was making sure his presence in the neighborhood was duly noted.

He continued hobbling in the direction of the soup kitchen. It was closed up tight. *See you tomorrow* was written with a blue marker on a sheet of paper tacked to the door. He tried the knob anyway and jiggled it a little for the benefit of anyone who might be watching. Then he checked out the line of garbage cans. He took small bits of food out of a couple of the cans, and stuffed them in his pocket. Inside, his stomach churned at the abominable things he was doing.

Love endureth all things.

He poked around the outside of the building until he found a slight inset in the wall. About three feet deep and four feet wide. Immediately he laid claim on the space. Carefully opening his trash bag, he took out the blanket and the pillow and spread them in the small alcove. Then he curled up in the space and feigned sleep. From his comfy spot, he was able to case the neighborhood.

About five o'clock that evening, a young man rode by on a bicycle. He had a grocery bag hanging off each side of the handlebars. And a pizza box tied on the rack over the rear wheel. He glanced around to see if anyone was watching before he ducked into an opening between two trees. He was swallowed by the overgrowth in seconds.

Thirty minutes later, several of the kids from the apartment house walked by hooting and hollering. One of the guys nudged Rob with his foot. "Hey, who told you that you could sleep here?"

Rob pulled his blanket tight around his head and tried to ignore the intrusion. Two more guys joined in. "Get outta here . . . your reservation's been cancelled." Followed by laughter, and a couple more sandaled feet to the groin. Rob grit his teeth and received their jibes and blows in silence.

"Leave the old guy alone. He ain't hurting nothin'." It was the girl's voice. The tall skinny girl who'd said "Bumpkin" had left with a guy.

Rob longed to jump up and grab one of the guys by the throat and throttle the truth out of him. But in the long run, this plan would bring him more information—if he could just be patient.

As they departed, Rob heard one say, "Let's go pay a visit to the honeymooners." That idea was nixed by the others quickly. Amid much suggestive talk.

Rob wondered if the honeymooners were Sarah and the guy she ran off with.

And had she really left with him willingly?

A dark shroud seemed to settle over him and the demon of doubt whispered in his ear. "Sarah has made her choice, and it's really none of your business. Go home to your wife."

Chapter 23

It wasn't the first time Rob had heard the voice of a demon. And it probably wouldn't be the last. He lie awake on the hard cement surface. Cold crept clear into his bones, and the only good thing he could say about it was, he wasn't really old. He was only thirty-five and in excellent health. He'd live through it, whereas an old homeless man might not. With an aching heart, he made a mental note to give more to their church ministry to the homeless.

A few fitful hours of sleep ended before sunrise. It would be many hours before he could continue his investigation into Sarah's disappearance. His mind turned back to the young man on the bike over and over. It was like the Lord was trying to tell him something.

"Father," he prayed, *"please give me supernatural insight into this situation. Please guide me by Your wisdom and Your mighty power. This child I'm seeking to find and save needs me. But more than that, she needs You. Help me, Abba Father. Go before me and lead me to her, wherever she is. In Jesus's name, I pray. Amen.*

He saw the young man on the bike emerge from the woods around 10:00 a.m. Apparently on his way to work. It was still too soon to take any action, so Rob feigned sleep a while longer. At long last, it was time to go into the soup kitchen for lunch. He was genuinely hungry. And pleasantly surprised at the quality of the food heaped on his plate as he worked his way through the line.

God worked it out so most the seats were taken except for a few vacant spots close to the kids from the apartment house. Rob had excellent hearing, but he had asked the servers to repeat themselves, many times—pretending to be nearly deaf. He heard several cracks from the kids about his deafness.

"No wonder he didn't move last night. He probably didn't even hear what we said," one of the guys remarked.

Another came back with, "Must be numb too. Didn't even flinch when we kicked him."

"Well," came a third voice, "if he wasn't numb before, he is now." This remark was met with much laughter.

Rob kept his misfit, grubby glasses on during the meal. They made him a little dizzy, but that only added to the effect of his advanced age and demented condition. He didn't take his eyes off his food. And ate like he hadn't had a meal in days.

And he listened—undetected.

"So," the skinny girl began, "exactly what did Chance say about him and Bumpkin when you asked why he never has us over anymore?"

Chance. Now Rob had a name. But was it Chance who rode the bike into the woods?

The guy with the brown crusty hair answered. "He said his old lady is sick all the time. Having a rough pregnancy." He laughed sarcastically. "Guess he's finding out being a daddy-to-be ain't all that much fun. Anyways, she don't want no company, and he's so exhausted from waiting on her, he don't feel like partying. Sad state of affairs."

Everyone started talking at the same time. "I don't see Chance falling for her anyway. It happened too fast. And we all know he's not the homebody type."

"Yeah, kinda wonder what he's up to myself."

"You guys see him every evening bringing home the bacon—on his bike? Riding it a mile back into the sticks to feed his crabby old lady has gotta be getting old."

His bike. Thank you, Lord.

"You know, right before he met Bumpkin, he told me he had some sort of a deal going that was going to get him outta that shack for good. Then all of a sudden, he's Mr. House-Husband. Something fishy going on, if you ask me."

Rob was eager to look for the shack, before this Chance guy got home. But if he rushed out right now, he might arouse suspicion. So he dawdled over his food, performed a pretty convincing coughing spell, and pretended to doze off a time or two.

Finally, he felt a rough hand on his shoulder. "Wake up, old man. And see if you can't get yourself a bath somewhere. You about ruined my lunch." The kids tumbled out the door, laughing uncontrollably.

Rob waited until he didn't hear them any longer. Then he ambled out the door carrying his ever-present black trash bag.

From out of nowhere, someone snatched the bag from his hand. He let himself be hustled around the corner of the building, his feet dragging. With one kid holding his arms behind his back, another searched his pockets.

"Please don't hurt me," he begged.

This earned him a jab to the kidneys.

"Yuck. Three stinkin' wadded up dollar bills, lots of lint, half a cookie, and a piece of hamburger with mustard on it. I think I'm goin' be sick."

Rob was begging, "Please don't hurt me. Don't take my stuff. It's all I got."

"Who'd want your junk, you stinkin' old man?" The biggest one of the punks threw his black trash bag into the middle of the street. "You want it, you go get it."

THE TRINITY QUILTS

A black belt in karate since high school, it was all he could do to keep from mopping up the sidewalk with the punks. When they became bored with pushing him around, they pocketed his three dollars and released him. He slipped to the sidewalk like a rag doll. Scooting along as fast as he could into the little alcove he'd slept in last night, he covered his head with his arms and waited until they were out of sight. Then he crept, head down, into the street to retrieve his bag of treasures and slinked back into his niche.

He'd noted of the location of the opening where Chance slipped into the trees yesterday. There was a pile of trash just feet from the spot. Rob limped over to the trash pile and began sifting through it.

Apparently he'd already become enough of a landmark that people paid little attention to him. When no one was in sight, he ducked into the opening in the trees and moved swiftly into the brush. When he was far enough in that his movements couldn't be seen, he took off his spectacles and began looking for bicycle tire tracks.

He was elated when he spied them. *I always knew my Boy Scout Indian badge would come in handy someday.*

The tire tracks were fairly easy to follow. Though he was constantly looking behind himself for fear the bicycle and rider were about to overtake him. It was a very long way into the woods. Much farther than he'd anticipated.

The trail, only wide enough to accommodate a bicycle, opened abruptly into a clearing. And there it was, a hundred feet ahead. A run-down old shack. It looked deserted, but for a small trail of smoke coming from the cracked and sagging chimney. Rob had a strong feeling there was a frightened young woman inside. Now that he saw the place he supposed her to be, he couldn't help but wonder why—if she was in there against her will—she hadn't simply walked out while

Chance was at work. The place didn't look sturdy enough to hold anyone in who truly wanted out.

She's a tramp and she wants to be with him. That's why. Go back to your fine home, and leave her alone. She's happy here.

He was hearing the disparaging voices again. Reason enough to believe he was on the right track. Rob asked the Lord for help in knowing what to do next. He could knock on the door. But if she answered and told him she was perfectly content where she was, could he just walk away and forget about her and her baby? Did he have any other choice?

He crouched down and peeked in the front windows. There were dishes in the sink and a few smoldering logs in the fireplace. But there was no sign of an occupant. He crept around the back. There was one window. Crouching down he looked in.

What he saw struck his heart like a knife.

Her dark curly hair had grown some. Tousled yet beautiful. She was wearing a thin shift dress, lying barefoot on a dirty mattress plopped carelessly on an old metal bed. There were no sheets and one thin cover. Her back was to the window, and her right arm was raised above her head—*handcuffed* to the metal headboard. Her hand hung limp.

Oh, Lord, please. Let me be in time.

He tried the window, but it was painted shut. He ran around the front to try the other windows, but they, too, had been painted so many times they couldn't be opened. The door was locked with a heavy bolt. He fiddled with it, but soon realized it couldn't be cracked without tools.

He thought he heard her stir. He ran back to the bedroom window and peeked in.

She was looking straight at him. Forgetting for a moment how he must have looked to her, he put his forefinger to his lips. *Shhh.* Her mouth formed a perfect O, but the sound of her screams didn't register in his mind for a split second. Then he realized, because of his appearance, she could only see him as a threat. So much unlike himself that his own mother wouldn't recognize him, his wife had said. He ducked back out of sight to rethink the situation.

———

Sarah's worst nightmare had come true. There was a filthy, dreadful-looking man skulking around the shack.

He suddenly dropped out of sight.

Where'd he go? Oh God, it there another way in? Did Chance lock the door when he left this morning?

She shouted, "I have a gun, and I know how to use it." Even as she said it, she knew how ridiculous it sounded. He'd seen her predicament and knew very well she couldn't defend herself.

He was back at the window.

It was only a matter of time until he found his way in. Then she'd be at his mercy.

His lips were moving. He was probably thanking whoever had chained her on. She was helpless. His for the taking. All he had to do was get in. He began clawing and prying desperately at the window, with a rusty piece of metal that had been laying behind the house.

Fighting the urge to faint, Sarah cried out so loud the angels must have put their hands over their ears. "Leave me alone. Be gone in the name of Jesus."

He wasn't blown away.

He didn't disintegrate.

Because he was no demon. He was a dirty, evil, flesh and blood man.

Tapping.
Scraping.
Prying.
Determined to get to her.

Rob could see every move Sarah made. She looked around for something to throw at him, but there was nothing in the bare room but her bed and a chair that was too far away for her to reach, and far too heavy for her to throw anyway. She was trapped like a frightened animal. With the window closed tightly and Sarah screaming hysterically, nothing he yelled was getting through to her.

Her shackled wrist was beginning to bleed again. And her belly was showing the first plump signs she was carrying a baby. He had to calm her before she hurt herself.

Inside, a chunk of paint fell from the window casing to the floor, and Rob was able to open the window a few inches. He reached his hand toward her.

"Sarah, Sarah," he began yelling. It's me, Dr. McKinley."

"Go away, whoever you are. Leave me alone. My husband will be home any minute."

He hoped she'd only said that to frighten him away. He was making progress with the window.

"I'm Dr. Mac, Sarah. Remember. It's me. I won't hurt you. I'm here to help you."

"You're no doctor. You're a tramp and a nasty, toothless pervert. Get out. Don't you dare touch me. I swear my husband will kill you if you come close to me."

Rob had to think fast. Chance could be home at any moment. "Noodle soup, Sarah. Noodle soup and crackers at the hospital."

She stopped screaming momentarily. She stared at him with a questioning look in her eyes. However, it was soon replaced by the look of panic. "How do you know these things about me? Who are you? Go away. Please . . . leave me alone." She sank onto the bed, sobbing.

"I told you I'd be back the next morning, but I was in an accident. But I'm here for you now. Please believe me. I only want to help."

"Dr. . . . Dr. McKinley?" She drew a deep, shaky breath. "No. No. You're lying. Why would Dr. McKinley be looking for me?"

"Listen to me, Sarah. Your last name is Blake, and you're pregnant. They brought you to the hospital because you fainted at the bus station."

She wrinkled her brow and examined his face. Recognition kindled in her eyes.

"But . . . but why do you look like that?'

"To find you. No one would talk to me when I was a doctor. I had to become a homeless man to fit in. Now I've got to get this window open. When will Chance be home?"

"I don't know. He was mad at me when he left this morning. He may come home early to mete out some kind of punishment, or he may stay out real late to frighten me." She reached her free hand in his direction. "Please hurry, Dr. McKinley. I'm so afraid of him."

The window was hopelessly stuck. Rob searched the ground for something hard and found an old brick. "Step back and protect your eyes, Sarah, I'm going to break the glass."

In moments, Rob was in the bedroom, holding Sarah close. She clung to him, breathing in gasps. Seemingly unable to stop trembling.

"You're okay now, Sarah, but we've got to move fast. Think hard. Where might he have hidden the key to the cuffs?"

"He puts it in his pocket, Dr. McKinley. He never lets it out of his sight."

"Then we'll just have to wait until he gets home. Is there any ointment in the house for your wrist?"

"No. He takes it with him too. He puts it on my wrist once in a while. Says he has to keep me and the baby healthy." She was gripping Rob's clothing with her free hand, as though she could keep him from disappearing.

Rob was stupefied. "So he loves you and the baby? And this is his way of keeping you from leaving him?"

"Oh, no. He wants to keep the baby healthy, because . . . because . . ." The words burst from her in an explosion of tears. "He's planning to *sell* it."

Rob's eyes must have revealed his complete disbelief. "*Sell it?*"

Sarah blurted out, "I don't know how I got myself into this. I promise. I moved in with him because he said he only wanted to help me. But he makes me stay here all the time. He won't let me look for a family for my baby. Then he insisted *he* wanted the baby. You know, like he wanted to be the father. When I got scared of him and told him I was leaving, he started chaining me to the bed. He started calling the baby his *investment*. Now he says I gave up all my rights to my baby in exchange for free room and board. And he has the right to do whatever he wants with it."

"You did no such thing, Sarah. That is not going to happen."

She leaned into his chest and moaned. "Dr. McKinley, he already has a buyer."

"Put it from your mind. You are the baby's mother and it's *your* decision who will raise it." Rob turned her face to look at him. "You have my word."

Both of them seemed to have had forgotten Rob's grotesque appearance.

Rob held her trembling, tiny frame for a long time—until she was able to gain control of her emotions. Very gently, he asked, "Has he violated you?" Rob was having a very hard time keeping his voice at a normal range.

"No. That's the only promise he's kept. Though he's hinted at breaking it. I think he's afraid he might hurt the baby and lose his investment. Oh, Dr. McKinley. He has a violent temper."

"You're safe now, Sarah. He can't hurt you anymore."

"But he's young and strong. What if he . . . what if he . . ."

"What if he hurts *me*, Sarah? He shook his head and smiled. I don't think that's going to be a problem."

They both heard Chance working to unlock the bolt at the same time. Rob backed up and stood against the wall where the bedroom door would hide him when Chance opened it.

Chance burst in holding up a nail clipper. "Okay, Bumpkin. You're about to get your nails chopped off. You better not struggle either. These things could take off the end of a finger."

Jerking his head to the right he did a double take, "What the . . . Who broke the window?" Jaws clamped and fire in his eyes, he shook a fist in Sarah's direction. Rob stepped out from behind the door. "That would be *me*, tough guy."

Chance's jaw dropped. "And who are *you*? Oh, yeah, the old bum that showed up in town yesterday. What the hell are you doing in my old lady's bedroom? I'm going to mop the floor with you, old man."

Chance pounced toward Rob with a vengeance. Rob met his attack with a roundhouse kick that landed the younger man flat on his back.

Chance pulled himself up, shaking his head. "What the . . ."

"Now get up and unlock the lady's handcuff. Leave the other end on the bed rail."

Chance didn't move

"Now!" Rob picked him off the floor by his shirt collar and belt and set him on his feet.

Chance reached into his pocket and whipped out a pocket knife, which Rob swiftly kicked from his hand. It landed on the other side of the room.

Stunned, Chance stuttered, "Who . . . who are you anyway?"

"I'm the homeless old bum who's going to clean the glass shards off this floor with your butt if you don't free Sarah immediately."

Chance produced the key from his pants pocket and, hands shaking, unlocked and opened the handcuff. Holding her wrist, Sarah dashed past him to stand behind Rob. She put her hand on his shoulder, as though to assure herself this wasn't a dream. She'd really been rescued.

Without taking his eyes off Chance, Rob reached up and patted her hand. "Now, give me the key, pizza boy, and put the cuff on *your* wrist. I'm going to give you a little taste of what it's like."

Chance's eyes flitted toward the door. He looked ready to make a break for it.

Rob moved in front of the door. "I can do it for you after you're unconscious, if you prefer."

Reluctantly, Chance gave Rob the key and slipped the handcuff on his own wrist, ratcheting it shut only a little.

"Oh, come on. I want you to enjoy this experience to the fullest." Rob reached over and squeezed it as tight as it would go. And stuck the key in his pocket. Right in there with the piece of hamburger and the broken cookie.

"Now, just take a little rest. I'll stop at the police station on the way home and let them know you're expecting them. I wouldn't try leaving by the window if I were you. The bed won't go through."

───※───

There were still a couple of hours of daylight left. Rob rode the bike down the wooded path, with Sarah balancing precariously on the handlebars. They emerged on the other side in time to see the sun set.

"I think that must be the most beautiful sunset I've ever seen." She sighed.

"Get used to it, Sarah. There are many beautiful sunsets ahead for you.

"Let's get out of this neighborhood and find a phone. I'll call my wife to come get us."

Rob sat on the curb and took off his right shoe to retrieve the ten-dollar bill Glenn had given him. "You hungry? I've got ten dollars."

Chapter 24

Sarah didn't turn off the lights right away. She wanted to lie in bed and just admire her surroundings. Last night she laid down on a filthy mattress, in a bare room, handcuffed to the bed. Tonight she'd already had a warm bubble bath and was wearing a cozy pair of pajamas, sharing an immaculate king-size, pillow-top bed with a giant stuffed dog. A private bathroom opened on one side of the beautifully decorated room. A walk-in closet on the other. Hanging in the closet were five tops and several pairs of jeans that belonged to Beth but looked to be about Sarah's size. Also multiple pairs of panties and bras were tucked in the bureau drawers. And this was only temporary they'd told her, until Beth could take Sarah shopping.

On the way home earlier in the evening, Dr. Rob—as he insisted she call him—and Miss Beth had been so happy to see one another, they drove right past the police station. She had to remind them Chance was handcuffed to the bed and would likely be more than happy to see the police arrive to arrest him. The Chief of Police knew Beth—he wouldn't have recognized her husband—so Rob waited in the car with Sarah. The cops had been to the shack before looking for a fugitive, so they knew exactly where to find Chance. It was agreed an officer would contact Rob in the morning for the full story.

This brought the whole situation to the forefront, and after taking care of that issue, the conversation was dominated by the horrific ordeal Sarah had been enduring for several weeks.

It was decided Sarah would stay with the doctor and his wife until some satisfactory arrangements could be made for her and the baby.

Sarah reached across the bed and turned off the light. She was asleep before her head hit the pillow.

The smell of fresh brewing coffee awakened her in the morning. She could hear Dr. Rob and Miss Beth talking in the kitchen, just across the wide hallway. She hurried into the bathroom to wash her face and brush her teeth—a new toothbrush and toiletries were a part of the guest package.

I didn't know anyone really lived this kind of life.

"Good morning, sweetie," Beth greeted her with a hug. "Do you drink coffee?"

"Yes, ma'am. I'd just learned to enjoy it when I made the mistake of moving in with Chance. And he would never buy me any. So I'd really, *really* enjoy a cup this morning."

"Cream and sugar?"

"Just sugar."

"Almost grown-up style." Rob turned from the coffee pot to look at her. He was fresh from the shower. Handsome, with clean clothes, clean shaven, and a beautiful smile. The *real* Dr. Rob McKinley was back. "Most newbies," he said, "have three or four spoons of sugar and lots of cream."

"Dr. Rob, don't you look wonderful. Well, I feel like I've grown up a lot in just a few weeks. Enough, in fact, to make wise decisions about my future . . . and the baby's."

Rob glanced over at Beth. She was looking down at her cup of coffee. Her face drawn with anxiety.

Rob's voice was a little shaky, but apparently Sarah didn't notice. "Are you thinking about keeping the baby after all, Sarah?"

"Oh, no, sir. I haven't changed my mind. I guess I've never explained the most important reason for my decision to you."

She took a long sip of coffee to steel her nerves. "But first I have to be honest with you. I'm sorry. I lied when I said the baby was my boyfriend's . . . and he'd died in an accident."

"I kind of suspected that. You're not a very good liar." He smiled at her.

Sarah looked down at her hands. "I was . . . I was . . . raped."

Beth jumped up from her chair, ran around the table to Sarah, and took her in her arms. "Oh, you poor baby."

Sarah clung to her for a moment, languishing in the love she'd never received from her own mother. Only to know for a short time from Vivi and now, this lovely lady.

She finally pulled gently away. "I . . . I don't know who it was. But I'm pretty sure it was a guy from school. I don't think I could handle it, should my baby be the spitting image of my rapist. I prefer to not even know who it was and pretend the baby was conceived in love. I think every child should believe it was conceived in love."

"But why did you lie to *me,* a doctor?"

"I have so much be ashamed of. My folks said I was asking for it." She shook her head. "Honestly, I wasn't. But I keep thinking there must have been something I could have done to prevent it. First Papa punished me, then they both pretended it didn't happen. They said I'd shamed the family."

Rob put his hand over hers but didn't interrupt her. "When I found out I was pregnant, I knew I had to find a good home for my baby. They would have made me have an abortion. But I was afraid if people knew what kind of girl I am and the baby's father was a rapist, no one would ever want it."

Beth opened her mouth to speak, but instead she just sighed. It wouldn't be fair to Rob for her to say what she was thinking without first discussing it with him.

I want it, Sarah. I want your baby and I'll love it until the day I die. I have no fear of the stigma of its father being a rapist. I know its mother.

Beth looked into Rob's eyes and saw a battle raging. Surely he didn't have any doubts about adopting the child. Did he?

Rob stood up, lifted Sarah from her seat, pulled her to him, and held her tight. He spoke softly in her ear. "And what kind of girl *are* you, Sarah? You're a brave, honest, beautiful, and innocent child of God." His shoulders jerked involuntarily for a moment. And the tears came.

Beth put her hands on their shoulders and prayed.

Father, You've given us a beautiful love for one another. Please help us work it out to Your honor and glory.

Chapter 25

Beth excused herself after breakfast. She said she had a few things to take care of before she took Sarah shopping. Rob was giving Sarah a tour of the house.

"I suppose the name 'Bumpkin' really is appropriate for me." Sarah laughed. "I mean, I've never been in a house like this. The nicest house I've ever been in is Uncle Sam's. And I think his whole place would fit comfortably in your living room."

"It's definitely more house than we need, Sarah. I guess we weren't thinking too clearly when we bought it. You see, I already had a practice when Beth and I met. She came from a wealthy family, and I didn't want my in-laws to think I couldn't take as good of care of her as they had. Besides, we had grand plans to have at least five children . . . so we'd need lots of room. That was ten years ago. And . . ." His voice tapered off.

"Have you not been able to have children, or did you change your mind?" Sarah blushed. "I'm sorry, it was very rude of me to ask."

"Don't be sorry. It's a rather difficult thing for Beth to discuss. She's had miscarriage after miscarriage. She's ready to give up. But I don't think she can ever be happy until she's a mother."

There was a long awkward pause between them and Rob looked away, realizing he'd just opened a can of worms. "Excuse me just a moment, Sarah. I need to see if Beth is all right. Make yourself at home." He bounded up the circular marble staircase two steps at a time.

When he opened their bedroom door, Beth was sitting on the edge of the bed, crying.

Rob kneeled in front of her, taking her hands in his. "So, darling, be honest. Do you want this baby?"

"Oh, Rob, I don't care what it's father did. That doesn't scare me. I want Sarah's child more than I've ever wanted anything in my life."

"Stay where you are. I'll see what I can do."

When he got to the top of the stairs, Sarah was gone.

"Sarah, where are you?"

"In here." Her voice was coming from down the hall, right there on the second floor. "In the nursery," she called out.

She was sitting in the rocking chair, looking out the window. "The view is lovely from here. I can just picture Beth rocking her baby, looking out over her backyard and garden." Her eyes were misty.

Rob walked over to her. "I don't know if that's ever going to happen, but I certainly pray so. I pray for her every night in bed, after she's gone to sleep. She's such a good woman. She'd be such a good mother."

Neither of them spoke for a moment. Then Sarah asked in a hushed tone, "Do you think she would even consider . . ."

"Yes."

"Are you sure?"

"Positive."

She laid her hand on her ever-so-slightly swollen belly. "We *are* talking about the same thing, right? My baby?"

"Your baby, Sarah. That precious child you're carrying. Beth and I would be so honored if you'd entrust its future to us. And I swear it would be the most loved child in the world."

Sarah shrieked with joy.

The master bedroom door slammed, and Beth came running down the hall. "What's wrong? What happened?"

"Nothing really." Rob grinned. "I just found out you're going to be a mother."

Chapter 26

Adam Liotta drew up all the papers.
Everything was legally pinned down. Rob and Beth would put Sarah up in an apartment for the duration of her pregnancy and pay all her medical bills. And she would relinquish her child to them within minutes of a successful delivery. Of course, Sarah had the option to change her mind at any time up until the exchange was made. After the exchange, there would be no further contact between Sarah and the McKinleys. It was all cut and dried.

That's how lawyers like things.

Not so with three people who have discovered a deep abiding love for one another. To them, the saddest part of the agreement was "no further contact." But it couldn't be helped. If the baby was to be raised the way Sarah wanted, she had to bow out and take her past and all her sordid baggage with her.

From there, she had no idea where she would go or what she would do. Uncle Sam and Aunt Vivi would welcome her with open arms. But that could only be a temporary fix. They had their lives to live. And she wasn't their responsibility.

***

Rob couldn't bear to see her go back out into the world with no skills to support herself. But law prohibited him giving her money over and above support. Otherwise, it could be construed as "buying" the child.

Adam tapped his pen on his desk. "Have you found an apartment for her yet?"

"Haven't even looked, Adam. She's so young to be living by herself."

"She's old enough to have a baby, Rob. And she's been through some pretty *maturing* experiences lately. The agreement was you were to get her an apartment and have regular visitations." Adam put his pen down on his desk. "I hope you and Beth aren't getting too personally involved. That will only make things more difficult."

"I think you're too late with that advice. We love the girl. And we're concerned about her future. Adam, there has to be some way we can be sure she's in a position to support herself after the baby's born. And we don't want her to merely exist. She's giving us the greatest gift we'll ever receive. We want her to have a successful, good life."

"This is against my better judgment, Rob. But how far did she get in school?"

"She's smart. She skipped a grade when she was in elementary school. So she was a junior in high school when she dropped out. Straight A's." Rob folded his fingers in front of his face, resting his chin on his thumbs. "She's as bright as they come, Adam. But she doesn't have a high school diploma. If she had it would help, wouldn't it?"

"I'm thinking more than high school, Rob. I have clients who are looking for tax write-offs. I'm pretty sure I could talk one into paying four year's college expenses for a needy child. I'd just need to get it approved as a write-off. And . . . she would have to have no less than a GED."

"She can handle that, I know." Rob stood and extended his right hand. "Adam, you're the man."

"Not so fast. Let me work on my end. You work on getting her a diploma or a GED certificate. Let's not celebrate until we get the ground work done." He stood up to shake Rob's hand. "You know she's lucky to have you and Beth in her corner."

"Well, she's never had anyone before . . . so her time to be blessed is past due. Call me when you know something." Rob turned to leave.

Adam Liotta watched pensively as his friend glanced back to give him a smile and a thumbs-up. Brow knit in a concerned expression, Adam returned to his desk and dialed the phone.

"Hey, honey, can you meet me at the club this evening for dinner? I've got something on my mind I need to discuss with you." He paused to listen. "No, never. No more bad surprises. No more surprises of any kind. You know everything there is to know about me . . . and I'm so blessed you decided to *keep* me." He smiled as he listened to her reply. "I'm hoping you'll like this idea, Gloria. It's a chance for us to help a youngster. Uh-huh. I thought you'd like that. How's seven o'clock?" He glanced at his watch. "Great, see you then. Love you."

<hr />

Beth and Sarah had just gotten back from the doctor's office when Rob got home.

Beth reached up to give him a kiss on the cheek. "What did you do today, Rob?"

"Visited Adam. We're trying to put together a deal to get Sarah in college after the baby comes."

Sarah's jaw dropped. "College? But how? I didn't even graduate from high school."

"We're taking it one step at a time. And we have a few months yet to accomplish this. Right now I want you to call around to see where you can take the GED test. I don't have any doubt you can pass it."

"Oh, by the way, Sarah, I checked lost and found. No cross pendant. I'm so sorry. We'll get you another."

"Not necessary, although I appreciate the offer. It had a lot of sentimental value. Vivi gave it to me." Sarah was visibly disappointed.

Rob put his arm around her shoulder. "I'm really sorry. So . . . what have you girls been up to today?"

Beth spoke up. "Been to the doctor. Good report. Everything is normal and on schedule." She grinned at him. "And Sarah and I have come to a decision. Hope you don't feel left out you weren't asked. But it would be so foolish to put her in an apartment all by herself and *support* her when we have four empty bedrooms. Sarah's going to live right here with us until the baby arrives."

"I think that's great. In fact, Adam and I talked about it today. He thinks we shouldn't become so close. I told him . . . *too late*." He reached out and ruffled Sarah's hair. "But why do you have to leave after the baby arrives? You could stay right here until it's time to start school."

Sarah's eyes darted to Beth and back to Rob. "No! That wouldn't work at all. I'm not coming back here from the hospital." She turned and hurried to her room.

Puzzled, he turned to Beth. "What was *that* all about?"

Beth sat on the couch and motioned for him to join her. "We had a long talk today on the way back from the doctor's office. She asked me if I was happy about the good report. I told her I was ecstatic. And I said 'how about you'? She said 'Yeah, I'm glad . . . for you, because this is *your* baby.'

"Then she went to great lengths to assure me she would never change her mind. I told her I believed her. But that wasn't enough. She went on to say she would never ask *anything* of us ever again because she wants us to be completely happy. *That*, she said, is the only way the baby can be completely happy. And that's all she wants. Ever.

"She doesn't want to see the baby or hold it after it's born."

Rob sat for a long moment. "Wow, I've never known anyone so selfless."

"I'm not selfless." Sarah walked in from the hallway. "I just want you three to be happy. And the only way that can happen is for me to be absent."

"I'm sorry, Sarah." Beth pulled her down on the couch next to them. "I didn't mean to be talking about you behind your back—but Rob needs to know your desires before he can honor them. And your desire is to—"

Sarah cut her off. "My desire is to give my child the most normal and loving life possible, without messing it up with a birth mother skulking somewhere in the shadows waiting to complicate his or her life."

Rob raised his hand like a child in grammar school. "I think I understand where you're coming from, Sarah. And we *will* honor your wishes. But while you're here . . . while we wait for the arrival of *our* baby, if that's the way you want to think of it, can't we be family?"

"Please, Sarah," Beth interjected, "if there's anything we can do to make you feel more a part of this family . . . please tell us."

Sarah stood and moved in front of them. Then sat on the floor, cross-legged, before them. "I do have one favor to ask. I don't want any pictures. I definitely don't want you to assume the obligation to keep me abreast of the baby's progress. But, if you would, let me do this one thing that will make me feel in my soul there's an unseen thread of connection between me and the baby . . ."

Rob and Beth both sat forward in their seats. "Yes?" they said, almost in unison. "What is it you want to do?"

"I know you like quilting, Miss Beth. I've seen you sitting in your garden the last few days cutting squares for a quilt."

"Oh, me. I'll probably never get beyond cutting squares. I don't think I have the talent to take it any further."

Sarah stared at the floor for a moment before looking up at them. "My grandma used to make quilts. She taught me a little about it one summer when my parents let me visit her for a couple of months. We started on a quilt for me, but it was never finished because Grandma died. I don't know what happened to the unfinished quilt."

She had to fight the tears back thinking of her grandma. It was the only time her parents ever let her spend any time with the old lady, in spite of Sarah's and Grandma's begging. She got to know and love her that summer, but Grandma died soon after. And her name was never mentioned in their home again.

"I know this is hard for you to talk about, sweetheart. You don't have to explain." Beth extended her hand.

Sarah took her hand briefly and released it. "Yes, but I must tell you. Or I should say, ask you.

"I'd like to make two quilts. Two identical quilts. One for me and one for the baby. I'll sleep under my quilt every night, starting the night of its birth. If you could find it in your hearts to cover your baby with the quilt I made every night, I know our souls will connect somewhere between here and heaven.

Beth was in tears. "What a sweet thought. Of course we'll do that for you. And one day when the child is old enough to understand, we'll tell the whole story."

THE TRINITY QUILTS

"When you do, you've got to promise to not reveal who I am or any of the ugly details of my life. Promise me, please. Or this is all for naught."

"We promise, Sarah. Your child will be brought up safe, happy, and loved." Rob stood and helped Sarah from her position. "You've got to stop worrying and concentrate on keeping yourself and the baby healthy. You can use my office and my drafting equipment if you need it to design your quilts. And you and Beth can shop for fabric. I'm anxious to see what you can do."

One evening, a few days later, Sarah called Beth away from her kitchen chores into her room. She was lying on her back on the big king-sized bed, with her hand on her stomach.

"Hurry, Miss Beth. You need to feel this."

Beth was drying her hands on a kitchen towel as she rushed into the room.

"Give me your hand," Sarah demanded. She grabbed Beth's extended hand and pressed it, palm down, against her stomach.

Beth drew in her breath. "Oh! Is that the baby moving around?

"Yes, it's still quite small, but it makes waves, doesn't it?"

Beth was wide-eyed. "It feels like a butterfly fluttering just beneath your skin. I . . . I . . . don't know how to express this, Sarah, but my heart is overwhelmed at the gift you're giving me . . . us."

"You don't have to say anything. This is *your* baby. You've taken a great load off my mind. I'll be able to sleep at night, because I'll know my child is loved."

Sarah hugged Beth and turned away before her tears became obvious. "I think I'll take a little nap now. I'm very tired."

Whatever Sarah was feeling in her heart, she kept it well hidden. She worked daily on the quilts, took long walks, and slept soundly. She'd found her niche in quilt-making. The design she'd created was very beautiful, and her stitching was precise.

She was quiet and helpful around the house. A very pleasant person to live with. Almost too good to be true. Then one day she handed a piece of paper to Rob.

"If there's ever an emergency where you absolutely must reach me . . . like if the baby needs a bone marrow transplant or a kidney or liver . . . here's the name and number of a family I will always be in touch with. But please, I implore you, don't contact me unless the baby's life is hanging in the balance. I love it too much to ever burden it."

Rob glanced at the slip of paper. "Sam Blake and Vivi Blake Harris," he read. "Uncle Sam and Aunt Vivi. I'm so glad you are going to stay in touch with relatives."

"Family, yes, in the spiritual sense. Not relatives. I'm not related by blood to Sam and Vivi. But they took me in without hesitation when my whole world was going down the tubes. Just like you and Miss Beth did. Only difference is, I can stay in touch with them without bringing heartache to my child. You and Miss Beth I will hold in my heart, but never will I betray you or my baby by showing up on your doorstep."

"So your name's not really Blake?'

"It is, Dr. Rob, only because I choose to claim it. I fell off the grid when I ran away from home. And I'm sure my

THE TRINITY QUILTS

parents are glad to be rid of me. No one knows or cares what happened to Sarah Horner. She is no more.

"But Sarah Blake? That's a different story. Some very wonderful people love her. And though she'll always miss seeing her child grow up . . . thanks to you and Miss Beth, Sarah Blake has a future." Sarah threw her arms around Rob. "Oh, I will miss you and Miss Beth."

"Well, don't start missing us yet, young lady. You have a few more months to stay with us, and we intend to make the best of it."

Sarah spent the beautiful early spring days sitting for hours on the bench in Beth's garden working on the quilts. On rainy, chilly days, she sat in the rocking chair in the nursery. One day Rob joined her in the garden. He was carrying a brand-new Bible with Sarah's name imprinted on it in gold.

"You know, Sarah, just as you're making a sacrifice by giving us your child, God gave us His Son in order that we might have eternal life." He sat on the step next to her. "I've heard you make mention of the Lord. But never with any claim you've accepted Jesus as your Savior. If you don't mind, I'd like to talk with you about Him. My hope is you'll accept Jesus, and when this life is over, we can all be together again, in glory. The baby, you, Beth, and me."

Sarah had been thinking a lot about God. And reading about His plan of salvation in the little pamphlet, Sasha had left on the bus. Even hoping her baby would get to know Him early in life and by-pass all the bad stuff. But she thought it was far too late for her to have a relationship with Him. She just couldn't get her head around the thought God forgives all the bad stuff, if you'll just ask.

Rob and Beth and Sarah began having a Bible study in the evenings, and within a few weeks, Sarah had accepted Christ as her Savior.

Now when she needed a break from her quilt making, she'd pick up her Bible and read God's word. It was such a comfort. Yet it raised questions. And provoked deep prayer.

> *Jesus, Dr. Rob and Miss Beth had to know having You in my life could change my attitude about raising my own child. Yet, they cared so much for me, they took that chance.*
>
> *Lord, I believe You've made me whole . . . and capable of raising my baby. But I will never break my promise to these two beautiful people, no matter how much it may break my heart to say goodbye to my firstborn. I just ask that You watch over Dr. Rob, Miss Beth, and their child. Keep them in Your loving care. Amen.*

Rob's mom and dad had moved to Texas from their retirement home in Arizona shortly before Beth had her second miscarriage. Wanting to be close to their only grandchild and handy in any emergency, they'd bought a home in the same subdivision as Rob and Beth. Two blocks away and around one corner. Their house was smaller, but just as lovely.

Rob's mom was an avid gardener, and their yard was ablaze with bright blossoms from early spring to fall. Her big kitchen always smelled of something delicious. Adele was a storybook grandmother in every respect. Rob's dad, Roger, was a tender-hearted, gentle man, and a Southern gentleman as well. They insisted Sarah call them Gram and Granddad. Sarah couldn't believe her good fortune in finding not only a wonderful mother and father for Emily . . . but the perfect set of grandparents as well. She could dream the rest of her life and never conjure up a more idyllic existence for a youngster to grow up in.

Chapter 27

The day finally arrived when the doctor asked Sarah if she would like to do a sonogram to find out the gender of her baby. She'd come to the doctor alone for the first time, because Rob and Beth had taken a couple of days to drive to Galveston and relax on the beach. She decided against asking Gram or Granddad McKinley to take her to her appointment.

Rob and Beth had left her in charge and reminded her to keep the house locked. It was almost frightening to be alone in that big house, but she was thrilled and excited they thought she was mature enough to handle it. And now she'd proved her maturity by going to the doctor alone. To her, this was a major milestone.

She knew nothing of sonograms. "Can we do that so soon?"

"Sure," the good doctor said, "and I, for one, am curious. Aren't you?"

"I guess I am, although it makes everything become so real when you can actually start calling a baby by name."

Dr. Blount knew Beth and Rob well. "Has Beth decided on a name?" He immediately blushed. "I'm sorry, I just assumed Beth and Rob would be naming the baby."

"Don't apologize, Dr. Blount. As a matter of fact, Dr. Rob and Miss Beth decided on a very, very long list of names . . . both boy's and girl's . . . and told me I could make the final choice." Sarah grinned.

"Well, then, let's get busy."

Dr. Blount rang his nurse, who prepped Sarah for the procedure. The three of them watched closely as the doctor brought the baby's image into view.

The sound of the baby's heartbeat reverberated through Sarah's consciousness.

A little life, actually living within me.

"Lookie there. I think it's a girl. Wait a minute. Let's get that view again." Dr. Blount was grinning. "Hold it, little lady, quit your kicking and let me have a good look. Yes!" He turned to Sarah. "It's definitely a little girl."

Sarah squeezed her eyes shut. And tears forced their way through her eyelids. "Thank You, God." Then looking back at the screen at the little figure, who now seemed to be flinging her arms in all directions, Sarah whispered, "Hello, Emily."

Chapter 28

The Texas Panhandle

Sam came home that night to find Vivi sitting at the kitchen table crying.

"What's wrong, sis? The kids okay?"

"Yes, yes, yes. They are all okay. Oh, Sam . . . even Sarah's okay."

Sam took both of her hands in his. "You heard from her? Oh, thank God. Where is she? What's she doing?"

"Sam, you're not going to believe it. She's been through hell and back, but she's now living in Dallas with a doctor and his wife, who are going to adopt the baby." Vivi stood up and started fidgeting with the coffee pot.

When she opened the flour canister instead of the coffee canister to fill the basket, Sam took the spoon from her hand. "You sit down and tell me everything. I'll handle the coffee," he chuckled.

Vivi related the whole story about Sarah's kidnapping and being chained to a bed, all the way to the luxury home she was now occupying. Sam listened with his mouth hanging open. He had to laugh when Vivi described how Dr. Rob looked as a homeless man. And how he man-handled Sarah's unsuspecting kidnapper.

"Now for some really good news. The doctor has arranged for Sarah to get a college education after the baby comes. All paid for. They've bought her a beautiful new wardrobe and a dependable used car. It just looks like everything has turned around for the good for our little one."

Sam shook his head. "I just can't believe it. It's just too good to be true. Is there a chance, now that her life has turned around, she may keep the baby?"

"Not a chance. And here's why. She made a promise. To the doctor's wife—whose name is Beth—and to Jesus."

"To Jesus? Has she . . . has she . . ."

"Uh-huh, I was getting to that. She gave her heart to Jesus—and she said her promise to the doctor and his wife is more binding now than ever." Vivi got up to pour two cups of coffee. She placed one in front of Sam and carried the other to her side of the table. "She cried a little and said she thinks she could raise the baby on her own. But Beth has been through a lot, and she could never hurt her like that . . . by changing her mind now. By the way, the baby is a little girl. Sarah named her Emily.

"She's grown up a lot, Sam. She's not a little girl anymore. But a determined and compassionate young woman."

Sam added sugar to his coffee. Took and sip and added more. "This is a lot to take in. Did she say when we might see her again?"

"As soon after the baby—Emily—arrives as possible. Maybe on Thanksgiving break from school."

"Hope she hasn't changed too much."

"Not our Sarah. She may grow older, she may get a degree, and someday, Sam, I suspect she'll marry. But she'll never change. Not our Sarah."

Chapter 29

When Sarah got home from the doctor, she double-checked the calendar. Rob and Beth weren't due home until the next afternoon.

She got out her embroidery thread and needles. Picking up the baby's finished quilt, she carefully located the center of the right border where she embroidered a name—"Jesus Christ." Then on the top border, in beautiful script, she put "Father God." She added the words "Holy Spirit" on the left border before putting the quilt up and taking a few minutes rest.

She had one more name to add. The baby's. Her hands shook slightly as she ran them over the names of the three persons of God. Then with a prayer on her lips, she began working on the bottom border.

She held the finished work up to admire.

Emily.

Sarah had dinner ready to serve when Beth and Rob walked in the door from their mini-vacation. Lasagna, garlic bread, and a green salad. She was becoming quite proficient in the kitchen.

"Oh, something sure smells good." Beth laid down her small bag and grabbed Sarah for a long hug. "We've missed you. Hope you enjoyed yourself just hanging around the house."

"Well"—Sarah grinned—"you forgot I had a doctor's appointment..."

"Oh no. I'm so sorry. Did you reschedule?"

Sarah sat on the couch and patted the seat next to her. "Why no. And I wasn't about to remind you. I was afraid you'd call off your trip. So I went by myself."

Rob gave Sarah a semi-stern look. "You should have asked Dad to take you."

"I had to prove something to myself, Dr. Rob. I need to know I can take care of myself when I go to school and then out into the world. Truthfully, I was rather proud of myself."

Beth sat on the edge of the seat and faced Sarah. "What I want to know is . . . did we get a good report?"

"The best. Dr. Blount verified—as much as it's possible to—the baby should arrive around September 1. It seems healthy. I seem healthy. I don't see how I could have gotten a better report." Sarah reached behind her and picked up the baby's quilt from the library table. "I wanted to show you the finished product. One down and one to go."

Rob still had some luggage in his hand. He laid it down to take a good look at the quilt. "Now that's what I call a beautiful quilt, Sarah. You've done a superb job on it." He put his hand on Beth's shoulder. "It's beautiful, isn't it, baby?"

Beth had unfolded it and was examining the edges. She noticed the "Jesus Christ" embroidery first. "Oh, look at this, Rob." Turning it around by the edges, she traced "Father God" with her fingers. "Oh, Sarah, this is so lovely. You do such good work. And . . ." Her fingers now rested on the words "Holy Spirit." "And to dedicate it to the Holy Trinity. That's just . . ."

She froze midsentence.

She was staring at the bottom border. She held it up for Rob to see.

Rob spoke first. "'Emily?' Who . . . Emily—Emily—is that the baby's *name*?" He lifted Sarah to her feet. "That's one of the names we chose for a girl . . . are you telling us we're having a little girl?"

Biting her lower lip to hold back the emotion, Sarah nodded.

Rob threw his arms around her. Starting to swing her around, he caught himself. "Oh, no more of this until the baby arrives. Gotta be careful."

Sarah laughed. "I'm not that fragile *yet*. You should know *that* . . . you're a doctor."

"Oh, but, Sarah, this is a very special baby. I feel like I should be carrying you around on a satin pillow."

Beth was still staring at the quilt, repeating the name—Emily—over and over. Her eyes flooded with tears.

Rob dropped down next to Beth on the couch and they hugged and cried until Sarah finally touched them both on the shoulder. "Emily and I are hungry—and supper's getting cold."

Sarah was home alone when Emily decided to come—a week early. What felt like it might be a labor pain hit her as she stood in front of her bathroom mirror. A mild pain . . . but it took her by surprise and caused her to double over. Straightening out, she began putting the last touches on her makeup. She was trying to decide if she should call Rob about the pain when she suddenly realized her legs and the floor beneath her feet were wet.

Rob had put his phone number in her phone on speed dial. Within seconds, she had him on the line. "Everything all right, Sarah?"

"I think so. This is my first baby, so I don't know how much time we have, but I think my water just broke."

"Hang on. Dad's on standby. I'll call him right now."

"I'm pretty sure I can drive myself."

"Bite your tongue! Like you said . . . this is your first baby. Don't even *think* about doing that. Dad can get there faster than I. He's just around the corner. Your bags are by the door. All you have to do is sit down and wait."

Granddad and Gram McKinley had taken Beth's miscarriages almost as hard as Rob. And they were ecstatic Sarah had chosen Rob and Beth to bless with her baby. From their first meeting, they treated her like their granddaughter. Sarah was indeed going to miss this exceptional family when time came to leave.

And it looked like the time was drawing nigh.

The day when she would give up *everything* precious to her had arrived. *I don't know if I can do it. Give up my own flesh and blood? What was I thinking?*

Sarah heard a key turning in the front door lock. Granddad McKinley stuck his head in the door and reached around to disengage the alarm at the same time. "Sarah, are you all right, darlin'?"

The sight of his gray hair and precious old face brought Sarah back to reality. She had nothing to offer Emily. This family was everything a child could ask for. Everything Sarah had ever dreamed of. For herself—which didn't work out and never could now. And for her baby—and *that* was within her power to make happen, simply by keeping her word.

"I'm fine, Granddad. Just sitting here at the dining room table waiting for you. You must have already had the engine running."

"Just about, sweetheart. Looks like this is the big day we've all been waiting for." He held out his arms to receive Sarah's genuine hug. "I just wish you'd change your mind and stick around after Emily arrives."

"You don't really wish that. It would lessen Beth's joy of motherhood and make Emily's life complicated. But I know what you mean." She stood on tiptoe and kissed his cheek. "Leaving will be the hardest thing I've ever done. Staying away . . . even harder. But we're doing it for Emily, right?" She turned her head momentarily to gain control of her emotions.

Turning back, she saw Granddad was having the same problem. Wiping a tear from his wrinkled cheek, she smiled. "Come on. You'll make me start crying. And this is a time for nothing but joy. Emily's on her way!"

The words were barely out of her mouth when another pain hit. This time there was no doubting the baby meant business. Granddad, a retired doctor himself, put his hand on Sarah's tummy. "Oh yes, little girl. Emily is making her presence known. We'd better get this show on the road."

The drive to the hospital was a time of true soul-searching for Sarah. She kept her hand on Emily and prayed silently. *Father, I've tried to do right by Emily, and now there is no turning back. I'm leaving her in Your tender care. I know it was Your plan for Dr. Rob to find me in time. You've provided her with a family like no other. A family that loves You and Emily. And, yes, even me. I promise I'll always keep my word to them and never hurt them by butting into their lives.* She swallowed hard on the last sentence. It was going to be very, very hard.

But now she'd promised God, so there could never be any turning back.

By the time they reached the hospital, the pains were getting very close together. Granddad pulled under the entry pavilion and switched off the engine. "Stay put, darlin'. I'll be back with a wheelchair."

A nurse ran out the door with the old gentleman and helped Sarah into the wheelchair amidst another contraction. It was Barbara . . . the first nurse she met the night she fainted at the bus station.

"Oh, Barbara," she moaned through clenched teeth. "Nobody told me it was going to hurt this much."

Barbara squeezed her hand. "You'll do fine, baby."

Dr. Rob stood holding the door open. He kissed Sarah quickly on the forehead as she was wheeled by. And trotted along with Barbara and his dad as they hurried down the corridor.

Rob put his hand on Sarah's arm and gave it a little squeeze. "Beth is on her way. I hope she gets here in time."

She grabbed his hand, "Oh, Dr. Rob. I think the baby's coming. I gotta help her."

Barbara entreated Sarah, "Hang on, baby. Don't push yet."

"I'll try. But . . . ooooh." Another wave of pain.

Emily was coming.

Ready or not.

Chapter 30

Adam Liotta sat in a comfortable tufted brown leather chair and surveyed the typical exquisite trappings of a college dean's office. Books—lots of books. Trophies and pictures of the dean with various celebrities.

Wow, a picture of him with then-president Gerald Ford's arm around his shoulder. He's been walking in some high cotton since I went to school here.

Adam had managed to get Sarah enrolled in his alma mater due to his financial influence and academic prowess. He certainly couldn't have done it on his behavior record. He spent more time in this very dean's office than he did in the classroom. The dean never seemed to care for him, for obvious reasons. Adam regretted he'd been so wild in his youth. He still managed to graduate magna cum laude, but it would have been even better had he graduated with the respect of his professors. Especially the dean.

The door opened, and Dean Evans entered. The set of his brow revealed he had not forgotten Adam Liotta. Not even after twenty-two years.

Adam stood and held out his right hand.

The dean looked at him from head to toe and shook his hand briefly. "Hello, Mr. Liotta. You haven't changed a bit."

"Good afternoon, Dean Evans. Nor have you." *You looked a hundred years old then, and you look a hundred years old now.*

"What can I do for you?" The dean made his way behind his desk and sat down.

Adam sat down and cleared his throat.

"I've come to talk to you about one of your newly enrolled students. Her name is Sarah Blake, from Dallas, Texas."

"Yes, I seem to recall seeing that name. What's your interest in her?"

"I'll be responsible for all her expenses."

"Oh, really. And may inquire of your relationship to her?"

"I'm an attorney in Dallas, Dean Evans. I've handled some legal matters where Sarah is concerned. And I'll be handling all her expenses while she is getting her education."

He settled way back in the plush armchair, his eyes fixed on the old dean's returning gaze. "Sarah is never to know who's footing the bill. As far as she knows, one of my clients is using her education as a tax write-off."

"I'll see it's handled discreetly." The old man displayed little approval of Adam—and no affection. "What do you propose I do if she has a problem, financial or otherwise?"

"She shouldn't have any financial problems . . . the bank will be depositing ample funds to her account to handle all her personal needs. And I'll be sending quarterly checks to the school to cover her tuition. But if anything unforeseen comes up, you can get in touch with me without her knowledge. As I said, she thinks one of my clients is . . ."

"Yes, yes, I got that," Dean Evans interrupted. He showed little patience for Adam.

Evans reached for the humidor and held it open to Adam, who reluctantly took one. After selecting one for himself, the Dean trained his eyes on his former student. "There's one thing I can't help but ponder, Adam, and you may tell me it's none of my business. But I feel I have a right to know. What is your interest in this girl? Is Sarah Blake your illegitimate daughter?"

Adam took his time answering, tending to the ritualistic lighting of his cigar before he even met the old man's eyes. "You remember me too well, Dean Evans. But I'm not that person anymore. My wife, Gloria, and I have been married twenty years, and I've not even looked at another woman. Not that I suddenly turned into an angel. I think I was just too scared to cheat. Afraid I'd lose her. She's an awesome woman."

Evans rolled his eyes.

Adam chuckled. "I don't blame you for doubting, sir, but it's true."

"Then why the financial sacrifice, if you have no personal connection?"

Adam took a long draw on the expensive cigar and breathed it out languidly. "I'm not bragging, sir, but I've done quite well for myself. I have no children of my own. Sending one deserving child to a good college is not going to break me. And Sarah deserves so much more than she's ever received in this life."

"For me to believe that, I'd have to believe you've done a total about-face since we last met some twenty-two years ago."

"It wasn't instant, sir. My wife and I have been on enough vacations and cruises in our twenty years to satisfy ten families. We've got houses, cars, a boat . . . you name it. We've actually been quite selfish. Me, much more so than Gloria. She wanted children, but I didn't. And I saw to it that she wouldn't conceive . . . if you know what I mean."

"Vasectomy?" The word dripped contempt.

"Yes. If I had it to do over . . ."

THE TRINITY QUILTS

Adam snuffed out his cigar. He hadn't smoked in some time and he wasn't enjoying it. "No children and no elderly parents to worry about. It's been all about us."

"Sarah came into the life of one of my clients . . . homeless and pregnant. Needless to say, that's strictly confidential." Adam took a deep breath. "She gave her baby up for adoption to my friend and his wife, who have been trying for years to have a child.

"She asked for nothing in return. She says knowing the baby will be loved is all she wants. She obviously loves it very much. Anyway, while waiting for the baby, they became like family."

Totally engrossed in Adam's story, Dean Evans stood and came around his desk to take a chair closer to him.

"But she refused their offer to stay and be a part of the family because she wants her daughter go have a normal childhood . . . and for my friend's wife to have a normal and happy motherhood, without the stigma of a *birth mother* hanging in the shadows."

Adam balled his hand into a fist and pressed it against his mouth in an attempt to keep his emotions in check.

"As much as he wanted to, my friend—who's a successful doctor—couldn't give her money because it would have endangered the adoption agreement. That's where I come in. Seeing such selflessness on the part of a child who's never had as much as a new dress to call her own made me realize how self-centered I've been my whole life."

Evans cleared his throat and leaned forward to put his hand on Adam's arm. "Forgive an old man for judging, son. You're right, you are *not* the person I used to know. I'm proud of the person you've become."

"Thank you, sir. I have a lot to make up for. I started by telling Gloria the truth about my vasectomy. It took her several weeks to come to terms with it, but she forgave me." He managed a small grin. "I told you she was awesome."

Dean Evan leaned back in his chair. "Forgiving *and* awesome. No wonder you love her so. Please go on."

"Since that time, we've tried to be more mindful of the needs of others. Children, especially. When the opportunity to help Sarah came up, Gloria was all for it."

Adam reached in his vest pocket and produced an envelope. "Would you keep this in Sarah's file. It's an insurance policy on me. It should cover all her expenses until graduation, should something happen to me."

Dean Evans took the envelope and Adam stood to go. "Thank you, Dean . . . for your help in this. And keep an eye on Sarah for me, will you? She should be an excellent student—bright as a new penny."

"Of course. Goes without saying. But I have one more question before you go, Adam. Why did you choose this school, all the way up here in Tennessee? It's so far from Dallas."

"Two reasons, sir. I think the distance from her baby will make it easier for Sarah to make a life of her own. *And*, to my knowledge, there's no finer school she could attend. Although I didn't appreciate it at the time, I credit this school, and *you*, sir, for any success I may enjoy." With a sheepish grin, he added, "I guess your lectures weren't a total waste of time on me after all."

Dean Evans rose and did a surprising thing. He put his arms around Adam and hugged him for a long time. "You know, son, you've made this whole miserable job of mine worth the while. Now get outta here!"

Chapter 31

> *Dear family, today our baby is three. There's no doubt in my mind she's a happy little three-year-old. And probably quite beautiful, don't you think? Sometimes I'd like to write her mother and dad and ask for a picture of her. But I'd be opening a door I may not be able to close again. And breaking a solemn promise. I've made it three years. Surely I can make it the rest of my life.*

Sarah laid the pen down.

She was writing a letter to Sam and Vivi. She wrote and called them often but made it a special point to write every year on Emily's birthday. They were her only family now, and even though she hadn't seen them since the short visit she'd made on her first Thanksgiving break from college, she knew the rock solid love they shared would never change. They called her every Christmas. Even asked her to come visit for the holidays last year. But Sarah felt the need to close this present chapter in her life before she moved on to another. One more year and she'd have her coveted college degree. Then she'd begin looking for a job. Perhaps even in Amarillo where she'd be close to Sam and Vivi.

But, on second thought, that may be too close to Emily. Her love for her child never waned, not one little bit. And the temptation to plan a trip to Dallas to try to get just a glimpse of her was always at the top of her mind. But she could never succumb to it. Staying here in Tennessee might make the constant battle she fought a little easier.

Birthdays were the hardest. Most of the time, she managed to stay busy and keep her mind otherwise occupied. But today, she was in the doldrums. Even though it was Sunday she hadn't gone to the morning service in the cafeteria like she usually did.

An after-service get-together had been planned. Maybe it would get her through the day.

I think I'll go. Gotta get my mind off my troubles. I can finish this letter later.

She pushed away from her desk and checked her hair in the mirror. *Good enough.*

The music could be heard from outside the cafeteria building. But she couldn't make out the tune until someone from the inside burst through the double-doors past her. She stepped in, heard the crowd singing, and stopped dead in her tracks.

"Happy birthday to you. Happy birthday to you. Happy birthday, dear Jacob. Happy birthday to you."

She turned to leave, but someone touched her arm. "Don't leave. It's not a private party."

She looked first at the masculine hand resting on her arm, then turned her face up to look at the owner of the hand—a ruggedly handsome man, several years her senior.

"I . . . I really need to get back to my room to study."

"Please stay. If you go now, I'll feel like I caused you to leave."

Sarah felt her face grow hot. "Why would you say that? Are you the birthday boy Jacob?"

"No, that would be my son. He's three today. I couldn't leave him at home with a babysitter on his birthday, now could I?"

This man's child is three years old today. And I've come to get my mind off Emily because today is her third birthday. What a joke. What a really bad *joke on me.*
Her legs were suddenly made of Jell-O.
His eyes grew concerned. "Are you all right?"
"Just need to sit down for a moment, please."
He grabbed the nearest chair and directed Sarah to sit.
"Don't move. I'll get you a glass of water."
When he returned, he had a small child with dark curly hair in tow. He lowered himself on his haunches in front of Sarah. The child stared jabbering about today being his birthday. "Wait just a moment, son. The lady isn't feeling well."
Jacob leaned in close to her face, tilted his head, and put his little hand on her forehead. "She's not hot."
All the maternal love Sarah had been stuffing for three years bubbled to the top and she let out a gulp that was somewhere between a laugh and a groan. "Oh, Jacob, I bet you're going to be a doctor when you grow up."
Jacob slowly scratched a spot on his arm with only his index finger and shook his head. "Nope. I'm gonna be a preacher like my daddy."
Jacob's daddy held out his hand. "By the way, my name's Todd Webster. And, of course, this is my son Jacob."
Sarah took his hand briefly. "Hi, Todd. I'm Sarah Blake." She brushed her hair back from her eyes. A habit she'd picked up when she was flustered. "I'm sorry I missed church. Did you bring this morning's message?"
"Yep. I pastor a small church. I asked our associate pastor to bring the message today. He's been anxious to take to the pulpit and I thought it was a good time to give the congregation a little break from me." He grinned.

"And like I said. I couldn't leave the young one at home. When the students found out today was his birthday, they insisted on making this get-together into a party for him. Hope you're not disappointed."

Sarah shifted in her chair. Suddenly she felt short of breath. "No, not disappointed at all." She'd never met anyone who affected her breathing before.

"Are you meeting someone here, Sarah?"

"N-n-no."

"Perhaps Jacob and I could keep you company for a while. They'll be serving lunch shortly."

With the fingers of her heart crossed, Sarah asked, "Will your wife be coming later?"

With only the slightest hesitation, Todd stood and held out his hand to help her up. "I'm a widower, Sarah."

"I'm sorry. It was thoughtless of me to ask."

"Not at all. You have a right to know before accepting our invitation."

"We don't often get to hang out with a pretty lady, do we, Jacob?" Todd smiled down at his son. "So, Sarah Blake, will you celebrate Jacob's birthday with us?"

The little tot's bright eyes watched her expectantly.

The hopeful eyes of a motherless child beckoned to her, and although she wanted to turn and run, she heard herself say, "It would be my pleasure."

"Yay!" Jacob and Todd shouted in unison.

I hope you don't mind if I pretend Emily's celebrating with us.

Chapter 32

"I don't want to be nosey, but I'm afraid I'll say something hurtful or wrong in front of Jacob." Sarah was sitting at Todd's kitchen table—for the fourth time that week. And the umpteenth time that month. "He's so young. Does he remember his mother?"

"No, Sarah, he doesn't remember Della. You see, she only got a chance to hold him once before the Lord took her home."

I guess someday—if we continue to see each other—I'll have to tell you, Todd, I never got to hold my baby at all before I gave her up.

Sarah put her hand over Todd's. "How awful that must have been for you."

"Awful, yes . . . but it wasn't a surprise or anything. Della was very fragile woman. She'd been told as a teenager, because of her health issues, she should never get pregnant. But she wanted a baby so badly . . . she didn't tell me of that warning when we married. I was so happy we were going to have a baby. I didn't suspect a thing until one day I realized, Della wasn't looking at all well. She was refusing meds her body needed, because they would have been bad for the baby."

Sarah's throat was hurting from holding back the tears. She knew all about a mother's love and how powerful it can be. "She must have been a fine woman, Todd."

"Yes, she was. There was a time, early in her pregnancy, she could have aborted the baby and returned to relatively good health. Instead she ate and did all the things to make the baby strong . . . at her own peril."

"How much of this can Jacob understand? What have you told him?"

"Only that his mother was a wonderful woman who loved him more than anything. And the Lord called her to heaven on the day he was born. I don't think he could grasp the whole story. One day . . ."

He moved his chair a little closer to Sarah's. "I know this is rather sudden, Sarah. But we've know each other for seven weeks . . . tomorrow. And it's been three years since Della died. I don't think it's too soon for me to move on. Would you like to hear the last words she spoke to me?"

"Of course. That is, if you want to share it with me."

Todd lowered his head and in a very soft voice repeated Della's last words. "Promise me you'll find a good mother for Jacob . . ."—Todd's voice broke—"and I can die happy."

Sarah put two fingertips over her lips, because she knew she couldn't speak. She tried to comfort him with her eyes, but they were filled to the brim with liquid emotion.

"I'm not trying to put you on the spot, Sarah. I just want you to know I care very deeply for you. And I've seen what a fine mother you would make for Jacob. But you should complete your education first. Maybe by that time I will have won your heart."

"You've already won my heart, Todd. And I can think of nothing that would make me happier than to be your wife and Jacob's mother. But I owe it to a lot of people to finish my education and get a degree. Then I think . . . if you still feel the same . . . well . . ."

THE TRINITY QUILTS

"If? Did you say *if*, silly girl? I'll hang by my toes until then if that'll help. I love you, Sarah Blake." Todd stood, causing his chair to fall backward. The clatter didn't even slow him down as he zeroed in on her lips.

She received his first kiss willingly—even anxiously—but pulled away when his arms began to tighten around her waist.

"Before you make any commitment based on who you *think* I am, I need to tell you *my* story, Todd. But not today."

He retrieved his chair and sat down, his elbow on the table and his chin resting on his fist. He shook his head slowly. "Nothing you could say would change my mind. Please tell me what you're talking about. It's not even supper time. We have the whole evening to talk."

"No, Todd, I don't want to take a chance on losing you. Not today."

⁓⁕⁓

It was Friday night, and Sarah's roommate had gone home for the weekend.

Their room, which they'd decorated so cheerfully, seemed dull and drab tonight. Sarah flipped on her bedside lamp, but it did little to alleviate the gloomy atmosphere. She seemed to be sinking in the doldrums and didn't know why.

I'll listen to some praise and worship music. That'll lift me out of this mood.

But their shared boom box was nowhere to be found. Apparently her roomy had taken it with her when she left town.

So Sarah sat staring out the window at the campus grounds below. And her mind wandered to Todd's ministry. He was so happy serving the Lord. And his congregation seemed to love him dearly. He does need a wife to help him in his ministry and to raise his son. But that should be a woman with a spotless reputation, shouldn't it?

What would it do to his career if it was ever found out his wife got pregnant out of wedlock and gave the child up for adoption? She hitchhiked halfway across Texas, then lived in a dump and got her meals from a soup kitchen. And, for a time, she shared a shack in the woods with a half-crazy, career con man.

What would his congregation think of *that*? He might want to forgive her, but if she cared for him—and she did—it was her responsibility to not let him throw away everything he'd accomplished.

All the great things that had happened in her life since meeting Dr. Rob and Beth suddenly seemed sleazy. She was a terrible person. Nice clothes and an education couldn't change that.

Wanting only to fall asleep and put these thoughts out of her mind, Sarah pulled the shades and slipped out of her clothes. Glancing at her naked body in the mirror as she entered the bathroom, she felt a white-hot flush of shame. She was attractive. But she was "used goods" as Papa had said. Being attractive was not an asset. It made her all the more likely to be coveted and desired by men of low character. She was not good enough for a decent man—certainly not good enough for a man of God. She could only make a train wreck of his ministry.

A hot shower did nothing to improve her spirits. She slipped into her pajamas and crawled between the sheets. As soon as her head hit the pillow, a droning voice began chanting, "*Harlot . . . harlot . . . harlot.*"

Sarah sat straight up in bed and demanded, "Leave me alone."

Quiet reigned.

Until the moment, she laid her head down again.

"You forfeited your opportunity to be of use when you swung your hips and tossed your long ponytail for a young man bold enough to call your bluff. You got what you deserved." The voice seemed to come from every corner of the room.

"Okay." Sarah raised up on her elbows and spoke aloud. "You've made your point." She lowered her voice to a whisper. "I don't deserve a life of happiness. I don't deserve to raise Todd's child. I gave mine away. What kind of a woman gives her child away?"

"Certainly not a pastor's wife."

She stifled a sob. "I'll refuse to see him again. He'll get over me and find someone who won't bring shame to his calling. I'll stay single and serve God from the shadows where I won't shame Him either."

She laid back down. Silence. The voices were gone. They'd made their point. Now she remembered why she never dreamed of getting married. No good man should be stuck with her. *It's all I can do. I can't undo the past. But I can protect Todd's future.*

With aching heart and determined mind, Sarah succumbed to a fitful night's sleep.

She was awakened by her cell phone the next morning. She glanced at the clock. *Eight thirty.*

The phone call was from Todd. He was probably calling to remind her he was bringing the church service in the cafeteria this morning at nine. After that, he'd want her to accompany him to his church for the eleven o'clock service.

She let it ring. When it finally stopped, she made a call to the dorm office before turning her phone off. Trying to sound like she had a cold, she implored the acting dorm mother, "Please don't let anyone disturb me today. I'm going to try to get some sleep."

The sweet elderly lady who manned the office on Sundays was concerned, so Sarah promised if she wasn't better by Monday morning, she'd check in at the infirmary. Sarah took a couple of sleeping pills. Anything to shut out the world and any possible contact with Todd.

"You missed a good church service. So what's up with you?" Kerstin, Sarah's over-the-top roommate, made no attempt to be quiet. Anyone still asleep at 1:00 p.m. on Sunday deserves to be rudely awakened to Kerstin's way of thinking.

Sarah stretched and yawned, then glanced at the clock. "When did you get home?"

"Yesterday evening. You were asleep then too. But I decided to let you alone. Is there something wrong?"

"No, I think I just needed a long rest. I tossed and turned for hours last night. So I took a couple of sleeping pills. How come you came back early?"

"Woman, you know those sleeping pills hit you hard. What were you thinking? Me? I got an overdose of hominess. I can only handle so much of 'The Waltons' before I start screaming. Thought I'd get back a little early. Maybe you and I could do something. Fat chance with you sawing logs like a big dog. So how about us going out for a bite now . . . or do you have a date with Todd?"

"I'm sorry, Kirsten. I don't feel like going out today. And Todd and I are kinda . . . well . . . I don't think I'll be seeing him anymore."

"Whoa—"

The pay phone in the hall rang, interrupting Kirsten. She ran for it and answered before Sarah could object. "Yeah, she's right here." With a look somewhere between curiosity and aggravation, she dropped the receiver and shuffled back in the door. "It's Todd."

Sarah shook her head and glared at her. Turning her head to the side and covering it with her pillow, she muttered, "Tell him I must have gone to the bathroom."

Kirsten sighed, kicked one of Sarah's shoes under the bed, and went into the hall again. Sarah could hear her, loud and clear. "Sorry, Todd, she must have slipped into the bathroom. I'll have her call you. Bye." Returning, she slammed the door behind her and jammed her hands to her hips. Standing over Sarah, she demanded, "Okay, what's going on anyway?"

Sarah turned on her back and put her pillow under her head. "I don't want to talk about it. Just this once, can you give me a break and not demand an answer. I'll explain later. Now let me go back to sleep." She turned her back to her frustrated roomy and pulled the covers over her head.

Kirsten slung her purse over her shoulder headed for the door. "Well, excu-u-u-u-se me, your highness, I'll let someone else enjoy my company for lunch." Slamming the door extra hard behind her, she strode down the hall.

Sarah wanted to run after her. Kirsten was acting a bit cranky, but they were best friends, and it hurt to see Kirsten so upset. But Sarah wasn't prepared to tell *anyone* about her past, and her past was the one and only reason for her strange behavior. *I'll think of some excuse before she gets back, and I'll beg her to forgive me, if necessary.*

At 4:15 p.m., there was a knock on her door. Sarah went to the door reluctantly. "Who is it?"

It was the lady from the reception desk. "Sarah, there's a young man to see you. He's been here for an hour and he said he won't go away until you talk to him. Shall I send him up?"

"No! Tell him I'm sick and I'll call him when I feel better."

There was a pause. "He's pretty adamant about seeing you right now."

"Well, I'm adamant that he *can't* see me now. Please get rid of him."

Sarah stared at the door until she heard receding footsteps, then threw herself back on the bed and cried herself to sleep.

At 9:00 p.m., her tummy awoke her to remind her it had been nearly forty-eight hours since she'd eaten anything. She slipped out of bed. She was alone—apparently Kirsten had not come home yet. After a hot shower, avoiding the bathroom mirror that had set her on this course, she put on a pair of sweats and her running shoes, having decided to jog the two-plus miles to the nearest fast-food restaurant.

The lobby was always deserted at this time on Sunday evening. The desk clerk nodded, motioned her thumb toward the door, and mouthed the words, "*He finally left.*"

Sarah tiptoed silently down the wide, winding staircase and headed for the rear exit. She sighed with relief. At least she wouldn't have to face Todd tonight.

Once outside, she spied a lone figure in a hoodie sitting on the right side of the bottom step. Heart pounding, she kept as far to the left as possible as she sped by him. Even at this upscale university, there was always a tinge of fear—especially for a young lady, alone at night—at the sight of a male, face hidden by a hoodie. Because of her past, Sarah may have been more susceptible to panic than most.

She headed down the path toward the main road at a full-out run. She relaxed and slowed a little when she heard no sound behind her.

But a quick glance revealed the stranger in the hoodie was indeed following her at a considerable distance. He seemed to be loping, pacing himself until she reached the park. Once in the park, he'd have a full mile through the heavily wooded area to catch up to her. Sarah picked up speed.

Glancing behind her periodically, she seemed to lose him from time to time on the curves, only to see him again on the straight stretches. Each time a little closer.

The demon of fear was enjoying this. *Can't turn around and can't run fast enough to outrun him, can you, harlot? Exciting, isn't it? Kinda reminds me of that night four years ago. You remember, don't you? The Frederick's shack?*

Sarah tried to run faster, but she was losing strength. He, however, seemed almost relaxed. Soon he was right on her heels. She whimpered in fear, expecting the inevitable touch. Would he cover her eyes, like the last time? Without thinking she balled her fists, preparing to fight for her life.

"Wait up, Sarah," a familiar voice huffed.

She stopped and swung around to see Todd. Panting, he flung the hoodie back off his head, revealing his generous crop of dark hair. And a tentative smile.

Sarah bent over and dropped her hands to her knees to catch her breath. "Todd, what on earth are you doing here? I told them to tell you I'd call when I felt better."

Todd's smile faded. "What's going on, Sarah? I thought at first you were playing with me, running from me like that. But this was no game. You were terrified. I called out to you."

"I didn't hear you."

"I'm not surprised. You ran like a frightened animal . . . not like a sick woman. I thought we had a close enough relationship that you'd tell me if you were sick. Not just suddenly become unavailable." He stepped closer.

Sarah backed away. "I . . . I . . . just didn't want to see *anyone* right now. Where's Jacob?"

"I left him with the babysitter. He wouldn't understand what I'm about to do."

With that, Todd reached out and pulled Sarah to him. With one hand on the side of her head, he pressed her to his chest. "I've never seen this side of you, Sarah, and it frightens me. Your heart's beating like it's about to explode. Sarah . . . I love you. I want to take care of you the rest of your life. Nothing you can tell me will ever change that."

"Oh, Todd."

Before she could say any more, he found her lips with his and kissed her firm, but gentle. She struggled briefly, then relaxed against his chest, her heart and mind doing battle. When he released her, she pulled her hand back in a rather half-hearted attempt to slap him. Todd caught her wrist and lowered it to her side.

He held her firmly by the shoulders, "Now, Sarah Blake, you're going to tell me what has come over you. Why are you acting so strangely?"

She struggled against his firm grip. "Let me go."

"I've no intention of doing so. Not until I know what you're so afraid to tell me."

Todd took her hand and led her to a picnic bench along the path. "I'm waiting."

"You don't want to hear it, Todd. Please believe me. I'm not what you think I am."

"Sarah, we all have a past. I love the woman you are now . . . and I don't care what's in your past. Can you understand that?" He put one hand under her chin and lifted her lips for a brief kiss.

Todd sighed and looked down at their entwined hands. "Sarah, do you know God?"

"Yes, I do. I accepted Jesus as my Savior several years ago. I've already told you."

"Do you realize whatever those things are you did in the past, God forgave, and He *forgot* your sins the night you asked for forgiveness?"

"Yes, but . . ."

"There's no but to it. He's forgotten!"

Sarah couldn't hold it in any longer. "But, Todd, there's a child out there in this world *I* haven't forgotten. And never can." She tried unsuccessfully to wiggle from his loving hold. "I have a daughter Jacob's age. Born the same day, actually. I didn't know what to do except give her away, because I was homeless." She dropped her head into her hands. "But I love her so much."

Todd drew in a breath and seemed to release it with a prayer. Wrapping his arms around Sarah, he rocked back and forth. "Oh, my darling, you should have told me sooner. We'll get your baby back if we have to take it to the highest court in the land."

"I can't, Todd." Sarah shuddered and pressed her full weight against him. "I gave my word to the wonderful couple who took her I'd never, *ever*, bring that kind of sorrow on them—or her. And now I have to live with that promise the rest of my life."

༺༻

Todd pondered how this lovely young lady had gone from a homeless, pregnant waif to someone who appeared to be the product of an educated, successful family. Her manners and upbringing seemed impeccable. *God must have great plans for her to have blessed her with the means to turn her life around.*

Sarah's stomach rumbled.

Todd pulled away to look at her. "When did you eat last, sweetheart?"

"Um . . . two days ago."

"Let's walk back to my car, and we'll go get something to eat. And afterward . . . to my house. I want you to tell me everything, without ever giving a thought to losing me. That's not going to happen. Ever. We're going to take this to the Lord. He'll guide us in how to handle it—together.

With his arm around her, they walked back to the dorm parking lot to retrieve his car. He opened the door for her and leaned in to fasten her seatbelt, kissing her as he did so.

"Do you know your daughter's given name?"

"Emily. Emily McKinley. They let me name her."

"They sound like good people, Sarah. Have you told them about us?"

"We've not spoken since the day Emily was born. She was, maybe, fifteen minutes old when the doctor laid her in Beth's arms. Not mine. I never held her. I had to ask Beth and Rob to leave before I changed my mind and messed up everyone's life. We all knew we'd never meet or speak again. And that's the way it has to be, Todd—for Emily to have a happy life."

Chapter 33

Sarah and Todd were wed on the evening of her graduation day, in his church with his best friend, and associate pastor, officiating. Sam and Vivi attended and Sam gave away the bride. On his best behavior, with all his tattoos covered up, Sam cut a handsome figure. Well, perhaps handsome would be a slight exaggeration, but the ladies of the church found him totally charming.

The same ladies had taken Sarah under their collective wing and planned a wedding to be envied by a princess. They tidied the parsonage and, to the best of their ability, balanced Todd's typical masculine decorating with items from Sarah's cardboard boxes that had been stacked in the living room. The ladies oohed and aahed over Sarah's beautiful quilt. But it was double-bed size and much too small for Todd's king-sized bed, so they hung it over a quilt rack at the foot of the bed.

The quilt was the first thing Sarah saw when she walked timidly into Todd's bedroom for the first time—on their wedding night. No longer Sarah Blake, the girl who had to borrow a last name. No longer an abused waif. She was Sarah Webster. Mrs. Todd Webster. Pastor Todd's wife.

And this reminder from her not-so-distant past brought tears to her eyes. Todd was right behind her. He put his arms around her from the back. "Is this your Trinity quilt you told me about? It's outstanding. Where did you learn to quilt so beautifully?"

"A little from my grandma. Mostly, I was led by the Holy Spirit. I couldn't have done it—twice—but for His presence. There's another one just like it in Dallas."

"I know, darling." He turned her around to face him. "I don't know what plans God has for us. But He loves you more than we can even comprehend. And I feel so strongly someday you'll get to hold Emily in your arms."

"Perhaps, darling. But until that day I have the knowledge she's loved and cared for. And I have another child who deserves all my love and attention.

"Our son, Jacob."

Two couples bravely facing the future—each with a precious three-year-old child. One in an upscale suburb of Dallas. The other in a modest parsonage in Nashville, Tennessee. Both families leaning heavily on God to see them through the good times and the bad.

And known only to God, a fine golden thread of love that cannot be broken, binds them, one to the other.

Part 2

Chapter 34

"Daddy, my Sunday school teacher said God is my father. I thought *you* were my father." At nearly four years old, Emily McKinley was full of questions. Some of them difficult to explain to such a young mind.

Rob lifted Emily to his lap. "I'm your earthly father, darling. God is your Heavenly Father. You see, God is Father to every living being. Even me and Mama. He created us, and He loves us like a father."

"Sometimes stuff about God is confusing, Daddy. If God is your father, who is Granddad?"

Rob looked helplessly at Beth and shrugged his shoulders.

Beth held her arms out to the curly-headed youngster. "Come here, baby. Let me try to make it easier to understand."

Emily climbed down from her daddy's lap and loped over to where Beth was sitting, dark curls bouncing. She crawled onto the couch and snuggled up to her mother.

"Do you know what *creating* is Emily?"

Emily was very bright but struggled a bit with the word *mother*. "Yes, Motho, that's when you make something."

"That's right. And God created man—and woman—many years ago. He was their father. The first father in the whole world. The man and woman got married and had children. And the children grew up and got married and had more children. The first thing you know the world was full of people. Each person had an earthly father and mother. You know, a man and a woman. But everybody still agrees God started it all, so He is our *Heavenly* Father."

"Oh." Emily slid down off the couch. Shaking her head, she looked questioningly at Rob. "Why didn't you just say so, Daddy?"

Rob and Beth couldn't stifle their laughter. Emily looked from one to the other and started laughing with them.

Beth suddenly turned serious. "And I'll never stop thanking God for giving you to us, Emily. But now it's time for bed. Kiss Daddy good night."

Later, Rob and Beth enjoyed a cup of hot chocolate in front of the fireplace. Beth sat quietly gazing into the gentle, glowing flames. Her thoughts were of the young lady who came into their lives and blessed them, both with her presence and the beautiful gift of her own child.

"Penny for your thoughts, Beth."

She turned to face the man she'd loved for more than fourteen years. "I'll never get over what Sarah did for us. I wish there were some way we could repay her."

"We can, and we are, Beth. We're raising her daughter to be a loving, secure, happy little girl. That's all Sarah asked of us. It's the most important thing in the world to her." He nodded to the stairway where Beth had walked a few minutes earlier, hand in hand with a little angel, escorting her to her room. "We're covering her every night with the quilt Sarah made for her. One day when she begins to wonder about where she got those beautiful dark curls, we may have to tell her about her birth mother. But not before she understands how deep our love for her is."

"I know you're right. But I worry about Sarah. I really grew to love her."

"Last time I talked to Adam, she was doing great in school. And he assured me her benefactor was committed to seeing Sarah all the way through school. In fact, I haven't talked to him lately . . . but I think she's about to graduate—with honors."

Rob's phone rang.

He pulled his phone from his pocket and checked caller ID. "I don't recognize the number."

"Hello." He paused, his brow knit. "Yes, it is."

He shook his head absently and shrugged.

"Who? Oh, yes, Mr. Shubert. I remember you. What can I do for you?" Rob grabbed his forehead. "Oh no. When? I'm so sorry. We were just talking about him. Is there anything I can do?"

His face was drained of color.

"Thanks for letting me know. Please call if I can help in any way. Goodbye."

Beth was standing by his side by the time he disconnected. "What's wrong, Rob?"

"There was an accident. Adam Liotta and his wife were killed."

Chapter 35

When Todd and Sarah had been married less than a month, there came a mysterious letter in the mail. It was addressed to Sarah Blake at the college. That address had been scratched through, with her new address and new name written below it in a very precise handwriting. Kirsten's handwriting. Kirsten would be graduating midterm. Sarah talked with her from time to time and found it strange she hadn't mentioned the letter.

The return address was a law firm in Dallas. Sarah's first thought was Adam Liotta was writing her something regarding Emily. And she was afraid to open it.

Then she realized the firm name on the envelope wasn't Liotta. And the street address was all wrong. She propped the letter, unopened, against the toaster. And stared at it.

She was still staring at it when Todd came bursting in the back door, excited about the pending plan to construct a gym on the church campus.

He stopped short when he saw the look on his bride's face. "What's wrong, sweetheart?"

She pointed to the letter. "I'm afraid to open it."

He followed the trajectory of her finger to see the ominous letter leaning against the toaster. "Why?"

"It's from a law firm in Dallas. I'm afraid it has to do with Emily. I'm afraid something has happened to her." She turned her eyes to her husband, tears lingering just below the surface.

"Sweetheart, I don't think they'd write to *you* if that was the case. Let me open it for you. We can't just stand here and look at it." He got a case knife out of the drawer and grabbed the letter.

"Let's pray first, Todd."

"We can, baby. But whatever it is, it's already been typed. I don't think God is going to change it now. We pray for Emily every day. Have faith."

Sarah nodded, and Todd slit the envelope open.

He read a few words to himself, then looked up at Sarah. "Was Adam Liotta a good friend?"

"Well, he's Rob's attorney. And the person who found the benefactor who paid my college expenses. He handled all my financial affairs. I don't know him very well, but he seems to be a nice man." She tilted her head to one side, her eyes questioning. "What do you mean, *was* he a good friend?"

"Well, baby, Adam and his wife were in a bad accident. Neither of them survived."

Sarah plopped down at the kitchen table. "Oh, dear, how awful. Do you think we should try to go to the funeral? But we can't, can we? We could run into Rob and Beth."

Todd took the chair next to her. "No, it's too late to attend their funeral anyway. This letter is to let you know at the reading of his will, you were mentioned. They're asking you if you want to come to Dallas to pick up a check when his estate is settled, or if you'd rather it be delivered by a representative of their firm."

"A check?" Sarah began nibbling on a fingernail. "Why would Adam Liotta leave money to me?"

"I don't know, honey. Let me read the rest of the letter, and see if it tells us anything."

"Sweet Jesus!"

"What?"

He didn't answer. His eyes were glued to the letter. "Oh, my Lord."

"Todd! What are you talking about?"

"Honey, they had no children. Mr. Liotta, personally, was the one who paid for your education. But he didn't want it known as long as he was alive. With his wife gone too, you're slated to receive twenty-five percent of their estate. They left the rest to various charities and distant relatives."

"It was Mr. Liotta paying my expenses?" Sarah put her head in her hands. "Oh, I wish I'd known so I could have thanked him."

"Did you hear me, sweetheart? A quarter of their estate."

She looked up at Todd, shaking her head. "I have no idea how much that would be."

"Well, here's a rough idea. They're estimating a little more than $600,000.00 when all debts are paid."

"Oh my gosh. Twenty-five percent of $600,000.00 is . . . is . . . why it's $150,000.00, Todd."

Todd leaned in closer. "You misunderstand, sweetheart. $600,000.00 is how much one quarter of his net worth will most likely come to.

"Honey. You. Are. Rich."

A few weeks later, another unfamiliar letter was forwarded, by way of the college. This one was from an insurance company. Kirsten's name and dorm room number were scribbled on the envelope in pencil.

This time Sarah ripped the envelope open without hesitation. *They probably want more detail about Kirsten's car getting smashed under a fallen tree last month. And I've told them everything I know. Over and over. They just don't want to pay her for the damage done to her car. It's so unfair.*

Her fingernail caught on something in the envelope, and it fluttered to the floor.

It was a check.

For $100,000.00.

I've got to get this to Kirsten right away. She'll be ecstatic.

She stuck the check back in the envelope and dialed Kirsten's cell phone. *Come on, come on . . . pick it up.*

Kirsten answered on the sixth ring, out of breath. "Hello?"

"Kirsten, your check came from the insurance company. It's for $100,000.00. How did you swing *that* amount?"

Kirsten's replying voice was incredulous. "What?"

Sarah answered somewhat impatiently. "You heard me. Your check came. But it's for a lot more than repairs to your car could possibly cost."

"I got my check for the car a long time ago. And even if I hadn't, why would they send it to you? What insurance company is it anyway?"

"I kind of wondered myself." Sarah glanced at the return address on the envelope. "Gregory Fidelity of Dallas."

"Oh, right. The school office tried to give it to me a couple of days ago to give to you when I saw you next. I gave them your address . . . again . . . and told them to forward it. It might be something important."

Sarah pulled the check back out of the envelope. "Well, it's made out to . . . oh, oooh. It's made out to . . . oh, dear, I'll call you back."

Sarah hung up and collapsed into the nearest chair. She turned the check over, as though that might give her some insight. She turned back to the front and looked at it again. Yes, the check was still—very clearly—made out Ms. Sarah

Blake. In the lower left-hand corner was the notation: Life Insurance Policy #4592410 / Adam Liotta.

―――❦―――

"I don't understand, Todd." Sarah was pacing the floor in front of the big picture window. "Why me?"

"Apparently Adam Liotta cared a great deal for you. This insurance payment was to carry you through to graduation should he die before you got your degree. That you got such a big inheritance also was just a fluke. He had left the bulk of his estate to his wife. He had no way of knowing they would die together."

Todd pulled her down on the couch next to him. "I called Dean Evans today, after you called and told me about the check. I think I understand now why Mr. Liotta favored you so. Dean Evans confided in me Liotta was not proud of himself. He'd had a vasectomy without telling his wife because *he* didn't want kids. She, on the other hand, longed for a child. He loved her. But was afraid to confess what he'd done. So he tried to make it up to her by spending a fortune on vacations, cars, homes . . . you name it."

"I'd gathered by what Rob said they lived a pretty lavish lifestyle."

"Very lavish. Then when Rob engaged his services for Emily's adoption, Liotta learned about what you'd been through, and how you kept on keepin' on, and it really shamed him. He determined to do what he could to make your life better. Without telling anyone. The rest is history. Here you are . . . college educated and wealthy. God is good, Sarah.

"You can afford anything you want now, sweetheart. Where do you plan to begin?"

Sarah shook her index finger at him, the way she often did. A habit he found adorable. "First things first, Mr. Webster. We haven't received anything from Mr. Liotta's estate yet, and I don't like to count my chickens before they hatch. As to the $100,000.00 check, we need to tithe on that first . . ."

"Wow, that'll make a good start on the gym. The folks are going to be so excited."

"Well, don't you dare dangle the tithe from the *inheritance* in front of them. I don't want them to get too excited over something that may or may not happen."

"Killjoy!" Todd called over his shoulder as he walked toward the kitchen. "I'm going to make a pot of coffee. Let's break out that blackberry pie in the freezer. Good with you?"

Sarah stared at his back as he walked away from her and spoke in a soft voice. "Honey, I don't think we should be celebrating our good fortune, considering it came at the cost of two lives."

Todd made an about-face. His countenance fell. "I'm sorry, baby. I never met Mr. Liotta. I know that's no excuse for being jovial. But all this seems so surreal. I'd almost forgotten the sacrifice that brought this all about. Please forgive me."

"I only met him twice, Todd. And I never met his wife. So I'm not exactly mourning. I didn't mean to make you feel bad. It's just that I'm feeling . . . I don't know. I can't explain it. Feeling sorry for him, I guess, that he . . . he missed his chance to . . ."

Todd put his arms around her just as she lost her voice to tears.

"It's okay, honey. He had a change of heart at some point. We'll just believe for him he had accepted Christ, and we'll get the chance to thank him someday, okay?"

Sarah put her arms around her husband and held him very tight. "I do know this, Todd. What's left after the tithe from this check I'd like to put up in a college trust fund for Jacob. That seems a long way off now—he's not yet four . . . but as they say . . . time flies."

Chapter 36

"So how do you feel about North Carolina, baby?" Todd called from the pantry where he retrieving a pound of ground coffee from the shelf.

"What do you mean, how do I *feel* about it? It's a beautiful part of the country. Or so I've been told. Never been there myself. Why do you ask?"

"Well, Asheville is a beautiful place. Surrounded by mountains. So lush and green in the summer. But I'm getting ahead of myself. Let me put on a pot of coffee before I hit you with this." Todd walked to the sink and began rinsing out the coffee pot.

"Hey, no fair. Hit me with *what?*" Sarah grabbed his shirt sleeve and almost caused him to drop the coffee pot.

Todd grinned. "Easy there, Mama."

"Yeah, easy there, Mama." Jacob echoed from the under the kitchen table where he was playing cars.

Laughing, Todd put the pot down and led Sarah to a chair. "There, it's two against one. You just sit here and stew about it for a minute while I fix coffee."

Sarah sat good-naturedly and drummed her fingernails on the tabletop while she waited. Her beloved languidly filled the pot with water and the basket with fresh grounds. Then he took two cups from the cabinet and carried them to the table. Next, the sugar and the creamer. Sarah knew he was deliberately stretching this out as long as he could. It must be something of importance to him and he was trying to figure the best way to present it.

Two can play this game. When Todd finally pulled out a chair across the table from her, she said, "Might as well wait until it's finished perking. Otherwise you'll just have to get up again to get our coffee."

His sheepish grin told her he was onto *her* game as well.

"Sorry, this can't wait another second." He plunked down in the chair and reached across the table to her. "I got a call today. An invitation from a church in a small college town near Asheville, North Carolina. They want me to speak one Sunday next month, in view of a call."

"Are you serious?"

"As a heart attack."

"Where'd they hear about you?"

"No idea."

"Would you actually consider taking it?"

"Depends on a lot of things. We don't have any family ties holding us in Tennessee, and I do love the mountains in North Carolina. I think you would too." He cast his eyes downward. "It would be a step-*down*, salarywise." He looked back up, seemingly hopeful of her approval. "But from what I was told today, the growth potential of this little church is awesome. It's in very close proximity to a college. Yet there are very few college students attending. Baby, there's such a vacuum of Christian influence in schools these days. The college is a whole big pond full of hungry fish."

Sarah leaned in closer. "Well, we both know salary isn't what your ministry is about. Besides, we always have my inheritance."

"Hopefully your inheritance will never enter the picture, sweetheart. I just need to know how *you* feel about a possible move."

A move to North Carolina will increase the distance between me and Emily. But neither time nor distance can ever alter my commitment to Rob and Beth. So it really makes no difference if I live in Tennessee, North Carolina, or Hong Kong.

Sarah put her hand over Todd's. "Todd, *you* are the one who was called to serve God in the ministry. *I* am the one who was called to stand by you, wher*ever* you're led. Does that answer your question?

⚜

Three months later, Bethel Baptist welcomed their new pastor. And Todd and Sarah Webster, along with their young son, Jacob, moved their belongings into a lovely, if small, parsonage directly across the street from the church.

When they were more settled and secure, perhaps they'd have more children and buy a larger home. The church could use this location to further their ministry. But for now, this was just fine. More than fine—it was home.

Looking out the large dining room picture window, the majestic mountains in the distance looked almost like a God-painted backdrop. A far cry from Sarah's early years in a small dirty West Texas town. So long ago and so far removed from her new life, she could almost believe it had never happened.

Except for one small thing. A child . . . never far from her heart and mind.

Chapter 37

"I'm almost ten, Dad. All the other kids have grown-up names."

Todd looked down at his son, who had nearly caught up with Sarah in size. But had quite a way to go before he would pass up his dad. "I don't understand. What's not grown-up about the name Jacob?"

Todd's son sighed a deep, condescending sigh and looked at him defiantly. "You called me *Jacob* when I was in diapers. And when I was in kindergarten. Dad, I'm in the fourth grade now. It's way past time for me to be called *Jake*."

Sarah walked into the room. "What's all the fuss?"

"Mom, could you talk some sense into Dad. He wants me to be Jacob for the rest of my life."

"Who else would you want to *be*?" Sarah looked from one to the other, puzzled.

"I mean he wants me to use that name. And I want to be called Jake. Bobby made everyone start calling him Bob." And Sammy goes by Sam. And you know Billy?"

Sarah was having a little trouble keeping a straight face. "Yes, I know Billy. Is he now Bill?"

"Not exactly. His real first name is Christopher." Jacob hesitated, trying to figure a way to explain the situation to his advantage. "People started calling him Chris, but there were two *girls* in his class named Chris, so his new name was worse than his old one."

Todd broke in shaking his head. "I don't understand what point you're making, son."

"The point is, his middle name is William, and Billy is better than Chris, so his folks said okay for him to be Billy. They let *him* make the decision."

By this time, Todd and Sarah were biting their lips to keep from smiling.

The very serious youngster continued pleading his case. "I promise I'll use Jacob on all my legal papers and stuff when I grow up, but I want you and Mom and my friends to call me Jake. Okay?"

Sarah looked at her husband. Jacob was like her own son, but in a situation like this, the call was strictly Todd's.

Todd drawled out his answer. "W-e-l-l-l, if it means *that* much to you, son, Jake it is."

Jacob—now Jake—jumped up and shot a pretend hoop. "And the crowd is roaring for Jake Webster." He made the sound of a roaring crowd.

"But you're going to have to do Jacob's homework for tonight. I see his name on the assignment sheet." Todd gave his beaming son a rather firm pat on the rear. "Get after it, Jake."

They never had any more children. Sarah never got pregnant again, and though they often talked about adoption, the time never seemed right. But they did move to a larger house, just a few blocks from the church. Jake kept the house pretty well filled with friends, Sarah held an occasional lady's tea, and of course, Todd needed room for a home office away from the hustle and bustle where he could study.

They led a quiet, pleasant life, centered around the church and each other. Jake followed in his father's footsteps as he said he would. And Sarah matured beautifully. Life was good.

Until Todd fell ill. Terminally ill at the age of forty-nine.

⁓∾⁓

Beth looked over at Rob, who was reading a novel by his favorite author. "We did a good job, didn't we, honey?"

"A good job of what?"

"A good job of raising a beautiful daughter."

"Yes, we did, Beth. And I give you all the credit." He patted the couch cushion next to him. "Want to talk about it a little?"

"I thought you'd never ask."

He took her hand. "What brought this up, anyway?"

"Just thinking how different our life has been since she's been in it." She leaned her head on his shoulder. "Seems like only yesterday we got her . . . and here she is, almost ready to graduate from high school. And she's been such a joy the whole time."

"Is this going to be about Sarah again, baby?"

"You read me like that book you're holding, don't you?" Beth got a faraway look in her eyes. "It's just in the last couple of years my health has been getting worse, and I want to say some things before it's too late."

"I understand, baby, but a promise is a promise. And we promised Sarah. No contact."

"Yes, I get that. But did we promise to not keep an eye on her from a distance? We wouldn't have to contact her in order to check up on her and make sure she's all right. We can afford to hire someone to trace her. She need never know."

Rob sighed. "Oh, baby. I just wouldn't feel right about it. If we can't contact her and there's nothing we are allowed to do for her, what good would it do to know where she is?"

Beth rose to her feet. "I guess you're right. It's just . . . it's just . . . in the grand scheme of things, I feel like Sarah and Emily should know one another. They're missing so much. And if we don't arrange it, who will?"

Rob took her hand and pulled her back on the couch next to him. Turning her head to face him, he said simply, "God."

"You think He will?"

"If it suits His plan. Or maybe if we just pray enough about it, He'll do it for our pleasure. He does want us to have the desires of our heart, you know. But are you really sure this is what you want? You won't feel betrayed or left out if they meet and love one another?"

"On the contrary, it's exactly what I want. I'm not going to be around forever. When I'm gone, I'd like to know my little girl still has a mother to call on. Mothers are important, you know.

"What's more, if God chooses to complete the circle without me, I'd like to think you'd be there for Sarah as well. There's no such thing as being loved by too many people, darling."

Rob stood and pulled her up beside him. He held her for a long time. It was true, Beth had never been especially healthy. And now, her little body was wearing out. The doctors didn't expect her to live long enough to see her grandchildren. It was going to be a very bad day for him when God took her home. But Beth—being Beth—wanted to have all her ducks in a row when that time came, and she expected him to accept the inevitable as easily as she had.

And what choice did he have other than to accept it? Life goes on. And because she expected it of him, *he* would go on. Still kicking, as they say, but not nearly as high.

Chapter 38

Home from college for the holidays, Emily was enjoying the family's traditional Christmas Eve meal of meat pie and mashed potatoes with her father. She often suffered guilt pangs over having chosen a university in North Carolina, so far from home. Daddy was alone now and apparently had no social life to speak of.

She became very quiet. Laying down her utensils, she put both hands in her lap. *I'll never get used to not having Mother sitting across from me. I pray Daddy can be happy again someday.*

Rob dabbed his mouth with his napkin and turned to look at Emily. "Is there something wrong, baby?"

"I miss Mother."

"Me too, baby. Very much. But we've got to muddle through. Someday we'll see her again." He laid his napkin on the table. "But I get the feeling there's something more bothering you. Will you talk to me about it?"

"Well, Daddy, I'm worried about you. You spend too much time alone. I feel disloyal to Mother in saying this, but I think you need to meet some ladies. Get out more. Maybe find one special one who could bring you happiness. I know no one could ever replace Mother. But there's more than one kind of love, Daddy."

"Would you listen to this? My little girl, giving me advice on love." Rob smiled and shook his head.

"Well, I'm serious, Daddy. And you may as well know I'm praying in that direction. So if God answers my prayer, don't you go and mess it up.

"And there's one more thing. I know my birth mother thought it was best she stay out of my life. But I'm not so sure she was thinking straight. I know you've made a promise to her, but if you ever get the chance to talk to her . . . tell her I said so."

Rob pushed away from the table and walked into the living room.

Emily followed him. Rob gathered his "little girl" in his arms. "Father," he spoke softly, "You know all things. You know . . . better than Emily's birth mother or me . . . what would be best for Emily. If it's Your will, we ask You to arrange a meeting of mother and daughter, in Your perfect timing. Amen."

In a voice so low even Rob didn't hear it, Emily murmured, "Amen."

After they'd settled back to the table and finished their meal, Rob served coffee. "Remember the way you used to drink coffee, Emily?"

"Yes, three-quarters of a cup of milk, three spoons of sugar, and a small splash of coffee." Emily grinned. "Now I take it black . . . no sugar. And lots and lots of it when finals roll around."

Rob sat back in his chair. "You've really made me proud with your grades, baby. Tell me, have you had any time for young men in your life?"

"Not much, Daddy. I figure I have plenty of time for romance after graduation."

Rob flinched at the word *romance*.

"Don't worry, Daddy. I'll be a very particular judge of my suitors." She snickered. "Listen to me, I talk like I'll have multiple suitors. I may be in for a surprise."

Rob laughed and rolled his eyes at the suggestion there'd be a shortage of suitors. "Yeah, right. I'll probably have to hire off-duty policemen to direct traffic when it becomes known you're accepting invitations."

"Oh, Dad-dy..."

———

It was assumed by both Rob and his lovely daughter that love and marriage would follow swiftly on the footsteps of graduation. But Emily had promised to wait for the man God had chosen for her, and he was nowhere to be found *yet*.

Much to her father's chagrin, Emily returned to North Carolina after graduating to get her master's. Followed by an offer from her alma mater to teach at the college. It was an offer much too tempting to refuse. She'd learned to love the countryside and the people of North Carolina. It was home. Leaving Daddy was the only drawback, and he'd made that as easy for her as he could by promising he'd soon retire.

And consider a move to North Carolina himself.

Chapter 39

It was 2:45 a.m. when Pastor Jake Webster's cell phone started twirping the little tune he'd chosen, because he couldn't find anything he really liked. And didn't have the time nor inclination to download something better. Technology wasn't really his thing.

He raised his head from his pillow and glanced at the alarm clock. *Two forty-five? Who would be calling me so early?*

His first thought was of his mother, Sarah. More than his stepmother, she'd been there for him since he was three years old, and few people even knew she wasn't his birth mother. He'd taken her to the cemetery today. And while she seemed to be fine, he always worried his father's untimely passing had left her more bereft than she let on. They'd all known he'd probably proceed her in death, because he was several years older. But certainly no one had expected him to die at the young age of fifty.

Before his death, Todd and Sarah had served the Lord side by side for twenty-five years at the same church—which had grown and prospered—as the Lord had promised. Their son, Jake, a seminary graduate was called to serve beside his father upon graduation. And then pressed into the full-time pastorate upon his father's death, two years ago. Sarah stayed on as the pianist.

Only forty-five years old, well-to-do, and quite attractive, Sarah was already receiving a great deal of attention from the eligible men in the congregation. But she made it quite clear she planned to devote her time to the Lord, to her son, and hopefully some future grandchildren.

Jake snatched up the phone. He'd not been called on for any emergencies since he accepted the full-time position. But he was well aware of how often his father had been called upon, in real emergencies—as well as imagined ones.

He flipped his phone open.

"Brother Jake, there's a fire at the college. One of the girls' dorms is in flames. Doesn't Sam Madison's daughter live in one of those dorms?"

Within minutes, he was dressed. The church parsonage was being used for a homeless ministry these days, and his mother was still living in the house she and his father had bought years ago, so Jake lived in a nice apartment only blocks from the college. As soon as he exited his apartment building, he could see the bright glow of flames lighting up the sky to the east. The road was blocked by sight-seers, so he ran the short distance.

Firemen were bravely entering the blazing building. Water from the hoses filled the air but seemed to have little effect on the flames. Quickly they emerged, leading or carrying young women in a variety of robes and pajamas, and settling them on the terraced lawn, out of harm's way, where EMTs were working furiously to make them comfortable, and checking for injuries. Jake didn't want to get in the way. But he went behind the medical techs to each of the women, inquiring of her condition and praying with her. Blessedly, none of them had been seriously injured.

The fourth girl he came to was Amy Madison. "Oh, Pastor, thank you so much for coming over. I need to call my folks, but my phone's in there." She pointed toward the flaming building.

"Here, use mine, Amy. But I think your dad's in the crowd out there, probably looking for you. Call him, but stay here, I'll see if I can find him."

He handed his cell phone to her just as the announcement came over the bullhorn. "According to dorm records, that's everyone, team. Thank you. We all thank you. Now let's see about getting the flames out. We may still be able to save part of the structure."

Before Jake could start his search for Sam Madison, one of the young women suddenly sat up and looked around. "Maria! Where's Maria?"

She struggled to her feet and ran toward the inferno. A man grabbed her arm as she flew by him, but she managed to free herself.

The bullhorn blared. "Stop her."

But she wasn't to be stopped.

Jake watched in horror as she neared the entrance of the building. *Stop her, Jake. She'll never make it out alive.*

Without thinking, his feet took on a life of their own. He raced her to the entrance but wasn't fast enough to catch her. He followed her in, flames on all sides.

He could see her a short way in front of him at the bottom of a flight of stars. She was wearing blue jeans and a light sweater. "Young lady, please, come back."

"I've got to find Maria," she shouted back. "She was visiting from another dorm and decided to spend the night in a vacant room."

He caught up to her. "What room number?"

"Two-twelve. Right overhead."

"Please get out while you can."

"I'll wait."

"Get out *now*. I'll go after Maria." He spun her around and gave her a gentle shove toward the door they'd just entered.

Obediently she headed toward the door. Swinging around, she turned to face him. "Please be careful."

"Out!"

Turning back, he surveyed the situation. The stairs looked to be still intact. He'd have to take the chance. Taking the steps three at a time, Jake's thoughts ran to his mother. *Oh, Jesus, please let me make it. For the sake of Maria and Mom.*

When he reached the second floor, he was met by a wall of flame on the other side of the hall. Praying the floor plan was similar to many dorms he'd been in, Jake turned to his right and entered the first door on the other side of the hall, where the flames had not yet reached. Once inside the room, he looked to his left for a door to the bathroom. There is was. *Praise you, Jesus.* Entering the bathroom, he felt his way along the basin to the other side of the room. God had arranged for a wet washcloth to be lying on the basin. *Thank you, Lord.* He grabbed it, and putting it over his nose, he took a couple of deep breaths. By the grace of God, he found the door out of the bathroom and into the next dorm room.

With one pink house shoe on and one clutched in her hand, Maria was lying unconscious on the floor of the smoke-filled room. Her mane of black hair fell over her face. Jake fell to the floor beside her. Brushing her hair to the side, he put the washcloth over her face. *Breathe, Maria, breathe.* He struggled to get his arms under her and pick her up. Then carried her to the window, where firemen were just putting a ladder to the sill. Turning their bodies from the window, he covered her face as the firemen broke the glass.

"How did you know?" he choked.

They pointed to the ground where Maria's friend stood, her arms lifted to heaven. She called out to him. "Thank you. Thank you. Now get *yourself* down here, Pastor."

Jake watched as they carried Maria down the ladder. Smoke billowed out the window and around his face. Until he couldn't keep his eyes open or draw a fresh breath. Heat from the burning wall behind him seemed to penetrate all the way to his bones. Engulfed in smoke and seized by uncontrollable coughing, Jake couldn't feel the top of the ladder with his foot. Drifting into unconsciousness, he fell forward.

Chapter 40

Superficial burns and smoke inhalation. That's what his hospital chart read.

He opened his lash-less red eyes to see his mother sitting at the foot of his bed. "Mom. Boy, am I glad to see you. Did everyone get out all right?"

Sarah breathed a prayer of thanks before she answered. "Yes, son."

"What about Maria? Is she okay?"

"Yes, Jake. When I got the call you were in the burning building, my heart seemed to fall from my chest, and I didn't know if I'd make it to see the sunrise this morning. Praise God He saw you through it safely." She lifted her hands to heaven. "Thank you, Jesus."

Sarah approached the head of the bed, where her son was attempting to sit up. "Maria is in about the same shape you are . . . except she has eyelashes!" She smiled down at the man who, up until last night, was still a little boy to her. Recalling the first time she met him, when he was three, she smiled to herself. He told her way back then, he was going to be a pastor like his daddy. Now, it was as though he'd always been a part of her life.

"Maria is a beautiful girl, Jake. Perhaps you two should get to know one another. You are *getting up in years*, you know."

"Only twenty-eight, Mom. Not exactly senile," he bantered back at her.

He stared straight ahead at a beautiful landscape picture on the wall. "I don't remember a thing after seeing them carry Maria down the ladder." He turned his head toward his mother. "What happened?"

"They were on their way back up when you fell across the window sill. I wasn't there yet to see it, but they said you were half in and half out. It was as though someone was holding you from the inside until a fireman reached you."

"God had his hand on me through the whole thing, Mom. No reason to think He'd let go at the last crucial moment, right? What about the girl who led me into the building? She was the only one who remembered Maria was in there." He scratched a spot on his face. "Ouch!"

"Keep your fingers off your face, son." She pulled his hand down to the bed, just like she may have had he still been a child. "Your skin is awfully tender. You look like you fell asleep at a Texas beach in the middle of the day.

"Not sure where the young lady went. Home with one of her friends who had local family, maybe. Those without local connections have been put up at the little motel on the edge of town, until the school can make other arrangements."

Sarah retrieved the chair at the foot of the bed, dragged it around to the head, and sat down with a sigh. "She stayed around long enough to see that you and Maria were going to be all right though. I wouldn't be surprised if she came around to thank you later today. The hospital is buzzing with visitors.

"In fact, I poked my head in Maria's room on the way here. We talked for just a moment. Remember what I said about how pretty she is? You really should get to know her, maybe . . ."

They'd had similar conversations before. But Jake was in no hurry to settle down. He was waiting for God's leading.

"Relax, Mom. You'll get your turn at grandchildren. But I have to be the one to pick out their mother. Of course, I love you for keeping your eyes open for me."

Sarah shook her head and smiled her still-cute dimpled smile. "Gotta go now. Call me after you see the doctor." She stood and gave him a quick peck on the cheek.

"Ouch!"

―⸱―

Restless and ready to get back to his busy life, Jake pressed the call button at his bedside.

Within minutes, a nurse poked her graying head in the door. She was a member and second-grade Sunday school teacher at Jake's church. "Hi, Brother Jake. That was a brave thing you did last night. We're so blessed you're all right. You need something?"

"Well, Ms. Lucy . . . I didn't realize I was on your floor."

"Yep. Got transferred here about three months ago. Are you doing okay?"

"More than okay. I'm chomping at the bit to get out of here."

Nurse Lucy laughed. "Well, then, I've got good news. They're talking about releasing you this afternoon."

"How about Maria . . . wow, I don't know her last name . . ."

"Montego. She'll probably be going home today . . . she's doing great. You ought to walk down to see her."

Hmm. Another hint to meet Maria. Maybe I should take the suggestion.

"Might do that in a few minutes. You'll let me know when I can leave, right?"

"Sure, the doctor should be in right after lunch. We'll know then if you can go today. Call me if you need anything." She slipped back out the door and closed it quietly behind her.

Can't go meet Maria in my hospital gown. I'll just go ahead and get dressed.

Sarah had brought him a set of fresh clothes. In twenty minutes, he was showered and dressed—ready to meet the girl whose life he'd saved.

Walking down the hall, he passed several young nurses going the other way.

"Going to look in on, Maria?" one asked. The others giggled like school girls.

"As a matter of fact, I am." Jake smiled at them, coming to a stop.

"She's awfully pretty. And unattached." More giggling.

Jake tilted his head and looked from one to the other. "Did my mother put you up to this?"

One nurse who seemed a bit older than the others spoke up. "Well, you can't blame her. She said you were making no attempt at finding a wife, and she's ready for grandchildren."

Jake had to laugh. "She's incorrigible. Been after me since I was twenty-one. But maybe it *is* time I gave it some serious thought." He gave the ladies a friendly wave and continued down the hall to room 440.

⁓⁂⁓

They had not exaggerated. Maria was beyond beautiful. Seeing her in the light of day for the first time, he couldn't ignore a pair of smoldering Spanish eyes looking up at him from under luxuriant black lashes—drawing him into the room. Like a small chunk of steel meeting the force of a mighty magnet, Jake allowed himself to be swept into her domain. But even as this small drama unfolded, he remained in control of his sensibilities. The Scriptures were never far below the surface of his mind. God had much to say about the relationship between a man and a woman.

"I was just thinking about you, Pastor Webster." Maria exclaimed when Jake introduced himself. "Sit down, please. I was wondering what you looked like," she demurred and turned her face from him. But not before Jake discerned a tinge of pink on her olive complexion.

She was really quite charming.

She modestly pulled up the neckline of her gown to conceal even a hint of the cleavage that on first sight had been so evident. Her sensual movements were calculated to make the memory of that first sight that much more enticing. But her calculations were lost on Jake. It wasn't the first time a beautiful woman had flirted with him.

"Please call me Jake. Right now, I look a lot like a baked chicken," he bantered. "How did you come out of it looking so lovely?"

"Makeup."

"That must have hurt."

"Yes, it did, and the doctor really fussed at me. But it's a very gentle makeup made for sensitive skin . . . and I couldn't let you see me looking like, well, a baked chicken." She paused as though trying to decide whether to speak the next words. "For the record, you're the best-looking baked chicken *I've* ever seen." She cast her eyes downward, as though she'd embarrassed herself.

Jake caught himself wondering how much of her behavior was sincere and how much was an act.

He smiled. "How did you know I'd be coming by, Maria?"

Maria looked down at the sheet hem she was rolling between two fingers. "I . . . uh . . . asked your mom to suggest it to you." Two pleading jade eyes focused on his face. "I'm sorry, Jake. I just had to see the man who saved my life.

"I mean, I owe you so much. I don't know how I'll ever be able to repay you."

"Maria, it was something anyone wouldn't have done under the circumstances. In fact, there was a young lady who tried, but I made her turn around. So forget the *indebtedness* idea. You don't owe me a thing for doing what comes naturally."

Maria looked up and smiled. Her teeth were perfect. Apparently everything about her was perfect. "Tell that to my mother. She wants you to come over to dinner the very first evening after we're released from the hospital."

"One of the nurses told me we'll both be released today, most likely."

"Good, then this evening it is." Maria picked up a piece of paper and a pen from her bedside table. She scribbled a few words. "Here's my address. Come around seven."

Jake took the note and glanced at the address. A very prosperous area about twelve miles out of town. "I'll don't think I can make it this evening, Maria. I have some things to catch up on for the church. I'm a pastor, you know."

"Anything you have to do, I'll help you with tomorrow, my knight in shining armor. Please don't disappoint my mother. Or Daddy. He's pretty used to getting his way."

"I appreciate your offer to help with church work, but it really isn't an option." Suddenly Jake wanted to be anywhere but where he was. Perfect is as perfect does, and Maria's controlling spirit had just become very obvious.

"Oh, you have to be there, Jake. You can't save a girl's life and then refuse to meet her grateful family." She stuck out her lower lip.

He could see he was not going to win this one. "Well, I want to meet your folks too, so I promise to come, but I won't be able to stay long." Jake knew how a fish must feel right after it chomps down on the bait.

She's a very beautiful young lady. And very spoiled.

"And I have much to do right now, so I'd better run." He held her extended hand for a moment, then turned to leave. "See you this evening."

He hadn't made it two feet down the hall before she called out to him. "Jake! Jake!" He turned around and peeked back into her room.

"Don't be late." She threw him a kiss.

Twang. The hook was set.

He hadn't been back in his own room but a few minutes when the doctor stuck his head in the door. "How you feeling, Padre?"

"Past ready to leave, Doc."

Dr. Hanson strode toward his patient. "I can see you're dressed and ready to ride. Just let me have a quick look at your throat."

Jake complied with the usual commands: breathe deep—open wide—cough.

"Can't find any reason to delay you any longer, Padre. Just take it easy for a day or two, okay?"

As Jake walked out the front door of the hospital, there was only one thing he wanted to do. That was to go home, lock all the doors, and plunge into the Word. But it wasn't to be. He had a seven o'clock date at the Montego mansion.

Chapter 41

"Maria tells me you're a pastor. Is that so?" Mike Montego hunched over his dinner plate, a piece of rare steak impaled on his knife. His penetrating eyes scorching the distance between them.

He only used his fork to immobilize the meat while he viciously stabbed it, as though it was trying to get away. It went from the knife to his mouth. Odd eating habits for a man who lived in a virtual palace. His wife and daughter, however, were the picture of propriety.

"Yes, sir. That's right. Following in my father's footsteps."

Montego didn't beat around the bush. "Any money in that gig?"

"Not enough to get wealthy, sir. Unless your goal is a television ministry. That's not for me, but there's apparently a lot of money in it." Jake concentrated on his food, not really liking the direction this conversation was taking.

"Well, just asking. I need to know a little about a fellow who's come to court my baby."

Jake's fork stopped midway to his mouth.

Montego laid down his knife and fork and leaned forward. His expression demanding Jake's full attention. "We're beyond grateful for what you did for Maria. However, I don't agree with your casual outlook on the need for money. I wouldn't want Maria to have to do without. You're nice looking, Jake. Educated. You've got the potential to make it in the *big time*."

He picked up his tools to resume eating. "Well, maybe in time, I can make you see it my way." He returned to his steak with a vengeance.

In time? Courting Maria?

The hook in his cheek tightened as Mike Montego began to reel him in.

"Daddy, quit cross-examining every fellow I date. Mother, make him stop." Maria pretended to be upset by her father's manners, but Jake had the feeling this was a regular routine in the selection of possible mates for Mike Montego's little princess.

Maria's mother spoke for the first time since introductions had been made. "Just ignore my husband, Pastor Jake. Making money is all he thinks about. Maria takes after me. We're romantic souls. I perceive you are as well." She blotted her lips.

"Maria, why don't you show your fellow around? I know you're too excited to eat anyway."

Alarm bells were going off in Jake's head. *What have I gotten myself into?* Apparently all three of them assumed only a crazy man would not jump at the chance to marry Maria. The last thing he wanted to do was offend someone—anyone—especially a person who may not know the Lord. But how was he going to get out of this *without* offending?

Maria had a firm grip on his hand. He eased it away from her. "Allow me to help clear the table, Mrs. Montego."

Mrs. Montego was a tiny woman with expressive hands and a rather hawkish face. It occurred to Jake to wonder where Maria got her exceptional looks. The missus kind of twittled her fingers in front of her mouth when she spoke. "Oh, heaven's no . . . may I call you Jake? The maid will see to it. Now you two run along." She made a shoving motion with her beautifully manicured hands.

THE TRINITY QUILTS

Maria snatched his hand back and began pulling him. "First a tour of the house, then we'll go down to the lower level kitchen and make a malt or something."

Jake stopped abruptly. "I don't mean to be rude, Maria, and I hate to eat and run, but I have so much to catch up on. And studying to do. I'll be back in the pulpit on Sunday. I really have to leave now."

"I told you I'd help you."

"This isn't something that can be done by two."

"Will I at least *see* you tomorrow?"

"I . . . I . . . doubt it, Maria. I really have to work."

Maria looked disappointed. "Well, okay, my hero. There's always the next day."

On the drive home, Jake prayed. "Father, Maria is a sweet girl. But she's not the girl You have for me . . . of that, I'm fairly sure. Please give me the wisdom to put an end to this nonrelationship I'm in, without hurting her or offending her parents."

Chapter 42

When Jake got home, there was an envelope stuck in his door. In it was a note:

> I'm sorry I missed you, Pastor. I went to the hospital to visit you, only to find you'd already been released. Praise the Lord! Just wanted to thank you for taking my place in that inferno. I know now I'd have never gotten out alive, nor would Maria, if you hadn't stopped me and gone after her yourself. I hope someday I'll get to meet you. Thank you again.
>
> In His love,
> Emily McKinley

There was a return address on the envelope. For one of the nicer apartment houses near the college. Apparently she'd already found a place to live until the dorm was rebuilt. Jake put the note and envelope in his desk. After Sunday service, he would make it a point to visit the brave young college student.

At seven o'clock the next morning, while Jake was enjoying his first cup of coffee, his cell phone rang. *Maria.*

"Good morning, Sir Galahad. I'm on my way to class. Though I'd see how your day is going so far."

THE TRINITY QUILTS

Her voice was sweet and concerned, but at this point, it almost made his blood curdle.

"Good morning, Maria. I'm doing fine. Just getting ready to dig into some church office work. Our secretary has been on vacation this week, so it kinda falls to me to keep it up."

"I'm a wonderful secretary . . . why won't you avail yourself of *my* services?" She sounded slightly miffed.

"Maria, I've no doubt you are wonderful at anything you undertake. But it would be unethical to involve anyone other than church employees in private church affairs. I do appreciate the offer, however. You'd better get on to class, or you'll be late. I'll talk to you later, okay?"

Jake heard her loud sigh. There was no doubt he was intended to hear it.

"All right, but I'd much rather be there with you than in a dry, old math class. Are you sure I can't help you?"

"Very sure. Wouldn't be proper."

"Okay. See you after while. Kisses."

Jake disconnected and stared at the phone. *After while? Kisses? Oh, Lord. What am I going to do?*

He bundled up all the paperwork he'd brought home to work on and carried it to his car. He'd have accomplished more at home where there'd be no interruptions. But if there was any chance Maria intended to "drop in" on him, he'd rather it be at church with other folks milling the halls.

~~~

Maria did drop in that afternoon and Saturday afternoon. And on Sunday morning, there she was in the pews. Center and second row back. She had plans for them for Sunday evening—at her house, of course. After service he walked her to her car, in the back parking lot, which was now empty of cars, except for her Tesla.

She displayed her too familiar pouty lips. "You have to come, Jake. Daddy wants to show you his latest plans for an apartment building he's planning . . . right close to campus. It will be close to the church too. And he thinks you might benefit from it." She smiled up at him. "And I want to make you the malt I promised. I put in a secret ingredient. You're going to love it."

Jake's shoulders dropped. How could he stop this avalanche of attention?

"Maria, I . . ."

"Don't tell me you have to work. It's Sunday. A day of rest. Besides, you're family now. You and I have a bond few people share." She stood on her tiptoes with her face close to his. And invitation to kiss, if ever there was one.

She was a real beauty, and, being human, Jake was tempted to taste her lips, but he turned his face from hers and tried again. "Maria, you don't understand . . ."

"Oh, but I do. You have a calling and you don't think it would be proper to move too fast in our relationship. I understand. And I'm a patient girl. But fate has thrown us together, Jake. And I, for one, will not try to deny it."

Why would a girl this beautiful be so desperate to establish a relationship with a plain guy she barely knows?

A loud outdoor bell rang, startling Maria. She threw her arms around his neck.

Jake took her hands in his and lowered them to her side. "It's only the church phone, Maria. We have an outdoor ringer for church personnel who may be between buildings." He glanced at his watch. "I'd better get inside and answer it."

"I'll call you after while," he shouted over his shoulder as he sprinted toward the main building.

Chapter 43

Jake checked the lights, windows, and doors throughout the building, adjusted the thermostat to meet the evening's requirements, and walked through the vestibule to the front door. Securing the lock on the wide double-doors, he took off at a trot toward his home. He often came to church on foot when the weather was good. This was an especially beautiful day.

He glanced at his watch. *Hmm, it's almost one and I have to pass Miss McKinley's apartment building on the way home. This would be a good time to stop and pay her a visit.*

Emily answered the door in jeans and a casual top. "Oh, hi, Pastor. Come on in."

"Hope I'm not coming at an inconvenient time, Miss McKinley."

Emily stepped back and waved him in. "Not at all. I just changed from my church clothes and was getting ready to make myself a tuna salad sandwich. Will you join me?"

"Well, I *am* hungry. Skipped breakfast this morning. So . . . if you're sure you have plenty."

Emily laughed. "I always have plenty of tuna salad. It's kind of my standby meal when I don't have time to cook."

The apartment was well-appointed but not pretentious. Pretty nice for a college girl. Even more impressive for a college girl who'd just lost everything in a fire.

Emily was busy making sandwiches. "What would you like to drink" I've got coffee, 7-Up, or water."

"Coffee, please. May I help?"

"You could get the plates down out of the cabinet, if you will," she said, pointing.

He couldn't help but notice her fingernails were short, in comparison with the current fashion. Neatly filed and natural colored. He liked that.

He got down two plates and set them on the table.

"Two cups too. Next cabinet over on the left."

Jake followed her orders. *She sure knows how to make a fellow feel at home.*

The conversation over lunch naturally turned to church. Jake learned Emily was attending a nondenominational church a couple of miles away. Her folks had always attended a nondenominational, and she'd just fallen into the habit—although she certainly had no problem with the Baptist denomination.

She shared that her mother had passed away, and Jake told her he'd lost his father a couple of years ago and had, in fact, filled the vacancy in the pulpit left by his father.

The conversation hit a lull and Jake took his first really long look at Emily. Strange. Her otherwise beautiful dark curls were unevenly trimmed.

"Uh . . . your hair is, uh . . ." He tried to indicate with his hands at the side of his face that her hair was longer on one side than the other.

Emily laughed. "You noticed. It got singed on the left side. I trimmed the burnt hair off and tried to even it out as best I could. But I quit when I realized it wasn't happening. I'd have been bald before I ever got it even." She grinned. "Couldn't get an appointment with my hairdresser until Tuesday."

Jake grimaced. "I'm sorry. That was rude of me."

Emily shrugged. "Think nothing of it." With a perfectly straight face, she retorted, "It's the kind of thing one would expect from a man with no eyelashes."

Jake's jaw dropped. Emily shot him a humorless look.

But she couldn't hold the look for long. She chuckled. "Gotcha!"

They both laughed heartily. And when they stopped laughing, they held up their coffee cups in a toast.

"Touché," they burst out in unison.

"On a more serious note, I really want to thank you, Pastor, for what you did for me, and for Maria, the other night. We both owe you our lives."

"No, please . . . let's not go there." Jake smiled. "I've been slightly overwhelmed with gratitude already. It was nothing anyone else wouldn't have done. And by the way, just call me Jake."

"Okay, Jake. May I take you to dinner tonight, just as a *thank you*?"

"I wish."

"What does that mean?"

"I seem to be in a relationship not of my own making. And apparently I'll never have a free night again, as long as I live."

Unsuccessfully stifling a grin, Emily continued, "I'm afraid you'll have to be a bit more clear. Does this mean I can never treat you to a meal?" Her countenance slipped a little when she apparently realized another possibility. "Or does it mean you're married?"

"Heaven forbid, Miss McKinley . . ."

The grin returned. "Whoa. If you're *just* Jake, then I must be *just* Emily."

"All right, *just* Emily," he cleared his throat. "Here's my problem. It seems a young woman has staked her claim on me—I can't imagine why—and short of hurting her feelings,

I'm afraid she's heading me straight for the altar." Jake deliberately didn't mention Maria's name.

Emily laughed aloud. "Is her name Maria?"

"How did you know?"

Emily was shaking her head, presumably in pity. "It was inevitable. Sweet though she is, Maria is a bit overbearing . . . and she has the irritating habit of falling head-over-heels in love with every good-looking guy she meets. And her father wants so badly to marry her off well—before she makes a terrible mistake—he comes on pretty strong to any man he considers worthy of his daughter."

"Good-looking? So the truth comes out. You find the lash-less look attractive."

"Don't let it go to your head. I've seen worse than the likes of you. But I've seen better." Emily accented that statement with a wink.

Jake grinned, but quickly turned serious. "What can I do about her, Emily? I've tried to explain to her, but it's like she's not listening."

"Jake, I've seen her fall in and out of love a dozen times since I've known her. She's a hopeless romantic. And I'm afraid you've come on the scene in the most dramatic way *yet*. I mean, rescuing her from a burning building. What could be more romantic? I'm afraid in her eyes, it's fate . . . destiny . . . that you two be together."

"You're. Not. Helping. I need some sage advice here."

Emily moved closer and spoke in a whisper. "Have you kissed her yet?"

Jake whispered back. "No, I haven't . . . and why are we whispering?"

"Sorry, I got caught up in the drama of it all. You wouldn't lie to me, would you? I mean, do you promise you've not kissed her?"

"I promise. Cross my heart. And it's not because she hasn't tried to maneuver a kiss."

"Then, there's hope. All Maria wants is romance. Marriage, yes. But it has to be the most romantic courtship imaginable. If you want to get out of this *relationship* unscathed, I'd advise keeping it strictly platonic." Emily sat back in her chair, effectively dismissing the subject.

"And what about her family? Daddy's already talking *future* with me, in respect to making money."

"Don't worry about Daddy." Emily shook her head. "As soon as she dumps you, so will Daddy."

"I don't like the sound of being dumped." Jake grinned helplessly.

"Take your choice. Dumped or wedded."

"You are wise beyond your years, Emily. It will be interesting to see how long I last as an unromantic clod. Maybe we could have dinner together after all . . . after I get dumped." Jake pushed away from the table and stood. "Come on, let's do the dishes. Then I'd better head home."

Emily laughed. "Not this time. I'll catch you another time, when there's more work involved."

She walked him to the door and gave him a friendly hug. "You get on out of here. Go home and prepare for tonight's service. And call me when you're a free man."

Jake was anxious for Maria's crush to be over. He had to keep reminding himself what damage one romantic move could do to his plan. It wasn't easy to avoid her at every turn without feeling mean. But the only other way to discourage her was even meaner. He would have to destroy her belief in *destiny*.

The wait lasted two weeks. Two weeks of dinners in her home, lectures from her father, malts, and the strain of remaining platonic while Maria tried to initiate intimacy.

Finally, success crowned his efforts. He was in his office, studying when there came a weak knock on the door facing. He looked up to see Maria standing in the doorway.

"Jake, I have to talk to you." Her words hung heavy in the air.

"Come in, Maria. Is something wrong?"

"Well, yes and no." She stepped toward him. "I'd rather fight a tiger than hurt you. But I'm afraid we can't continue seeing each other."

Trying to look appropriately concerned, Jake led her to a chair. She dropped into it like a rag doll. She looked so sad. Jake got down on his haunches and took her hand.

"I've come to the conclusion, Jake, we're what you'd call star-crossed lovers. I know how much you care for me, but our relationship isn't going anywhere." She turned to face him. Their lips almost meeting. Jake backed away. "See? You're afraid to kiss me. Your calling won't allow you to be the man fate has chosen for me. And I understand your calling is the most important thing in your life. That's why I've decided to set you free."

He felt like an absolute heel. He'd remained impervious to her advances and had literally "worn her down" with his strictly platonic attitude. Worse yet, he was letting let his ministry take the blame. She'd expected so much more of him. But he couldn't do anything *now* that might change her mind . . . like giving her the tender hug he felt coming on. She might misinterpret it.

"I'm sorry I've been a disappointment to you, Maria. I am what I am. But your knight in shining armor will come. Give him time. You're a beautiful girl. And God has already chosen the right man for you. Wait on God." He stood and held out both hands to help her up.

THE TRINITY QUILTS

To be reminded of her beauty seemed to cheer Maria. Or perhaps she was just relieved to have this moment behind her. But her sad demeanor had evaporated. She stood on tiptoe and kissed Jake on the cheek. "Goodbye, Sir Galahad."

Jake walked into the hall and watched her leave by the door to the back parking lot. She turned around and threw a kiss as she walked down the brief set of steps. Jake waved back, then turned and dashed to his office. He could see the parking lot from his window.

Maria opened the passenger door to a recent model, dark-blue BMW sedan. A young man was in the driver's seat. She leaned toward him, and he pulled her close. They exchanged a few words, then kissed. A long romantic kiss.

Jake took a deep breath and smiled. Had he been sure he was alone in the building, he'd have done a happy dance.

Immediately his thoughts turned to the brave college girl who'd asked to take him to dinner. He'd thought of her a lot these last two weeks. They seemed to click. She was very mature for a woman so young and she had a terrific sense of humor. He was sure they'd be good friends, at the very least.

He picked up his phone and dialed.

"Hey, Emily, are you still buying?"

"That depends, Jake Webster. Have your eyelashes grown back in yet?"

Chapter 44

Emily insisted on buying. To save her money, Jake suggested they eat at a fast-food restaurant.

"I'd rather have a Whataburger than the finest New York strip," he insisted.

Emily shook a finger at him. "You, of all people, should know lying is a sin."

Jake shot her a quick glance from behind the wheel. "How about exaggerating? Is that mentioned in the Ten Commandments? Aha! I thought not."

He pulled into the Whataburger lot considering the subject closed.

Chatter between them was almost constant. Jake had never known anyone with whom he felt so comfortable. And so quickly. Second meeting, and they were bantering back and forth like old friends.

"You know, Emily, the thing I find most amazing about you?"

"Amazing? No, what?"

"Our minds are so in tune. That's unusual, considering our age difference."

"And just how old do you think I am, Jake?"

"Well, you're a college student. I'd guess you're between nineteen and twenty-two."

Emily laughed aloud. "I don't know whether to be flattered or insulted. It's nice being thought to be so young. But

THE TRINITY QUILTS

I'm not a student, Jake. I'm a professor. I got my masters here four years ago."

Jake put his hamburger down and sat back against his seat. "Oh. My. You're even more amazing than I realized. So we're close to the same age."

"Probably. I'm twenty-eight. How about you?"

"Same. Now I know why you have such a nice place. You're all grown up! But what were you doing at the dorm the night of the fire?"

"I was relieving the regular dorm mistress. She took a few days off to visit her new grandbaby. That's why I happened to know Maria was visiting the dorm. I had assigned her the room for the night." Emily pushed her burger away, folded her arms on the table, and leaned forward. "And why were you there?"

"A member of our church called to tell me about the fire. And, as you know, I only live a few blocks from there."

Jake put his hand over Emily's. "Em, this puts a whole new light on things. You know, I felt a bit like a cradle robber, going out with a college student. Now, I feel I can ask you for a real date. Take you somewhere special."

"I thought Whataburger *was* special."

Walking back to the car, Emily asked, "When is your birthday?"

"August thirtieth. How about you?"

Emily's jaw dropped. "You are not going to believe this. August thirtieth. Jake, we were born on the same day.

"Who knows, our mothers could have been roommates in the maternity ward." Jake laughed. "So *where* were you born?"

"Dallas. And you?"

"Nashville, Tennessee. My family moved here when I was four." He started singing in a nice voice. Not outstanding, but nonetheless pleasant. "From Nashville to Asheville, wherever the four winds blow . . ."

Emily laughed. "I'd sing you a chorus of 'Deep in the Heart of Texas' except you don't want to hear me sing."

"I bet you have a beautiful voice. Why would God stop at hair, face, and soul? And not give you a beautiful voice as well?"

Just weeks after their first date, Emily began to realize this adorable and amusing young pastor had become the center of her life. It was hard to believe a person so serious about the Lord and so steeped in the Word could have a fun side that kept her happy heart laughing. She told her father about him with every call and every letter home.

"Dad"—she wrote—"we have so much in common, it's uncanny."

Rob McKinley was pleased and couldn't wait to meet this Pastor Jake Webster. As long as she'd been away from home, first to college, then to go on to earn her master's degree, Emily had never shown any interest in romance. When she decided to stay in North Carolina and pursue a teaching career at the same university where she'd earned her degrees, well, it began to look like he may never have the grandchildren he'd been patiently waiting for.

Rob walked over to the mantel to look at a framed snapshot of Emily and Jake. *Look at them, they even look a little bit alike. Same color hair. What a beautiful family they would be. I'm going to ask her to bring her young man with her when she comes home for Christmas.*

He dialed his daughter's number and waited to hear her voice. Sometimes he gave serious thought to moving to North Carolina to be close to her. He had no strings in Dallas anymore. And heaven knows she nagged him to do it enough.

"Hi, Daddy." She always sounded so happy these days.

"Hi, baby. Do you and Jake have plans for Christmas? I thought maybe you could bring him home with you."

"Oh, Daddy, remember—he's a pastor. He can't leave his church at Christmas time."

"Oh drat. I forgot. When is a good time for a pastor to take a vacation?"

"It may be a while before he can take some time off. Why don't you come up for Christmas? I have plenty of room."

Rob was disappointed. But that might be a good idea. He could look around and see what's available in the way of housing.

They talked a few more minutes, then said their goodbyes.

But the seed had been planted.

Chapter 45

"Jake, I've been thinking . . ." Sarah had something serious on her mind. Jake could tell by the set of her mouth. He could always tell. Ever since he was very small, that certain expression warned him if he was about to be scolded.

"What's on your mind, Mom?" Confident she wasn't going to scold him, he sat down at the kitchen table and patted the chair seat next to him. "I'm all ears."

"Well, you know the old house we used to admire in Possum Hills, about forty miles from here? Dad always said if it ever came up for sale he was going to buy it for a get-away."

"Sure, we used to drive past there sometimes on Sunday afternoons when we went for a drive. Seems it was pretty run-down, even back then."

Sarah sighed. "Well, it's not anymore. The last owner had it partially refurbished. Didn't change much in the way of design. Which, to me, is a plus. Anyway . . . it's for sale. And I'm thinking of buying it."

"Oh, wow . . . you *have* been thinking. What would you do with this place?"

"That's kind of up to you. I'd probably sell it, unless you want it. It's not like I need the money."

"I appreciate your generosity, Mom, but if I took it, I would pay for it. What I'm really concerned about is—would you be happy out in the boonies, forty miles from a decent-sized town?"

"I honestly think I'd be very content. I've wanted to have a vegetable garden and a few animals for a long time. But I couldn't ask your dad to move out somewhere inconvenient to the church." She stood up and turned her back to Jake. "Son, living here has been a drain on me since your dad's gone. Too many memories." She swung around to face him. "I think the change would do me good.

"And I *don't* need the money for the house. Dad handled my inheritance with such wisdom . . . I have need for nothing. I'd only turn around and leave it to you in my will. So you may as well enjoy it now."

Jake leaned back against his chair. "Well, it's a lot to take in. But if it's what you want, Mom . . . I say go for it. What's the first step in buying the old place?"

She shot him a sheepish glance. "Signing a contract . . . which I've already done. In fact, since I don't need financing and the owner has already moved out, it looks like a matter of a couple weeks until I can move in. As soon as all the inspections are completed."

"It doesn't need any work done on it?"

"A little bit of paint here and there. But you know me. It will be my pleasure."

Jake stood and put his arms around his mother.

"Mom, what am I going to do with you?" He laughed.

"Jake, it's been wonderful living so close to you. Especially with Dad gone. But I feel like you're ready to move on to a different phase of your life, perhaps with the young lady you're seeing."

Jake was genuinely surprised. "How did you know I was seeing someone?"

Sarah crossed her arms in mock offense. "It's pretty obvious. I almost have to have an appointment to see you these days." Loosening up, she smiled. "Should you marry any time soon, you'll have this house—if you want it."

She took his hands in hers. "And I'm ready for a change. Forty miles is nothing. We'll see each other often. And I'll continue to bug you daily on the phone." Sarah grinned and kissed him on the cheek. "I'm so blessed to have such a good son."

Jake was pleased with this development. He and his mom had been very close. Best friends, even. But he was spending more and more time with Emily. She occupied his every thought. To the point he found himself apologizing to God for thinking about her so much.

God, You know all about this feeling between a man and a woman. You created us to have these feelings. Please forgive me for wanting to be with Em every waking minute. And, Father, if she is the woman You've chosen for me, please let her feelings for me by as strong as mine for her.

Jake had hoped to introduce his mom to Emily before Sarah's move, but teaching and preaching schedules just didn't allow. The week of Mom's proposed move, Emily was going to be at a seminar in Raleigh.

Jake was watching Emily pack for the trip, wondering just how much longer he'd be able to wait before popping the question to this amazing woman. He'd come over specifically to fix a leak in her kitchen faucet before she left town. But caught himself making any excuse, just to be in the same room with her.

THE TRINITY QUILTS

Emily looked up from her packing. "Jake, I wish I could be here to help you move your mom's things. But this seminar in Raleigh is something I simply cannot miss."

"Don't fret for a moment, Em. Mom hired movers to do the heavy stuff. I'll only be helping her with personal items. And if I know Mom, she'll have everything in order before the sun goes down." He leaned over and gave her a peck on the cheek. "I'd better get my plumber's hat on if I'm going to get the leak fixed before it's time for you to go."

She grabbed him by the arm as he turned to go. "You can do better than that."

"Meaning?"

Emily grinned. She was holding a makeup case in her right hand. "I mean that little peck on the cheek. Surely you don't expect that to tide me over for three days."

He took one long stride in her direction and pulled her into his arms. "Oh, Emily, I'm going to miss you so much." He kissed each closed eyelid, then the tip of her nose, and finally her waiting lips. His arms tightened around her. And Emily's left hand found its way to the back of his head. She dropped the makeup case and with both hands pressed him in closer. Jake responded with a moan.

Abruptly, Emily pushed away. "Okay. Okay. Okay. *That* should hold me." She gasped.

Jake stood rigid in front of her, his eyes downcast. "I . . . I'm sorry . . . I . . ."

Emily eased down on the side of her bed and looked up at him. "No, Jake, I'm the one who should apologize. Seems we've had an unspoken agreement to not let something like this happen. And I crossed the line."

Jake took both of her hands in his and pulled her to her feet. "Em . . . darling . . . when you get back, we need to have a long talk."

"Uh-huh. Now go fix the leak, love. Before I . . . well, just go fix the leak."

Chapter 46

Jake and Sarah had a marvelous time moving. Yes, marvelous. They laughed and joked. Reminisced and shed a few tears. They chose a beautiful dogwood tree near the house to dedicate to Todd Webster, Jake's dad and the love of Sarah's life. And made plans to buy a beautiful marker to lay at the foot of the tree.

Jake spent the first night in his mom's new home. He told her it was so she wouldn't be frightened in her new surroundings. She laughed at him and told him she was not yet ready for the role-reversal thing. And she certainly felt no fear in living alone in the country.

"But I would like to start my menagerie as soon as possible, with a dog. I was thinking a German Shepherd or a Doberman. What do you think?"

"Both great breeds, Mom. I lean toward the Doberman personally. Doesn't require as much grooming."

"Doberman it is, then."

"You want a pup? Male or female? Give me a hint. Santa might just have one in his bag of goodies."

"Truthfully, I wish I could find one that's unwanted. One that's been rejected. I don't care about the gender or the purity of its bloodline. That's how I'd like to acquire most of my animals. They'll make me happy, and I can return the favor."

"Consider it on your Christmas wish list, Mom."

After all the furniture had been arranged and all of Sarah's personal items had been put away, they sat at the kitchen table for a midnight snack and a mother/son chat.

"I wish Emily could have been here. She wanted to help. Mom, she is such a blessing to have around."

Emily.

Sarah's sandwich caught in her throat as she choked down the memories the very name of her son's girlfriend forced to the surface of her heart, but she managed a grin. "She sounds like a wonderful girl, Jake. Will I ever get to meet her?"

"I'd hoped you could meet before the move, but it just didn't work out. She's at a seminar in Raleigh for a few days. Mom, do you remember what I said not too long ago . . . I get to choose the mother of your grandchildren?"

"A couple months ago, in the hospital. How could I forget? You kind of put me in my place. I'm sorry I was such a nag."

"Look at me, Mom. And take a deep breath. I've chosen her—if she will have me."

"Emily?"

I'll have to live with a constant reminder of my own Emily whom I gave up? Sarah took a deep breath. *Oh, God, forgive me. I've prayed for his happiness. If this girl, Emily, makes him happy, that's all that matters.*

"Yes, Mom. She's a professor at the college. Very smart, very sweet, and oh-so pretty. I know you'll like her." Jake took his mom's hand in his. "No, you won't *like* her, you'll *love* her."

Sarah kissed the back of Jake's hand. "She only has one requirement to fulfill as far as I'm concerned. She has to make *you* happy."

"Oh, that she does, and that she will. Hey, *you* know what makes a *woman* happy. You can give me pointers, any time you want, on how to keep Em happy. Because that's all I want to do. I hope soon I'll have two girls to look after. You and Emily."

⁂

Emily returned from Raleigh to find Jake sitting on her steps.

Pulling her suitcases behind her, she called out, "What happened to you, little boy . . . are you lost?"

"Not anymore." Jake rushed to her, grabbed her, and twirled her around in a big circle. "Gosh, I missed you, sweetheart. Here, let me take your bags."

When he closed the door behind them, he dropped the handles to her suitcases and swept her into his arms again. "Em, I don't ever want to be separated from you that long again."

"It was only three days, Jake." She looked at him with a puzzled expression on her face.

"That's three days too long."

He put his hand under her chin and tilted her face upward. "It only took one day for me to realize the single kiss we exchanged before you left would not tide me over. Not even close." With that, he pressed his lips to hers. He felt Emily's body go limp in his arms. She was clinging to him as though she would collapse without his strong arms around her. He released her reluctantly—and gently. "I think it's time we had that long talk."

They sat across the table from one another in Emily's kitchen. Exhausted from excitement. Content that neither could conceive of spending their life with anyone else. But a little bit at odds about the wedding.

The last thing Emily wished right now was to be practical. Jake had just asked her to marry him, and all she wanted to do was shout it from the housetops so the whole world would know they were in love. But someone *had* to be sensible.

"You know I love you, Jake. But we haven't talked about any of the practical aspects of being married. Like where will we live, who will handle the money, and shall we pool our funds or have separate accounts?"

Jake grinned at her. "You're kidding, right? We'll live wherever you want to live. And we'll handle the money however you want it handled."

His expression turned somber. "There is one thing that troubles me, though. Even though my mom inherited quite a sum of money and Dad handled their investments well, we were never a part of the social set. We never traveled abroad or hob-knobbed with the elite. I suspect your upbringing was quite different . . . your dad being a successful doctor in Dallas and all. I suppose a formal announcement and an engagement party in Dallas would be in order."

Emily touched his face with her fingertips and breathed a sigh. "Well, we did have an awfully big house and some very rich friends. But, believe me, my folks were not the uppity kind. Very laid-back. My mother's health was always a bit delicate. I had no 'coming out' party—although most of my friends did—because she was very ill about then." She laid both of her hands in her lap and looked down at them. "She passed away not long after."

Jake remained silent. But reached his hand toward her in a gesture of sympathy.

She seemed to not notice. "I'm sure Daddy would be happy to forgo the engagement party. As far as going abroad . . . we did, only once. My parents wanted me to see Europe, but they were hopeful I wouldn't want to go by myself—or with a bunch of young people—after I graduated high school, as so many graduates do these days. So they took me the summer before my senior year. We spent a month touring Europe. As they'd hoped, it satisfied my desire to travel abroad. I was very happy to get back to the States." She looked up and smiled. "And I'll be happy to remain here the rest of my life. We are very blessed in this country."

Jake extended his hand to her. "Em, I'd planned to have a ring to offer you before I asked you to marry me. But the time just seemed right tonight. Maybe you and I can shop together."

She put her hand over his. "Jake, I'm not much on wearing a lot of jewelry, as you may have noticed. Especially diamonds. If you really want to make me happy, buy me a real wide gold band. I've always wanted one. They make you look so *married*. On second thought, my mother had one. Daddy's just liable to offer it to us. That would make it even more special."

"Wow." Jake smiled at her across the table. "I think we've been very practical, don't you? Let's decide which parent to tell first. I've already hinted, very strongly, to Mom I was going to ask you to marry me."

"Oh my. What was her reaction?"

"Well, at first I thought she was going to argue with me. But what argument did she have? She certainly couldn't say I was too young."

Emily chuckled.

"I told her how smart and beautiful you are. But she said the only thing she requires of you is that you make me happy. I told her that was a given."

Emily stood and walked to the sink. She turned and leaned against the counter, facing Jake. "Well, since your mom's the closest and she's already been prepped for the news, I think it makes good sense to tell her first. You agree?"

Jake followed her to the sink. "There's one person who needs to know before either of our parents."

"Who?"

"Me. You never actually said yes."

"Oh, yes, Jake. Yes. Yes. Yes."

Chapter 47

The drive through the country to Sarah's house was beautiful. The air was crisp and cold. In a valley surrounded by snow-capped mountains, a thin coat of ice had formed on the tree branches during a brief sprinkle the previous night. Trees glistened like diamond broaches against a vivid blue sky in the bright morning sunlight.

The road was clear and dry.

They'd come in Emily's car because Jake's was in the shop. Emily's classes were dismissed for the Christmas season, and Jake didn't have to be back until Saturday. He'd already put in hours on his message for Sunday. All he needed to be prepared for the service was a good night's sleep on Saturday night. They were looking forward to a couple of days with Mom to give her and Jake's bride-to-be some time to get acquainted.

Next week they'd drive to Dallas for Jake to meet Emily's father, the doctor. Life was good.

Sarah met them at the door with an apron on. "Jake. Oh, Jake. I'm getting used to it, but I miss being able to walk over to your house or the church to see you." She pulled them close to her in a group hug. "And you must be Emily. Oh, dear, he's told me such wonderful things about you. I'm so happy to meet you."

Jake looked around at Christmas decorations on the porch and in the entry hall. "Mom, you have the place looking like you've lived here forever. How do you do it?"

The house smelled of fresh coffee and apple pie in the oven. One would never know Sarah had only lived there two weeks. "Time on my hands, I guess, son. Why don't you bring Emily's things in and put them in the guest room?

"Emily, you come on in and make yourself at home." Sarah took her hand and led her into the living room. "You drink coffee? I just made a pot."

Emily sat down on the couch while Sarah fetched the coffee. *I must be dreaming. I'm in love with the perfect man, who has a mother who is amazing. I already feel like part of the family.*

After a cup of coffee and a slice of delicious apple pie, Jake and Emily took a little walk around the grounds. Emily had never been around horses, ponds, ducks, and dogs. It was a storybook adventure in the country. They marveled at how Sarah had assembled a full-blown farm on such short notice. And Emily was overwhelmed with the old-fashioned charm of it all. When they returned from their stroll, Jake broke the good news to Sarah.

"Mom, we haven't set the date, but I promise it will be soon. We're not planning a big wedding. Just family and a few friends. We still need to make a few decisions about where to live and stuff like that."

Sarah pulled Emily to her and hugged her. "It's not really a big surprise, dear. Jake told me while you were at your seminar he'd found the woman he wants to marry. He's been so blessed to find you, out of all the women in the world."

Turning to Jake, she added, "You know you have my place just a couple of blocks from the church, if you want it. Permanent, or for the duration. Whatever you decide."

Later that evening, after supper, Sarah showed Emily where she would be sleeping. Sarah took her hand. "I do hope you and Jake will come often, Emily. I feel like I've known you forever."

"So do I, Mrs. Webster. I know now why Jake turned out to be such a fine person."

Sarah stepped back from Emily. "Well, I guess 'Mrs. Webster' will do for now, but I hope you'll soon be comfortable calling me 'Mom.' And you can start practicing any time you want."

Sarah's heart was about to burst. Nothing she'd said or done during this traumatic day had been insincere. She *did* find Emily to be a lovely girl. And Emily and Jake seemed to be very much in love.

She had every reason to be ecstatic, but the pain of welcoming a girl named Emily into her family—knowing she'd given away a girl named Emily, never to see her again—was tearing her apart. And it was a pain she had to bear alone. Todd was the only one who knew her secret. And he took it with him to the grave. No one else must ever know about her past. Not even Jake. Especially Jake. He'd grown to be like her own son, *yet* if he knew she'd given away her only-born child, would he still feel the same about her?

Emily laid in her comfortable bed in the guest room thinking of Jake. His room was next to hers. Her headboard and his headboard shared a common wall. Shortly after going to their separate rooms, Jake had tapped softly on the shared wall. Emily tapped back. Four taps. *Good night, my love.*

She was surrounded by comfort, gentleness, and love in this delightful home. Yet sleep wouldn't come. She could think of nothing but when she and Jake would share their own home. Out her window, she saw the clear night becoming brighter as the full moon rose in the sky. Brighter and colder. The promised freeze was not far behind. And her covers proved insufficient to quell the chill that enveloped the house. Not wanting to wake the household in a search for more cover, she pulled her covers more tightly around her.

She heard her door knob turn and her heart froze in her chest. *No, Jake, don't come in my room. I couldn't turn you away. And we'd regret it the rest of our lives.* The door creaked open. A figure entered and approached her bed.

It wasn't Jake. Too small. Emily stifled a scream and pretended to be asleep.

The figure bent over the foot of her bed and began unfolding something large. Emily relaxed her taunt body and smiled to herself when she realized her future mother-in-law was covering her with another quilt. *What a lovely, thoughtful lady.* Emily reveled in the tenderness of Sarah's deed and continued to feign sleep as Sarah tucked the quilt in around her body. Only then did she murmur a sleepy-sounding "Thank you."

"I've turned up the thermostat a couple of notches," Sarah whispered. "But the heat pump was never replaced, and the old thing is kinda slow." She patted Emily on the leg and slipped out of the door without another word.

With the warmth of the quilt and the pleasure of Sarah's kindness enfolding her, sweet sleep finally came to Emily. And brought with it happy dreams of her future as Mrs. Jake Webster.

THE TRINITY QUILTS

Three soft taps on the wall. *Tap. Tap. Tap. I love you.*

Emily opened her eyes to an overcast sky outside the bedroom window. And for a split second couldn't remember where she was. Remembrance and sheer joy flooded her heart when she realized the tapping came from the next room. Jake's room. She knocked back four times. *Knock. Knock. Knock. Knock. I love you too.*

She looked at the dark sky and pulled her treasured quilt around her shoulders. The quilt her birth mother had made her. With her fingers brushing comfortingly over the embroidered name "Jesus Christ," she snuggled deeper into the bed. *It looks like snow. Wish I could just lie here and bask in this euphoric mood all morning.*

She was about to doze off when her eyes shot open and she sat straight up in bed. *My quilt! How did it get here . . . at Jake's mom's house? I didn't bring it. And Jake didn't sneak it into the car. Why would he?*

Her eyes scanned every inch of the quilt she'd memorized as a child. It was hers all right. Bright colors, a crimson cross in the middle, gentle scenes of Jesus and the children, Jesus at Gethsemane, excellently crafted and lovingly sewn. It was an original. There was only one other like it in the world. An exact duplicate—and it belonged to her birth mother. On the bottom hem of Emily's quilt, her birth mother had lovingly embroidered the name "Emily"—months before she was born.

Daddy had told her the whole story about her birth mother's sacrifice, and about the quilts, shortly after her adoptive mother died. He was afraid it would cause her to love her adoptive mother less. Or to hate her birth mother. But she insisted she had a right to know. As a doctor, he had to agree she had that right. As a father and a Christian, he could only hope it was in God's will he do so.

He told her, "Emily, she loved you from the moment she knew you existed. She used to lie on her back in bed with her hand on her tummy waiting to for you to move. She said it felt like a butterfly fluttering just beneath her skin. Sometimes she'd call your mother into her room so she could feel the movement. She knew how much it would mean to Beth."

Rob wiped an eye. "She named you, you know. We had a list of, probably, twenty girl's names for her to choose from, and she choose *Emily*."

He told the entire story with so much compassion, Emily tried to convince herself she could love two mothers equally. But she kept her feelings for her birth mother deeply hidden in her heart. She treasured the quilt—and the story behind it. And she longed to believe her birth mother was truly the selfless person her parents thought she was. But how could she ever know for sure unless she met her face-to-face.

Still wondering how her quilt ended up at Jake's mother's house, she painstakingly worked her way down the border of the quilt, as she had so many times in the past.

On the bottom hem of the quilt her birth mother made for *herself*, she'd embroidered her own name. *Mother and Daddy never told me her name. They felt it might be a betrayal of her trust.* Emily's fingers moved over the different textures—each one so familiar to her touch.

She closed her eyes as she neared the bottom. Only her fingers moved. *Jesus, please let it say 'Emily.' I'd rather be losing my mind than . . . than . . .*

Her fingers touched the embroidery. It didn't feel right. She jerked her hand away from it as one might wrench their hand from an open flame. Opening her eyes slowly, she forced herself to look at the name. Through a veil of tears she read it.

Sarah.

<hr>

Emily's world flew off its axis. The roaring in her head drowned out any rational thought.

She'd spent the night in the home of her birth mother.

She'd spent the night in the home of her fiancé's mother.

She and Jake shared a birth date.

She and Jake shared a mother.

Her mind couldn't grasp the horror of it. She was in love with . . .

She stuffed a fist against her mouth to keep from screaming. Jake was knocking at her door. "You decent? Breakfast is almost ready."

I've got to get away. I can't even look at him—or his mother—ever again.

She recalled Daddy's prayer that she would meet her birth mother in His timing. *God would have no part of something like this. Oh God, forgive me. I didn't know. I didn't know.*

Struggling to keep her voice normal, Emily responded, "Go have your coffee. I'll be there in a moment."

"I love you, baby."

Emily's stomach lurched. "Uh-huh. Go on now. Let me get ready."

She checked to be sure the bedroom door was locked and stripped off her pajamas. There was no time to waste. She had to get out of this house while Jake and Sarah were in the kitchen. She stuffed everything but the clothes she wore yesterday into her suitcase and scraped her belongings off the dresser into her purse. She'd stop and brush her teeth somewhere along the way.

Along the way to *where?*

After slipping into yesterday's garb, she grabbed her suitcase in one hand, and her car keys in the other. *Thank God we came in my car.* She opened the bedroom door as quietly as possible and made a dash for the front door. Once out the front door, she ran like the wind to her car, slipping and sliding across the icy front lawn. Throwing her bag across the seat, she jumped in and started the engine in one movement. Gravel flew, pinging against the living room windows, but she didn't slow down.

A thin coat of ice on the road caused her car to careen from side to side, but somehow she managed to keep it on the road. A glance in the rearview mirror revealed Jake running across the front lawn in a vain attempt to stop her. She returned her gaze to what lie in front of her and never looked back. When she was reasonably sure they could no longer see her, she slowed to a more reasonable speed. It wouldn't do to have an accident right here in Sarah's neighborhood. She took a left and then a fork to the right and another left. Hopefully they would not be able to follow her tracks.

When she'd calmed down enough to think, the horror or it all invaded her soul, filling every corner and crevice. *Born the same day to the same woman.* They were more than brother and sister. They were *twins.* No wonder they thought alike and enjoyed the same things.

Just last night as she lay in bed, less than twelve inches from him—through the wall—thoughts of marital bliss had thrilled her heart.

She stopped the car to get out to relieve her rolling stomach. Guilt washed over her and she cried out to God.

God forgive me. I didn't know. I didn't know.

Chapter 48

Jake raced back into the house. He plunged into the kitchen to find Sarah gone. "Mom! Mom! Where are you?"

He barely heard her trembling voice. "In the guestroom, son. I'm . . . I'm . . ."

He reached her just in time to lower her to the side of the bed as she began to collapse. "What just happened, Mom? What in the world happened to make Emily run away?" He paced from one end of the room to the other. "She's not into drama. It had to be something really serious. Did you two have a disagreement?"

"No, we didn't, son." Sarah was fingering the quilt, running her fingers over and over the name "Sarah." "I may know what happened, Jake . . . but I don't know where to begin."

He sat down next to her. "You're as white a sheet, Mom." He felt her forehead, then put his arm around her shoulder. "What could you possibly know about Emily that I don't? You've never met her before yesterday.

"Yesterday . . . things were so right yesterday. What *happened*?" His voice rose more than he'd planned with the last word.

Sarah wilted against him and began sobbing.

"Mom. You've got to stop this. It couldn't possibly have anything to do with *you*. You were an incredibly super hostess yesterday. She felt so at home. She told me so."

263

"Jake. Please stop talking for a moment. I've got to explain something to you."

"Did you hear the phone ring during the night? Maybe she got an upsetting telephone call."

Sarah was staring at the floor, breathing hard. "Jacob. *Stop.*"

This got his attention. "What is it?"

"There are some things about me you don't know. Your father and I didn't see any point in burdening you when you were a child, and the longer we kept silent, it seemed the less sense it would have made to tell you." Her eyes pleaded understanding.

"What things, Mom?" He got on his knees in front of her and looked up at her. "Mom, *what* things?"

Sarah first told him about her family life as the daughter of a dirt-poor, vindictive man and his frightened wife, who was never able to stand up to him. Not even where their daughter's welfare was concerned.

He tightened his grip on her shoulder. "I'll always be here for you. Surely you know that."

"I know your heart, son. But sometimes circumstances can devastate even the most faithful heart."

She took a deep breath and let it out with a whimper. Jake returned to his position beside her and put his arm around her. Then, avoiding the sordid details, Sarah plunged into the story of her rape.

She expected to feel a loosening of his firm grip on her shoulder as she confessed her shame. Instead he held her tight and put his head against hers. *But I haven't gotten to the pregnancy part yet. That will alienate him for sure.*

She rambled on, trying not to think of what life would be like without her precious stepson. He continued to hold her and comfort her. Little by little, as she released one dark secret after another, her heart began to lift from the depths. And she realized this young man she'd raised loved her beyond her sins and shame. Just as his father believed in her—so did his son.

"They gave me a home, an education, and hope for the future. And I gave my baby to this wonderful family. I didn't want to—I swear I didn't—but I think had I changed my mind, it would have been more than the baby's adoptive mother could have borne. She'd been hurt so many times. I knew I had to keep my promise or destroy her. Even if it destroyed me."

Jake put his hand over hers. "Mom, you don't have to say any more."

"Oh, but I do, Jake. You have to know the whole thing, or you'll never understand what just happened."

She put her index finger to his lips when he tried to object. "I made two identical quilts. I called them my 'Trinity quilts.' I put her name on the bottom hem of hers, and my name on mine. You've seen it. *Well, here it is.*" She held it up by one corner. "In my ignorance, I covered her with my quilt last night. How could I have known she was my . . .

"And this morning she must have seen my name and . . . oh, this is not the way I've dreamed of finally meeting her. Not at all. She must be so . . . so . . . distraught."

She heaved a sign. "I've ruined everything for you."

Jake was stunned. "The one for the baby says *Emily* on the bottom hem. The name her adoptive parents allowed you to choose. Yes, Emily has told me about it. But I haven't seen it.

"But, Mom, you can't blame yourself. No one could have known she was the same Emily. What are the chances of *that* happening?" Jake held her close until she'd emptied her soul of tears. "We'll fix it. She'll get over the initial shock, and . . ." The blood rushed from his face as the enormity of the situation hit him.

"Son, I don't know if she'll ever forgive me. Your Emily is *my* daughter. And she's very, very upset at having found me this way."

Jake had his elbows on his knees and his face buried in his hands. "I'm afraid it's even worse than that, Mom."

"What do you mean?"

He turned his head toward her, without raising up. "Mom, I've never mentioned to Emily that you married Dad when I was three, and you're not my birth mother. It never came up. You're my mom, and the only mom I've ever known.

"And have I ever mentioned to *you* Emily and I share a birthday? We were born the same day, same month, and same year." He looked up at Sarah, tears filling his eyes. "But, of course, you'd *know* that, wouldn't you?"

"Only too well."

Jake took his mother's hands, and they together they stood. "So has it hit you yet, Mom?"

Sarah looked at her beloved son, and her demeanor changed from sad to stricken before his eyes.

"Yes, Mom. Emily thinks she and I share a mother. That would make me . . . her brother. *Her twin brother.*"

Sarah gasped. "And she's in love with you. Oh. My. God. What torture she must be going through right now. We've got to catch her."

"She's too far ahead of us, Mom. And we don't even know where she's going."

Sarah was already headed for the bedroom door. "If I had to guess I'd say she's running to her Daddy's home in Dallas. And I know where it is. Remember, I used to live there myself."

She hurried into her little office and began rifling through her file cabinet.

Jake stood in the doorway with a puzzled look on his face. "What are you looking for?"

"Your birth certificate, mine and Dad's marriage certificate, and—thank God we kept it—Dad's and your birth mom's marriage certificate. When we find her, we have to have the ammunition to prove her assumptions wrong."

Sarah threw a few things in a suitcase and called a neighbor to look after her animals. In less than thirty minutes after Emily's harried departure, Sarah and Jake were on their way to Dallas. They didn't realize because Sarah had rambled around in a daze before setting her sites for Dallas, they were actually leading the way.

Chapter 49

Her vision was blurred by tears that wouldn't stop. *Oh, Lord, forgive me. I didn't know. Oh, God. What am I going to do?*

Emily sped helter-skelter down the highway with no earthly idea where she was going. She couldn't go back to her apartment. Not now. Maybe never.

How could any woman do such a thing? She gave away her own child. Gave one away and kept the other. How did she choose? And why did I lose?

Sarah had seemed like such a fine woman. *But there's a name for women like her . . . and my parents taught me to not use that name. She's my birth mother and she's despicable.*

Emily came to a small town with highways turning off in every direction. This brought her to a stop. *I must decide where to go. I can't keep driving with no destination in mind. But where . . . who can I turn to?*

Daddy.

I hate to bring sadness on him. But he's all I've got.

A highway sign caught her eye: TO INTERSTATE 81. KNOXVILLE 40 MILES.

Gotta change lanes. From Knoxville I can find my way to Dallas.

Emily blinked away tears and made a swift lane change to take the exit. *Tomorrow I'll put on my big girl pants, but right now, I need Daddy.*

Emily stopped in Little Rock for a bite to eat and lodging. In the morning, she'd drive the rest of the way to Dallas.

After a sleepless night in Little Rock, it was all she could do to get out of bed, much less take to the highway. En route she stopped several times to be sick, even though she hadn't eaten for more than twenty-four hours.

After one particularly violent session with her stomach, she stood outside her car and looked out over the desolate winter-wrapped countryside, completely undone. There was not a building or a car in sight. She called out to the Lord in a loud voice. *Jesus, if I ever needed you, I need you now. I'm not sure I can make the rest of this drive under my own power. Guilt and shame are being heaped on me. Please help me rise above the accusations of the devil and get to my daddy's house.*

"Honey, that was one fine prayer you just offered up to the Master."

Emily swung around to face a small black lady with a cane. "Who . . . who . . . where did you come from?"

"I was just walking by when I heard you and saw you were all alone, honey. Thought you might like some company."

"Walking by? From where? We're miles from the nearest civilization."

"Oh, honey, you wouldn't believe me if I told you. But I'm trying to get to Dallas, and I heard you were headed that way. Mind if I tag along?"

While Emily watched, the little lady carried herself straight to the passenger-side door, opened it, slid in, and closed the door behind her.

Sarah jumped behind the wheel and looked across the seat at the nerviest woman she'd ever met. "Now you wait just a minute, Ms. uh . . ."

"You can call me Sasha." The old lady beamed. "That's not my name, but you can call me that." She broke into gales of laughter. "I've always wanted to say that. But I'm only joshing, Sasha's my name, all right."

Emily was not in the mood for humor. "Well, Ms. Sasha. Maybe I don't *want* company to Dallas."

Sasha put her hand on the door handle. "Okay. I'll just stand out there in the cold until someone else comes along, if you've a mind to leave me here all alone in the middle of nowhere. I'll probably get mugged and left to die. But that's your decision."

"Oh, okay, stay in the car," Emily grumbled. "How did you know I was going to Dallas?"

The old lady pulled a Snickers bar out of her purse and offered it to Emily.

"Thanks. I'll pass."

With a finger pointed to the sky, Sasha took a big bite. "He told me."

Emily started the engine. "Ma'am, I'm sure you're a very nice person, but I'm not really comfortable with this conversation. I don't even know you."

"Well, of course you don't. That's exactly why we need to ride to Dallas together, so you can *get* to know me. You see, I met your mother once. On a bus, when you were just a tiny thing, still in her womb. She's really a much nicer person than you're giving her credit for."

"You don't know anything about her, or me. If you knew . . ."

"Emily, stop." Sasha stuck her fingers in her ears. "I don't want to hear it."

"How'd you know my name?"

"I just do. I know everything there is to know about you." Once again pointing skyward, she said, "He brought me up to speed. So just sit tight. You're not going to get rid of me until I see you safely in your daddy's arms."

Sasha put her frail, dark hand over Emily's. "Now I know you've been through a lot. That's why I've been assigned the job of seeing you safely to Daddy's. Too much could happen to you in your delicate emotional condition."

"You couldn't know what I'm going through. It's unimaginable, even to me." Emily's shoulders shuddered and thrust forward as fresh grief clutched her heart.

"That's where you're wrong, little girl. I do know, and I *am* going with you. Now if you have a mind to make me sit on the roof, that's up to you. But I *will* be going to Daddy's house with you."

Chapter 50

Jake pulled in the drive and marveled at the size of the house. "It's a *mansion*. Are you sure this is it?"

"Yes, son. This is it. The doctor almost apologized to me once for the size of the house, as though he was embarrassed. But they'd hoped to raise a very big family in it. Until they had to accept the fact Beth couldn't carry a baby to term. That's why she needed Emily so badly."

Jake slid out of the car and timorously approached the door. He looked back at his mother who waited in the car. She nodded, and he rang the doorbell.

Rob came to the door with a dishtowel in his hand. He just looked at Jake. He seemed to be trying to remember where he knew the young man from.

"Sir, you don't know me, but I'm a friend of your daughter's. Well, more than a friend, I should say. You see, I'm in love with your daughter. My name's Jake Webster."

"Of course. She sent me a picture. Well, this is certainly a surprise. Emily said you couldn't come for Christmas because of your church." Rob extended his right hand. "Rob McKinley, Jake. Glad to meet you." After a brief handshake, Rob drew him in the door. "Emily's written and called a lot, and you're always the center of the conversation.

"Where is she?" He looked out the door and around the brick entrance wall at the car in the driveway. There was a woman in the front passenger seat. But it wasn't his Emily. "Isn't she with you?"

"No, sir. I was rather expecting to find her here. Have you heard from her?"

Rob's expression was skewed with anxiety. "No, I haven't. What's going on? Was she supposed to meet you here?"

"No, sir. There was a terrible misunderstanding, and she ran away. We assumed she'd come here."

"Ran away? That's not like Emily."

"How well I know. We figured she'd run straight to you."

"Who is *we*, son? The lady in the car and you?" Rob made another attempt to see who was waiting in the car.

"Yes, the lady in the car is my mother. My stepmother. I think I need to call her in, so you can understand this whole mess."

Rob walked out on the entrance porch. "Please do, she shouldn't have to wait in the car. What is your mother's name?"

"Webster, sir. Sarah Webster." Jake watched for a reaction from Rob at the mention of the name Sarah, but there was none. *Sarah's a rather common name.*

"And your father?"

"Passed away, sir. Two years now." Jake motioned to Sarah to join them.

When Sarah got out and walked around the front of the car, recognition lit Rob's eyes and he ran to her. "Oh, Sarah. Praise God, it's good to see you."

He hugged her and half lifted her off the ground. "I can't tell you how often Beth and I prayed for you and wished we could seek you out without breaking our promise." He swung her in a circle, then put her down and released her.

Stepping back to look at her, he shook his head in disbelief. Sarah was laughing for joy.

But the joy quickly dissolved, and her eyes expressed only concern. She turned from Rob momentarily. "Jake, perhaps you should put my car around back. It might be best if she didn't know we were here."

"Come in the back door, son," Rob called out as Jake sprinted toward the car. "It's open."

He turned his attention back to Sarah. "Please come in and tell me what's happened to upset Emily so. And where do you think she might have gone?" He led Sarah to the kitchen and began preparing a pot of coffee.

They sat around the table waiting for the coffee to perk. Slowly, in order to not leave out any important details, Sarah and Jake took turns bringing the good doctor up to speed on everything. Beginning with the way Sarah and Todd met on Jake's third birthday—which just happened to be Emily's third birthday. All the way to the terrible mistake Sarah made by covering Emily with her Trinity quilt.

The coffee sat forgotten on the counter.

Rob listened intently. When they'd finished, he got up from his chair and began to pace. "This is awful. There's really nothing wrong at all, but my poor baby thinks the world has come to an end. I can only imagine the horror of being so much in love, and then discovering you're in love with your twin brother. Or thinking you are anyway." Rob sighed. "I hope y'all are right in thinking she'll come here first. I'm worried because she hasn't already gotten here."

Jake fiddled with the empty coffee cup setting before him. "I feel in my heart she's safe. We drove straight through. Perhaps she stopped for a night along the way. Let's give her a little time."

"You're probably right, Jake." Rob got up and started pouring coffee in everyone's cups. "I'm sorry, son, you're having to go through this."

"Well, Dr. McKinley, my biggest worry right now is . . . will I be able to erase this horrible conception from her mind and make her see me as a husband and not a brother?"

"Oh, yes, that will happen. You have to know her mind is trying to reject the idea. And it hasn't had time to take firm root. It will wither quickly. Besides, God didn't bring us all this far to let it all fall apart because a well-meaning gesture on the part of your mother"—he sent a tender glance Sarah's way— "was snatched up by the devil and used for evil."

He patted Jake's shoulder. "In fact, I'm so sure everything is going to work for the good, I'm going to ask you to start calling me 'Pop' or 'Dad.' This Dr. McKinley stuff has got to go."

Rob's phone rang. He glanced at caller ID.

"It's Emily."

Sarah and Jake grabbed hands and prayed silently as Rob answered the call.

"Hey, honey."

Emily's voice sounded strained. But he was grateful to hear it.

"Yeah, yeah. You're on your way here? Great. Coming alone?

"Really? You picked her up where? Well, tell her she's welcome to stay with us, if she needs a place to stay.

"Oh, okay. But see if she needs money or something before she goes her own way. I'll pay you back.

"See you in a couple of hours. Bye, sweetheart."

Rob hung up and looked at the two of them. They were anxiously awaiting his report.

He put his hand to his chin and tapped his lower lip with his forefinger. "She'll be here in a couple of hours. Strange thing, though. An elderly black lady by the name of Sasha hitched a ride with her. Showed up on the highway in the middle of nowhere. She told Emily she wanted to ride with her to Daddy's house just to see she made it safely. That's weird. What do you make of it?"

Sarah let out a small squeal, found her way to the living room, and fell into an easy chair. She let her head flop back against the cushion. "I can't believe it. Well, I take that back . . . I guess I *can* believe it." She started laughing. Not a humorous laugh, but a joyful one.

Jake followed her and shot her a puzzled look. "You okay, Mom?"

"Yes, son. I'm fine. *And so is Emily*. Sasha kept me company on a bus when I was carrying Emily, almost twenty-nine years ago. She said God had sent her to watch over me. And kind of indicated she was one of many who'd been assigned the job. She disappeared into thin air, leaving me with a Gospel tract. A tract I read over and over during my imprisonment." Sarah looked toward Rob, who was hanging on her every word. "You remember the shack don't you, Rob? And your dramatic rescue?"

Leaning against the archway between the dining room and the living room, with his arms crossed, Rob—his thick hair now streaked with gray, for real—smiled and nodded. "How could I ever forget?"

Sarah signed. "Praise God. Emily is in good hands."

Chapter 51

They finally settled down to drink their coffee and talk while they waited.

Sarah laid her hand on Jake's arm. "You remembered to bring your birth certificate I gave you, right?"

"Got it right here." He patted his shirt pocket. "It should be proof positive to Emily I was born in Nashville, Tennessee, and not Dallas, Texas." He shot a grin at Rob. "Although I think *Pop's* assurance should do the trick."

Sarah began digging through her shoulder bag. "And I have your dad's and my marriage certificate, as well as proof of his marriage to your birth mother. I've no doubt she'll believe the facts. I'm more worried about the emotional effect this traumatic happening has had on her. It's not exactly how I'd hoped to see her again. I had imagined a joyous reunion . . . if it ever happened at all."

She unfolded the marriage certificates and laid them on the table.

"The joy will come, Mom. We'll look back on this someday and smile."

"Aren't you the optimistic one?" Sarah cast a sad smile at him.

"Yes, I am, Mom. Because Satan meant all this for bad, but God has a way of turning things around for the good, to His glory." He looked toward Rob, who nodded in agreement.

"Mom, this guy Chance, he held you captive? Did he hurt you?"

"He never mistreated me physically, except, of course, for chaining me to the bed. He was afraid to do anything that might hurt the baby." She put her hand over Rob's.

"And the day Rob, here, came peeking in the window at me . . . looking for all the world like a very dirty, homeless old man, up to no good . . . well, that really freaked me out."

Jake turned toward Rob. "That's so cool. Somehow I can't picture you looking that bad." Jake shook his head and grinned his admiration for his mom's hero.

"He went to a lot of effort. Took him weeks to perfect *the look*. Oh and you should have seen the moves he put on Chance when Chance started pushing him around."

Rob joined in. "Don't forget about . . ."

Conversation stopped when they heard a key in the front door.

"Daddy, I'm home!"

Rob jumped up and ran to greet Emily. But not in time to catch her before she rounded the corner and came to an abrupt halt. "What are *they* doing here?"

She pointed her finger accusingly at Sarah. "Do you know what *she* did? She had two babies and only gave you one. What kind of woman would separate twins? You'd have taken us both, wouldn't you, Daddy?" She glanced at Jake but couldn't make eye contact. "And what kind of woman wouldn't tell her son he had a twin sister running around out there?"

Rob let her spew it all out.

"Make them leave. She . . . she . . . let us think we were strangers. And we met and fell in . . . oh God. What am I going to do? Daddy, what am I going to do?" Emily collapsed into Rob's arms.

He held her and turned her body so she wasn't facing them, but looking him straight in the eye. "Honey, you've got this all wrong."

"No, Daddy, the quilt. She has the matching quilt. I *know* it's her."

"Yes, baby, it's her. Sarah is your mother. But Jake is *not* your brother. It's just a terrible mix-up."

"How else can you explain . . ."

"I'm a doctor, honey. I saw the ultrasounds. And I was there for your birth. Yours was not . . . I repeat . . . yours was *not* a multiple birth."

Holding her close, and not allowing her to turn around, Rob signaled to Jake. "Jake, I know this is hurting you, but would you lay your birth certificate on the table and leave the room for a few minutes. I want to talk to Emily and Sarah alone."

When Jake was gone, Rob turned Emily around to face her mother. Emily set her jaw and glared at Sarah. Sarah's eyes and cheeks were drenched.

"Daddy, I'm leaving. I'll come back when they're gone." She started to turn around, but not before she sneered at Sarah. "How did you decide to keep him and give me away? Did you flip a coin?"

With a moan, Sarah closed her eyes and dropped her head. But she held her silence. Rob would handle this situation with wisdom. There was no point in turning it into a shouting match.

Rob intervened. "Emily, I'll have no talk like that in this home. You will sit here and discuss this like the intelligent young woman I know you to be. Enough drama. You understand?"

Respectful of her father, Emily became quiet. But she set her jaw and looked defiantly at Sarah's contrite form.

Rob led Emily to the table and bid her sit down across from Sarah. "Do you want a cup of coffee, Emily?"

She barely opened her lips to speak. "Please."

He poured her coffee and set it in front of her. Sitting down beside her, he spoke softly. "Emily, this fine lady is your mother. Her name is Sarah Webster."

Sarah raised her head and trained her eyes on Rob, always her defender and friend.

Emily pushed back from the table. "I know her name. I'm not stupid."

"Then stop acting it." Rob pushed her chair back under the table. "You will sit, and you will listen to reason.

"When you were a happy child of nearly four—thanks to your birth mother's sacrifice—she married a pastor named Todd Webster, a widower with a son named Jacob." He moved the marriage certificate in front of her. She glanced at it briefly and pushed it away.

"No." He pushed it back in front of her. "Look at it, Emily. Look at the date and do the math."

Obediently, Emily studied the marriage certificate, apparently making note of the date. Then she pushed it back to the center of the table.

He then placed Todd Webster's first marriage certificate in front of her. "And this is the marriage certificate between Jake's dad and his birth mom. Look at the date on it, and you'll see they were married a year and a half before Jake's birth—a day which coincides with your birthday—very much by coincidence."

Rob continued, "I'm sure there were thousands of babies born in the world on your birthday. You cannot hold Sarah responsible for that."

Emily's stare was beginning to soften. Her lower lip quivered. Brushing back tears, she examined the birth certificate closely, touched Jacob's tiny footprint, and slowly pushed it back to Rob.

"Beth and I promised Sarah we wouldn't burden your life with stories about a birth mother until you were old enough to understand. *Really* understand. After Beth died, I told you what you demanded to know. How Sarah came to the decision to give you up because she had no home, no money, and no way to take care of you.

"Looking for the right family, at barely seventeen, she was kidnapped by a madman who planned to sell her baby . . . you . . . to a lawless family. She fought him with everything in her, only to end up chained to a bed, day and night. But God had plans for her . . . and for you. Someday you can hear the whole story if it's your wish."

The telling of Sarah's story was taking a toll on Rob's emotions.

Sarah reached out to him. "Rob, please, I can't bear any more. I'll leave. Just help Jake to make her believe. He loves her so much." She started to stand.

Rob gently held her down. "You're not going anywhere, sweet lady. *Our* daughter is a sensible woman. Give her time to let this all sink in."

Turning his attention back to Emily, he said, "What you need to get through your head now is Sarah was . . . and is a fine person. I happen to know when the time came to give you over to us, she suffered greatly. She wanted to keep you very badly, but if she'd backed out of the adoption—which she had every legal right to do—it would have broken Beth. Your birth mother kept her promise out of love for Beth. She asked only for the right to make those identical quilts. It was her comfort in life to know the two of you cherished matching quilts."

Emotionally spent, Rob leaned back in his chair and took Sarah's hand in his. "Emily, this woman—your mother—does not deserve what you're putting her through."

Emily's eyes were cast down and filled to overflowing with hot tears. Fidgeting with the handle of her coffee cup, she hesitantly raised her gaze to meet Sarah's. Sarah's cheeks glowed with spent tears and her eyes were filled with compassion. Slowly Emily reached her hand across the table toward her. "I'm so sorry. I've been very foolish."

Rob released his grip on Sarah's hand, and she leaned forward to meet Emily halfway. "I love you, Emily. I always have."

Their hands gripped tightly, they both stood and navigated the corner of the table until they were face-to-face. Neither spoke, both were trembling.

Sarah broke the silence with a gasp. "My baby." She pulled Emily close.

Emily put her arms around Sarah and held her tight. "M . . . Mom."

Chapter 52

Rob kept the tissues coming while Emily and Sarah got reacquainted. "Do you think we should let Jake come out of his room now?" he quipped.

"Wait just a few more minutes, Daddy. I want to erase the picture I had in my mind that he was my brother. And I think I need to freshen my makeup."

Rob smiled. "Well, I can assure you, you two do not share as much as one cell, and I don't think he's going to care about your smeared makeup."

"I want to hear it from Mom. Tell me a little about him growing up." Emily looked at Sarah waiting for just the right story. "I want to see him again, the way I saw him the first time when he was the hero of the night."

"Emily, he's always been my hero. He told me the first time we met, when he was three, he was going to be a pastor . . . like his daddy. We never used the terms *stepmother* or *stepson* because we were just *family*. He guided me through my grief when his dad died, checked on me daily even though he had a busy church congregation to lead. He's not the Superman type as a rule, although he sure did step up that night, didn't he?"

"Yes, he did. And I've never told him this . . . but I 'set my cap' for him that night. However, my adoptive mother wisely taught me to never be obvious. Always let the fellow make the first move. Oops, sorry, Daddy. Was that too much information?"

Rob rubbed his chin and grinned. "Well, it does make me wonder exactly when she decided we were getting married."

Sarah took Emily's hand and led her to the window. "Baby, Jake's love is a thing to be treasured. You see, he's never had another serious relationship. I know he would run into a burning building to save another person on a daily basis should the occasion arise. Because he has a very great love for people. Showing that love and telling people about the love Christ has for them is what he's all about. It's all he's ever wanted—to be like his dad.

"But his love for *you* shines from his eyes every time he speaks your name. And although that fire was a terrible thing and a great financial loss, God used it to bring you two together." Sarah smiled and slowly shook her head. "You didn't *set your cap* for him. That was *God* telling you the first time you saw him, 'This is the man I have for you.'"

Emily kissed Sarah on the cheek and rushed down the hall to get Jake. "Come out, come out, wherever you are, Jacob Michael Webster. We have some business to settle."

When the hugging, laughing, crying, and kissing settled down, Rob addressed Jake.

"Son, I thought I heard you talking to someone while you were back there waiting."

"Yes, sir. I'm glad you mentioned it. I was intending to spend the entire time in prayer, but I no more than got settled in a chair than there was a knock on the patio door."

Everyone was staring at him in rapt attention.

"Really? Who in the world? They would have had to climb the fence," Rob said.

THE TRINITY QUILTS

"I walked over to see a little old black lady with a cane getting ready to knock a second time. Seemed quite impatient to me."

Sarah started grinning.

Emily piped up. "Why that sounds like Sasha. I wondered where she'd gone. She disappeared while I had my back turned getting out of the car. What did she want?"

"Well, she wouldn't come in. Said she was in a hurry, they needed her at the hospital. But she wanted to tell *me* God was pleased with me. Can you believe that? And He'd gone to a great deal of trouble arranging Emily's and my meeting. And I better not mess it up—she giggled when she said that."

"Is that all?" Sarah was hanging on every word.

"No, Mom, she gave me this to give to you. Said you left it at the hospital, and you need to be more careful in the future."

He dropped something into Sarah's waiting hand. "She's quite a card."

The cross pendant Vivi had given her.

"I looked down at what she'd put in my hand, and when I looked back up, she was gone."

Rob laughed. "That's getting to be quite a habit with her.

Chapter 53

Rob closed up the house in Dallas for an undetermined length of time and made arrangements with friends to check on things periodically. He leased a large motor coach, and the four of them were headed for a little town just out of Amarillo. It had been years now since Sarah had seen Sam and Vivi, although they talked on the phone often. All Vivi's kids had married and moved closer to the city, but not too far away for frequent visits.

Emily and Jake had talked it over and prayed about it. After learning what a big part Sam Blake and his sister Vivi played in Sarah's life—thus also in Emily's—it was decided the wedding must be held where they could be present. Vivi wasn't in good enough health to travel. So what better place than their little West Texas country church, with their own pastor officiating.

When Rob turned off Highway 15, as directed by Sarah, she thought at first she'd made a mistake. *Did I miss their road?*

The little dirt road was free of potholes and ridges. The motor coach glided over it like it was riding on glass. There were no weeds, run-down shacks, or faded signs. Beginning a hundred yards or so into what was once the old Pleasant Acres tract, there was a neat split rail fence on either side of the road, enclosing a well-kept pasture. Round hay bales dotted the fields and several stout horses and cows grazed leisurely in the warm winter sun.

Sarah strained her eyes looking for Sam and Vivi's house in the distance. "You know, Rob, I may have had you turn down the wrong road." The motor coach crested a small rise in the road and a lovely log home appeared on the horizon. "Let's stop at that cabin and ask."

When Rob pulled into the driveway, before Sarah could get out the door of the coach, a tall, slightly bent man in overalls came bursting out the front door.

"Uncle Sam!" Sarah ran to him wanting nothing more than to jump into his arms. But as she got closer, she realized Sam had aged quite a bit. Jumping into his arms may not have been a wise option. So she threw her arms around him instead and hugged and hugged and hugged. She didn't release him until she saw Vivi come out the door. Then Vivi got her turn.

Sarah's heart did a flip when she realized how much they'd aged. But then, so had she. She owed them so much more than she could ever repay. She recalled how much Vivi had wanted to raise the baby herself. There's no doubt Emily would have been loved.

"Your place. It's beautiful. When did this all happen?"

Sam shrugged. "Finally got that great opportunity to use Angel Truck."

Sarah laughed. "You named it Angel Truck?"

"Actually, you named it Angel Truck. Don't you remember?" Sam turned her around to look toward the barn. "And there she sets. Doesn't get used much anymore, but I could never get rid of her. Too much history."

"So how did you get all this land?"

"Turns out it was all waiting to be picked up for back-due taxes. And thanks to Angel Truck, we could do that *and* have log siding put on the house. Bought an old tractor and cleared out the run-down buildings. Bought some critters to help us keep it mowed. And that's really all we've done.'

"That's *all*?" Sarah quipped. "Well, I'm so happy for you. It's lovely."

Vivi finally managed to get in a few words. "Who's the gentleman driving? And is the baby with you?"

Rob, Jake, and Emily had waited in the motor coach for Sarah to have a chance to catch up a little. When Sarah signaled them to get out, they all scrambled out the door, anxious to meet Uncle Sam and Aunt Vivi.

Sarah put her arm around Rob's waist. "This is the wonderful gentleman, who along with his wife, saved my life, took me in, helped to get my education, and most importantly raised my baby. Emily's father . . . Dr. Rob McKinley."

Sam's right hand shot out. "Doc, God knows what a pleasure this is for me and my sis."

Vivi stepped right up and threw her arms around him. "I wanted to raise that baby real bad . . . but we couldn't have done for Sarah or Emily what you've done. God bless you."

All Rob could do was smile and accept their gracious offerings.

Taking Jake's hand Sarah announced, with tears in her eyes, this is my son, Jake, an ordained minister and my personal hero."

More handshakes and hugs.

Then Sarah pulled Emily close to her. Visibly shaken by the awesomeness of the moment, Sarah drawled out, "A-n-d, this very special young lady is my son's fiancée, who also happens to be my daughter, and the *baby* you've been waiting to meet for twenty-eight years. Our baby, Emily. And I'm overwhelmed by . . . by . . ."

Vivi handed Sarah one of her ever-present tissues, and everyone started hugging and talking at the same time.

When Rob realized how much love these fine country folks had for Sarah—and how they would have gladly, even eagerly, raised Emily, he asked them to join him in giving the bride away.

Vivi spoke first. "Oh, Dr. Rob. We . . . we can't do that. You're her father. The one who gave her such a beautiful childhood and sent her off to college. We could never have done that."

Rob bent down to Vivi's short stature. "But your prayers and faith brought her to my doorstep. Please do this with me . . . for me."

When she nodded yes, Rob kissed her on the top of her head, raised to his full height, and stuck his hand out to Sam. Rob was fairly tall, but he still had to look up to meet Sam's eyes. Rob grinned. "So it's settled?"

Sam nodded. "It's settled, Doc."

If expensive flowers, elegant decorations, and high-ceilinged, steepled churches with majestic stained-glass windows are the essence of a beautiful wedding, Emily and Jake's wedding didn't make the grade. But if love, family, and the presence of the Holy Spirit are the determining factors in the eyes of God—Jake and Emily's wedding was the most beautiful one ever performed.

Time came to say goodbye to the Blake family.

Sarah knew she may never see them again this side of heaven. She and Sam, and Vivi hugged in a tight little circle and prayed for travelling grace, the newlyweds, and for Rob's need for family.

Rob's folks had passed away before Emily finished high school. He retired when Beth health started to fail. And since her death, he'd not had any family close by, and simply no social life at all.

Emily, Jake, and Rob took their turns saying goodbye to their newfound family. Sam pulled them aside, one by one.

"Jake, you take care of Emily, now. Or I'll come hunt you down."

"Emily, you've found a prince in the fellow you married. Be good to him."

And, lastly, to Rob, "Doc, it's none of my business, but you're all alone and Sarah is a fine woman. The age difference is not too great, and . . ."

"Say no more, Sam. I've noticed." The two guys exchanged knowing grins.

~~~

At everyone's insistence, Rob accompanied Sarah, Emily, and Jake back to North Carolina. The newlyweds drove Emily's car. Rob drove his Mercedes—a very happy Sarah sitting across from him—her compact vehicle being towed behind. At first neither of them had much to say. But as soon as Sarah broke the ice by telling Rob how much she'd always looked up to him, and he responded by saying she was an extraordinary woman who'd overcome unbelievable odds—well, a lengthy nine-hundred-mile "date" ensued. Talking, laughing, hand touching, and a few tears. Broken only by rest stops and meals.

At one point, Jake suggested they change partners to give the girls a chance to talk, or the parent-child teams. The suggestion was met with silence from Rob and Sarah. In fact, they didn't break eye contact long enough to respond. Jake looked at Emily and shrugged. Emily chuckled, and the idea was abandoned.

Late on the last afternoon of their journey home, they stopped at a beautiful rest stop near Gatlinburg. While the newlyweds bundled up at the picnic table munching on chips and sharing a soft drink, Rob and Sarah braved the chill to stroll forty or fifty yards beyond to see what was written on a monument.

"Em," Jake murmured, "we're stepsiblings *and* we're man and wife."

"Yes?"

"Not all that unusual of an occurrence, do you think?"

"Probably not. I imagine it happens fairly often, statistically speaking. Especially if the stepsiblings meet for the first time as adults."

"Right, but I'm just wondering . . ."

He paused for a long moment.

"Wondering what, love?""

"What would it make us if my mother and your dad fell in love and got married?"

Emily pulled away to give him a sideways glance. "I think you'd be your own grandpa." She laughed softly. "It would be neat, that's for sure. Just think, Daddy wouldn't have to buy a house in Asheville."

"And Mom wouldn't have to hire help around the farm."

Emily nodded. "And we could save postage on Christmas cards."

"They'd save money on weddings. We'd get them both married off for the price of one."

Emily jabbed him with her elbow. "Yeah, and our kids wouldn't have to learn so many names."

"Good one. Plus, we wouldn't have to put as many miles on the car visiting them."

Laughing, Emily reached for her purse. "I'm going to make a list. We can show it to them and maybe they'll consider such a proposition."

She had her head down, searching. "Now where is my pen?"

Jake tapped her on the shoulder. "You can forget about the pen. I don't think we'll be needing that list."

"Why?"

He nodded his head toward Sarah and Rob.

They were sitting on a bench in the lengthening shadows of the towering trees to the west. A chilly breeze ruffled Sarah's soft hair. Rob reached up to touch it, then trailed his finger down her cheek. And ended holding her chin in his gentle touch.

She raised her face to him. Rob whispered something to her that made her smile.

"The kids are watching. Let's give them something to think about."

Gently, he touched his lips to hers.

Jake and Emily began cheering. Hooting and hollering.

Pulling away, he whispered to her again. "Now, here's something for *you* to think about. Sarah Webster, I'm eighteen years older than you. But I love you. *Oh, how I love you.* Will you marry me?"

This time she pulled his face down to her and kissed him long and hard. They lost their balance and nearly fell from the bench. The kiss ended in gales of laughter.

"Is that a yes?" he asked.

"It is definitely a yes."

"*She said yes,*" he shouted to their awestruck audience.

About the Author

A second-generation clocksmith, Ms. Walding wrote her debut book on clock repair. This was followed by magazine articles on antique clocks. Her writing career in the field of horology seemed a sure thing.

But when she met the love of her life, a pastor, she put her writing career on the back burner for more than a quarter of a century. Only after they retired from the ministry did she again consider writing. But this time God gave her a much better subject to write on—Himself.

Everything Walding writes is pure fiction, but her years in the ministry have given her a keen insight into the kind of battles we all face, who's the evil perpetrator of our battles, and who is the only One who can bring us through victorious.

Being the perfect gentleman that He is, she says the Holy Spirit only gives her one plot at a time. Each story points the reader to a loving God who's always there for us through thick and thin.

Lynne and her husband, Dee, live on a bend in an old country road in East Texas with their dog, Sarah. They call their place Possum Bend. Although they're more likely to see deer at the creek each morning, the opossums are there. They come out after dark, as do the raccoons and armadillos. To be sure they stay around, the Waldings throw out seeds for the birds and squirrels each morning and scraps for the wild ones each night.

After all, they were there first.

Your correspondence is appreciated and encouraged. You can contact Lynne through her website: LynneWellsWalding.com, or her email address: lynne@lynnewellswalding.com